UP TO THE CHALLENGE

ALSO BY TERRI OSBURN

Meant to Be (An Anchor Island Novel)

UP TO THE CHALLENGE

AN ANCHOR ISLAND NOVEL

Terri Osburn

Montlake
Romance

Text copyright © 2013 Terri Osburn

Printed in the United States of America.
No part of this book may be reproduced, or stored in a retrieval system,
or transmitted in any form or by any means, electronic, mechanical,
photocopying, recording, or otherwise, without express written
permission of the publisher.

Published by Montlake Romance, Seattle

www.apub.com

ISBN-13: 9781477809686
ISBN-10: 1477809686

Cover design by Anna Curtis

Library of Congress Control Number: 2013908969

For Fran. You've been with me from the beginning.
Thank you for the push.

CHAPTER ONE

Sid Navarro considered calling a nurse to remove the stick of righteous indignation from Lucas Dempsey's ass. If he tensed up any more, the thing would snap off and put an eye out. Observing from the back of the hospital room, she couldn't help but pick up on the tension rolling through the broad shoulders of the man she'd been in love with for half her life.

Not that Lucas knew about her feelings, which was the way Sid preferred it. His type was the simple, friendly, girl next door, always smiling and ready to mingle. Sid wasn't overly complicated, but her unsociable nature along with an atypical job—foul-mouthed mechanic—meant she didn't fit his mold. Best to keep her feelings on the down low rather than face the humiliation of rejection.

Lucas stepped closer to the foot of his father's bed, waging what looked to be a battle between shedding a tear and tearing someone's head off. Her best guess for the head-ripping victim would be Lucas's older brother Joe.

Joe carried tension of his own where he stood four feet to Lucas's right, holding hands with his girlfriend. Beth Chandler had been Lucas's fiancée until six weeks ago, which justified the tension, but, since Lucas had supposedly given his blessing to the new couple, the blatant anger didn't make much sense.

Maybe the fiancée swap wasn't the problem. Since Lucas had bolted from Anchor Island the moment the tassel on his high school graduation cap switched sides, he and Joe hadn't seen eye to eye on much of anything. That made the rift ten years wide.

Sid and Joe had been working together on his fishing boat for just over five years and spent so much time together, the Dempsey family had more or less adopted her as one of their own. Except Lucas, of course. He didn't visit the island often enough to get sand in his shoes, let alone notice an extended family member.

Sid couldn't recall Joe mentioning anything about a new dustup with Lucas. Then again, Joe wasn't exactly a talker. One of the things Sid liked best about him. She wasn't one of those women who wanted a man to share his every thought and feeling.

In Sid's opinion, women were just asking for trouble with that nonsense. Raised mostly by her father and big brother, she had enough experience around testosterone to know the shit going through a man's head at any given moment should never be revealed for public consumption.

Especially not the female public.

"The nurse says five days in here, then six weeks recovery at home," said Patty, Lucas and Joe's mom. Technically, Lucas's birth mother and Joe's stepmom. She was talking about the boys' father, who occupied the bed around which they all hovered. Technically, Joe's biological dad and Lucas's stepfather, who'd given the younger boy his name when he'd married Patty.

The Dempseys were a complicated bunch even before the fiancée fiasco.

Tom Dempsey had suffered a near fatal heart attack while tending bar in the family-owned restaurant during the lunch hour. Eight hours later, here he lay, prostrate with translucent skin and a mess of tubes sticking out of each arm. Cables looped into the neck of his hospital gown, assumedly plugged into stickers glued somewhere around the vicinity of his heart. For a giant of a man known to be a pillar of strength and good health, Tom was doing a damn accurate imitation of a beached jellyfish. Sid fought a tear of her own, wiping the corner of an eye with the sleeve of her hoodie. She'd lost her dad to a heart attack when she was fourteen. Losing Tom Dempsey the same way would feel like having a four-sixty engine block dropped on her chest.

"But after six weeks he'll be good as new, right?" Joe asked. Beth leaned closer and he tucked her under his arm. Lucas's eyes narrowed, but he otherwise remained stoic.

Patty swiped away a tear, her voice cracking as she spoke. "I'm not sure 'good as new' is in the cards, Joe, but he'll be with us, and that's enough."

"Is there still a chance he could . . ." Beth let the question trail off. The group exchanged glances as if daring one another to say the word no one wanted to hear. Sid kept her mouth shut, as unwilling as the others to tempt fate.

"I'm not dying anytime soon," Tom said in a low, gravel-choked voice. His eyes were still closed, making it seem as if they'd all imagined the words.

"Tom? Honey?" Patty lifted his hand to her lips, pressing them against the tape holding an IV needle in place. "Can you hear me?"

"The heart might be on the fritz, but my ears still work."

Relief swept through Sid. His voice wasn't as strong as usual, but the words were so Tom, she knew he was going to be all right. The patient opened first one eye, then the other, licked his lips, then motioned toward a cup sitting on the tray to his right. After sipping through the straw Patty lifted to his mouth, Tom dropped his head back.

"Do I look half as bad as that look on your face says I do?" he asked.

Patty laughed as a tear slid down her cheek, unheeded this time. "Don't you ever scare me like that again, Thomas Dempsey. I thought I was going to lose you."

Sid nearly added a "Hear, hear!" to Patty's words. The man needed to take better care of himself, that was all there was to it.

Tom smiled, ran a finger along Patty's cheek, then shifted focus to his other visitors. "Now I know what it takes to get everyone in this family in the same room." He bounced a raised-brow look between Joe and Lucas, then addressed the latter. "Thanks for coming all the way down here."

"Not a problem," Lucas said, jaw tight with a smile that didn't reach his eyes. "Though you could have just asked. No need to get so dramatic."

Noticing Sid in the back of the room, Tom asked her, "You think you could modify this bed to power me out of here?"

Sid stepped up next to Lucas and tried to ignore how good he smelled. "Got my tools in the truck. We can have you doing thirty-five down the highway in no time."

"Don't encourage him, Sid," Patty scolded. "You'll stay here until they say you can come home, and then you're going to do everything the doctor says."

"I've got a restaurant to run, woman." Sid wouldn't put it past the Dempsey patriarch to leap out of the bed and stomp back to the island, ass cheeks shining through the hospital gown all the way.

"You're not running anything for at least six weeks," Patty said, sounding as firm as possible under the circumstances.

"Then tell me who's going to run the place. We can't close the doors. Not in July, for Christ's sake."

"We'll take care of it," Joe said. Leave it to Mr. Responsible to step up. He needed to remember he couldn't be in two places at one time.

"If you're going to run the restaurant, who's going to run the charters?" Sid asked. Joe couldn't afford to shut down his charter business any more than they could close the restaurant at the height of the season.

And there was the little issue of her own income. Sid was so close to having enough money to buy the garage that would house her future. There had to be a way to make it all work.

"I can find someone else to run the boat for a couple months."

Sid pointed out the obvious. "Every fisherman capable of running that boat is already running his own. And you've got charters booked for the next six weeks."

Patty interrupted before Joe could argue further. "You kids have businesses of your own. We'll find someone to run the restaurant through Labor Day, then reevaluate for fall."

"I'll do it," Lucas said.

He might as well have pulled a pin on a live grenade

and held it over his head. Everyone fell silent, exaggerating the incessant chirping of the machines monitoring Tom's every heartbeat.

"You'll what?" Joe asked, stepping forward. Sid stood her ground between the men. This was no time for Joe to do something stupid.

Lucas crossed his arms, revealing impressive muscle below the rolled up shirtsleeves. "I said I'll do it. I'll run the restaurant while Dad recovers."

"You heard the part about six weeks, right?" big brother asked. Beth tugged on Joe's belt loop and he stepped back.

"I may miss a clue now and then, but I got that part."

Sid wasn't sure if Lucas meant to take a shot at Beth, but that's what he'd done. Joe stepped forward again.

"As much as I want out of this hospital, I'm not getting kicked out because of you two." Tom hit a button on the bed rail, sending the mattress into motion. Once he was satisfied with his new position, he released the button. "Lucas, I appreciate the offer, but are you sure you can get away from the law firm?"

Lucas leaned on the bottom bed rail. "I'm sure. Do you trust me to run your restaurant?"

Tom frowned. "I won't dignify that with an answer." He turned to Joe. "If he runs the place while you run the charters, can you cover some nights?"

"I'll be there whenever you need me."

"Nights," Tom said again, as if passing down a final judgment. "Then it's settled. You boys will run it together. I expect the place to still be in one piece when I come back. Understand?"

Both brothers nodded but neither spoke. Tom's head dropped, the brief exchange apparently taking what little energy he could muster.

Patty gripped her husband's hand and turned to Beth. "You're running the art store, right?"

Beth straightened like a soldier called to attention. "Yes, but only until Lola and Marcus come back from New Orleans."

"How long is that?"

"Another month."

Patty nodded. "Sid?"

"Yeah?"

"I'm not letting Tom out of my sight, and that puts us two people down instead of one," she said. "Could you help cover for me?"

"If Joe recruits one of the high school kids to run the charters with him." Sid looked to Joe for his reaction and got a nod of approval. "Then I'm there. But I just need to be available for mechanic work if a call comes in."

"I'm sure we can work around that," Patty said. "It's all settled then. Beth can work with Joe to cover nights, and Sid will help Lucas during the day."

With Lucas? Sid hadn't thought that far ahead. She'd never experienced seasickness in her life, but the thought of working side by side with the guy for whom she'd secretly pined for more than ten years made her queasy. Or not so secretly, since Joe knew. And thanks to Sid's brother, Randy, Beth did, too.

Sid made eye contact with Beth, reading the unspoken question in her eyes.

This is good, right?

Then she turned to Lucas to catch his reaction. He looked like someone had just shit in his shoe.

Not from where I'm standing, she thought.

~

Life was about to become a living hell. Or rather, even more of a living hell than it had been since his fiancée had fallen in love with his brother. Lucas didn't regret having been the one to convince Beth and Joe not to become martyrs for his sake. Lucas had loved Beth, or thought he had the night he'd proposed. And he loved his brother for all they understood each other, which wasn't much.

Something had happened to Beth back in May when he'd left her on Anchor with his family to head back to Richmond for a case. The change could have been caused by Joe, or the island, or maybe the distance from Lucas and the law firm where they'd worked together. Whatever the reason, the Beth he'd left behind was not the woman waiting when he returned.

In fact, she'd been Elizabeth to him. He still struggled to call her Beth. Back in Richmond, he didn't have to call her anything. The gossip in the office had been a pain in the ass, but faded into ancient history as soon as Van Dyke got caught boffing his assistant in the janitor's closet.

Beth claimed she'd never set out to hurt him. She'd been living a lie for a long time, pretending to be someone else to make people happy, and somehow he'd become part of that lie. One more person she'd set out to please. The truth was, whether he'd brought her to Anchor or not, their life together never would have worked out.

Which drove him nuts, but he wasn't about to let Beth know that. Or anyone else. So she'd picked his brother over him. Nothing new there.

Through no effort of his own, and exuding no discernible charm Lucas could see, Joe had always come out on top. People *loved* him. More importantly, they respected him. They listened when he talked, cleared a path when he crossed a room.

Being Joe Dempsey's little brother was like playing second fiddle to a set of spoons, which was why Lucas preferred to live elsewhere. In Richmond, he was the star attorney. The up-and-coming counselor. Or he had been until Beth dumped him for Joe.

"Hey there," came a soft voice from behind him. Speak of the devil. "This is a really nice thing you're doing."

Lucas kept his eyes on the vending machine before him. "Yeah. Well. Mom and Dad need me. I'm here for them."

Beth leaned on the corner of the machine. "And you're sure this won't be a problem? Getting away from the firm?"

He should have known she'd wonder about that. "Not a problem." Lucas pushed the number-letter combination for barbeque chips, then watched the steel rod turn. The chips stayed put. "Damn it."

Beth ignored the expletive. "Leaving in the middle of a case isn't going to cause issues? No one wants you to jeopardize your career."

Lucas smacked the glass between him and the chips. Nothing. "I'm not in the middle of a case." Another smack. The chips didn't budge.

"Oh," Beth said. "Then you just wrapped one up? Did you win?"

Meeting her eyes for the first time, he blurted, "I'm on leave. I lost three cases in a month and Holcomb *suggested* I take a leave of absence until I've 'regained my focus,' as he put it." Lucas turned back to the machine to stare at the unattainable bag of chips. There was a metaphor in there somewhere.

His former fiancée stayed quiet, indicating she might hopefully be ready to drop the subject. No such luck. "I'm sorry. How long have you been off?"

"Two weeks."

"And you didn't tell us?" she asked. "Were you going to come down here?"

He shook his head, filtering through the possible replies. He picked honesty. "If what I need is focus, Anchor is the last place I'm likely to find it." Then before he could stop the words, he said, "That's more like returning to the scene of the crime."

Beth inhaled sharply and his gut churned. He'd sworn he wouldn't do this. "Look. I'm sorry. I didn't mean that."

Beth shook her head. "No, it's all right. We knew this was going to be a transition." She blushed. "That's not the right word. I mean—"

"I know what you mean," he interrupted. No reason to make this more difficult than it had to be. "Don't worry about it. We'll make this work." He tried a grin but his heart wasn't in it. "Six weeks. We can handle six weeks, right?"

Beth seemed to spot someone coming up behind him and straightened. "Right. Six weeks. I'd better get back in the room."

Lucas turned to see Sid Navarro coming down the hall. The pint-sized boat mechanic had been on the fringe of his reality since high school, but he wouldn't say they were friends. Not like she and Joe were. In fact, Lucas couldn't remember ever having a real conversation with the woman.

Every time he saw her, she was either snarling at someone, or covered in grease and cursing a blue streak. She had to be the least ladylike chick he'd ever met.

"How's it going?" Sid said, joining him at the machine. He expected an assault of diesel fumes but instead caught the scent of . . . watermelon?

"Hi."

Chocolate brown eyes met his for a brief moment, then turned to the display of junk food. "You getting something?"

"Trying to." He pulled his eyes from the smooth patch of olive skin exposed under her ponytail. "The machine is holding my chips for ransom, and I'm not paying. Guess I'll go without."

"I wouldn't say that." Sid stepped forward and pressed her ear to the side of the worthless box of bolts.

As she moved to listen at another spot, Lucas asked, "What are you—" but she shushed him with one finger in front of his nose. His mouth clamped shut.

Pulling back, Sid smacked the side of the machine with the butt of her hand, causing his chips to drop into the tray. He'd smacked the damn thing twice and gotten nothing.

"How did you do that?"

Sid shrugged. "I've got a way with machines. Are those the right chips?"

"Yeah." Lucas pushed the door to retrieve the snack as Sid pulled a wallet from her back pocket. "You don't carry a purse?"

She looked at him as if he'd asked if she had meth for sale. "Do I look like a purse carrier to you?"

He took in the hoodie, cargo pants, and work boots. "Guess not."

"You good with this working together thing?" she asked, falling into step beside him, after retrieving her candy bar from the drawer. Which fell on the first try.

"Fine with me. You probably know the staff better than I do. That should help until I get my bearings and the staff realizes I'm in charge."

Sid stopped. "*You're* in charge?"

Lucas crossed his arms, nearly smashing his chips. "It *is* my family's business."

She crossed her arms, mimicking his stance. Her head didn't reach his shoulder but she still managed to look like a badass. Must have been the boots. "I'm covering for Patty, who is as much in charge, if not *more* so, than your dad. So you may be in charge of everyone else, but you're not in charge of me."

Lucas debated how to handle the situation. He was used to being in charge, leading the team. Having a coleader would be something new. Running a restaurant wasn't the same as running a legal team, and deep down, he knew he needed her. He could always take the upper hand later if necessary.

"Equals?"

"That's right."

"We'll see." Not the strongest comeback, but for a tiny woman, Sid had a steady gaze.

"For a lawyer, you suck at this." Sid started walking again, then turned back to face him. "I hope you tend bar better than you argue, or I'm going to have to cover the whole damn place."

With that she disappeared into the hospital room, leaving Lucas in the hall with a bag of crushed chips and a bruised ego. Six weeks in hell had officially begun.

CHAPTER TWO

Thirty minutes later, the floor nurse announced visiting hours were over. After a brief round of good-byes, Lucas left his keys with Patty so she could use his car, then the younger generation headed for the parking garage. No one spoke until the elevator opened to Joe and Beth's floor.

"Do you guys mind if I ride with Sid?" Lucas asked, drawing blank stares all around. "It's a long drive and she shouldn't have to make it alone."

Sid tried to remain nonchalant about riding with Lucas. Alone. Her teenage self would have had a mental breakdown had this situation arisen all those years ago. But she was no longer a teenager, and this man had no idea he'd been the star of her fantasies for more than a decade.

She tried to be offended at the assumption she couldn't drive an hour in the dark alone, but Lucas's true motivation shone through loud and clear on his face. This had everything to do with his own mental preservation and nothing at all to do with Sid's safety.

She hoped the man didn't fancy himself a poker player.

"We don't mind," Beth said, giving Joe a *just agree with me* look.

"No," Joe said, catching on quicker than Sid would have expected. "No problem."

Beth dragged Joe away from the elevator and the doors slid closed. Sid waited until they'd stepped out at the next level before speaking. "If you think you can avoid them for the next six weeks, you've forgotten Anchor is the size of a postage stamp."

"I haven't forgotten anything. I'm just not in the mood tonight."

"So long as you wallow in silence, I'm good with it." Sid wasn't sure why she was provoking him, but it seemed a good enough way to keep a sort of distance between them.

Lucas stopped. "I'm not wallowing."

Sid kept moving. "Yes, you are."

"What do you know?" he said. Hard to believe this man argued legal cases in front of a jury. Good thing he was pretty.

"I know a man stuck in a pout when I see one." Distance shmistance, Sid had no intention of contributing to Lucas's pity party, especially not over another woman. She was more the snap-out-of-it type than the huggie type. Sid didn't hug as a rule. "Truck's over here."

"You like this with everyone or am I just special?" Lucas joined her next to the Chevy, looking like he might change his mind and run off to catch Joe and Beth.

Sid unlocked the passenger door, then turned to face her long-time crush. *Don't let it show.* "If we're going to spend our days together, we need to get something straight right now. I'm not a coddler. I'm not going to nurse that damaged ego of yours, and I'm sure as hell not going to tiptoe

15

around trying not to say something that might make you feel bad."

His full lips flattened. "I hope you're not on the island welcoming committee."

"What's that supposed to mean?"

"Oh, I don't know. That maybe your attitude would send a shark racing in the other direction." Lucas leaned on the truck bed, looking proud of himself for that one.

Sid gave him her best *fuck you* look and headed around the front of the truck.

"And another thing," Lucas said, following her. "You can drop that chip on your shoulder at the door."

"Screw you."

"You might be the first woman I've ever met with a Napoleon complex."

Sid stopped. No one made fun of her height. She counted to ten as she turned. The man was hurting, but he'd crossed a line.

"Unless you want to walk your scrawny ass back to Anchor, I suggest you shut your mouth and get in the truck. And walk around the back because I'm already tempted to run over you."

She opened the door and climbed up, struggling to control her temper. For fourteen years she'd longed to gain this man's attention. Talk about a case of careful what you wish for.

Sid tapped a thumb on the base of the wheel, waiting for Lucas to reach the other side. If she started the truck with him standing outside, the acoustics of the parking garage might damage his eardrums.

When he finally opened the passenger door, he said quietly, "I need to get my stuff out of my car." The temper he'd displayed seconds before had vanished.

"Didn't you give your key to your mom?"

"The lock is a combination. I don't need the key to get my bag."

Sid sighed. "Where's your car?"

Lucas looked around. "I'm not sure. What level is this?"

"Four."

"I parked on five."

"Fine." She turned the key and the engine roared to life. "Get in and we'll drive up."

As if noticing the truck for the first time, Lucas stared at the dash, blinking. "This is your truck?"

What the . . . ?

"No. I'm stealing it. Did you hit your head on your way over there?"

"What year is this?"

That did it. First thing was to check his bag for drugs. "Have you had this memory problem long?"

Lucas shook his head. "Not this year. The year of the truck."

"Oh. 1985. Restored her myself. If you ever decide to get in, I'll show you how well she runs."

He finally climbed into the cab, then skimmed a hand over the dash. "You did this?"

"I didn't build the dash," she said as she pulled out. "But I put her together." She swung the truck onto the ramp for the next floor. "Don't act so surprised."

"I knew you could fix boats. I didn't know you knew cars too."

"Anything with an engine. Dad had me fixing lawn mowers by age eight. Helped him build a go-cart when I was eleven."

Lucas continued to take in every detail of the cab. "I'm impressed."

A smile split her face. When she turned it on her passenger, he looked poleaxed. "What?" she asked, glancing in the rearview for something stuck in her teeth.

"Nothing," he said, rubbing the center of his chest.

"You're not having a heart attack too, are you?" That's all she needed. Though Sid worked out, no way could she carry Lucas back into the hospital. He had her by a full foot and though thin, his frame looked solid.

"A little heartburn. I'm fine." He squinted out the window. "My car's the second to last up here on the right."

Sid came to a stop behind the silver BMW. Too flashy for her tastes, but the vehicle fit Lucas's style. Expensive. Sleek. A statement on wheels. He'd always been a gem among pebbles, which was what had drawn Sid to him in the first place. Lucas was that brilliant, out-of-reach star she could admire from afar but never catch.

Sid's mother had shared the same quality. Removed. Special. Untouchable. Qualities Sid found mesmerizing, mostly because she was the complete opposite, best described as *nothing special.*

Within a minute Lucas had popped the trunk and thrown his duffel bag in the bed of the truck. If an expensive-looking leather bag could be called a duffel. They drove through the garage in silence, but not the comfortable kind, which made Sid antsy. Four blocks down Main she'd had enough.

"Took 'em all by surprise back there, didn't you?"

"Took who by surprise?"

"Your family," she said, jerking her head back as if his family were sitting in the truck bed. "No one expected you to step up and stick around."

"I may not come home much, but I'm still part of this family," he snapped. "Mom and Dad need me, so I'm here."

She'd found a nerve. "Sorry. I guess expecting you to turn tail and leave them flailing *is* insulting. You deserve more credit than that."

"No, I don't," he said. "I know how it must look, but I have my reasons for avoiding Anchor."

"I know why you avoid it now," Sid said, posing the question she'd been pondering for years. "But I don't understand why you didn't come around much before."

He ran a hand through his hair. "I suppose I should be ready for *the look*." He glanced over and Sid lifted a brow in question. "The one that says, 'Poor Lucas. How does he hold his head up like that?'"

Not exactly an answer to her question, but he'd opened the door for another. Sid couldn't resist the temptation; time to find out if there might be an ulterior motive to this visit.

"I'd be more ready for the gossipers assuming you're here to win her back." Sid held her breath, not sure if he'd answer. If she wanted to hear the answer.

"People can relax on that front. There's no winning Beth away from Joe. Joe always wins." Staring into the darkness to his right, Lucas added, "He always has."

Silence loomed again. Sid felt something shift, but not under the hood. The idea Lucas felt in any way inferior to

19

Joe had never crossed her mind, but it did explain his quick escape and long absence from the island. That he'd shared something so personal with her, in such close quarters, gave the moment an intimate feel. Which scared Sid enough to let the subject drop.

≈

Nothing like spilling your guts to a prickly boat mechanic with the bedside manner of a spitting cobra. Lucas didn't even know where the words had come from, but he appreciated his chauffeur's apparent willingness *not* to pursue the topic. Maybe Sid had a heart after all.

Time to change the subject.

"I'm about to run a restaurant full of people I don't know. Tell me about the staff."

"Sure," she said, keeping her eyes on the deserted road. "Where do you want to start?"

"Who does the cooking?"

"Day cook is Flynn O'Mara. He and Vinnie switch off now and then, but for the most part, Flynn handles the days."

"An Irishman and an Italian?"

"Hungarian."

"Excuse me?"

Sid turned right onto Highway 45, leaving the lights of Morehead City behind. "Vinnie is short for Edvin. Edvin Varga. First-generation American according to gossip. Doesn't say much so who knows for sure."

"A Hungarian named Vinnie?"

"Yep. Two sous-chefs. Chip and Nova. They switch off too, but I think Chip handles days most of the time."

"Okay, that's the kitchen. Up front?"

"Three waitresses are full time. Annie Littleton, Daisy Johannes, and Georgette Singer." Sid gunned the truck to shoot around a slow-moving Hyundai that appeared out of nowhere. "Annie is a native, but young. You probably wouldn't remember her. Daisy and Georgette are transplants, but have been on the island long enough."

Lucas knew what "long enough" meant. The natives respected the tourists because they kept the island afloat, so to speak. But anyone who showed up and stayed was subject to an unofficial probationary period, during which the islanders sized them up, asked lots of questions, and decided whether to accept them or not.

"Good to know everyone has approval." Lucas grabbed the dash as Sid swung around another car. He tried to check the speedometer, but couldn't get a straight view to the other side of the steering column. "I won't be running anything if you kill me before we reach the ferry. That pedal stuck?"

Sid coughed something that sounded like "chickenshit."

Ignoring his comment, she went back to the staff. "You've got two bussers. Mitch and Lot."

"Lot? Who names their kid Lot?" Not that he'd thought about naming kids of his own, but what the hell?

"His name is Brandon Sandoval. Kids called him Sand in elementary school and that rolled into Sandlot. At some point the Sand part dropped and Lot stuck."

Sid turned up the radio. An announcer was reporting on a hurricane working its way across the Atlantic.

"We've been lucky for two years," Sid said, "but this one is making me nervous."

"You think it's headed our way?" Lucas hadn't been in a hurricane since high school. "How much time do we have?"

"A week to ten days maybe. Might curve off, but I'm keeping my eye on the reports." The station went back to music and Sid lowered the volume again.

"So four in the kitchen, two bussers, and three waitresses. Not much staff for this time of year."

Sid shrugged. "Tom pulls in part-timers when necessary. Beth runs a section most weekend evenings, and I grab a tray now and then. Joe clears when it's really busy." She shot him one of those smiles that felt like a punch in the sternum. "We can handle it."

Lucas leaned on his door and rested one arm across the back of the seat. "You mentioned having to be available to fix the other boats around the island."

"If something breaks, they'll call. I'll let the guys know to dial Dempsey's if they need me." She leaned back, resting both hands at the base of the wheel. "Maybe we'll get lucky and nothing will break for a while."

Dark, silky curls brushed Lucas's hand. He couldn't resist rubbing a lock between his fingers. "Yeah. Maybe we'll get lucky."

The truck jerked.

"You all right?" he asked, bracing against the dash.

"Fine," she said, cutting her eyes his way then back to the road. "Foot slipped." She flipped the ponytail over her shoulder, out of his reach.

Interesting reaction. He wondered if her problem was being touched by him or by people in general. Might be worth exploring, if he ever felt suicidal.

CHAPTER THREE

L ucas struggled for a full minute to figure out where he was. Considering how much time he'd spent staring at the ceiling the night before, the fact he inhabited the guest room in his parents' house, the room he'd occupied for a decade before going off to college, should have been obvious.

But the room looked nothing like it had when he'd been a teenager. The dark blue walls now a muted yellow. The red plaid comforter usurped by a flowery afghan with feminine details around the edges. Frilly curtains matched the bedding, while watercolor beach scenes dotted surfaces once covered by Lamborghini posters.

Lucas had to give his mother credit. She'd waited until his junior year of college to wipe him from the room. After Lucas made it clear there would be no moving back home after school, she'd attacked the décor with a vengeance.

After donning a T-shirt and shorts for his morning run, Lucas tied his running shoes and wondered if his mom hadn't made the room as girly as possible out of spite, to prove she could move on too. Not that he doubted his mother loved him or would welcome him home any time, but Patty Dempsey was not the type to wallow or cajole. She preferred to adjust to the new reality and get on with things.

The way she had when Lucas's father had been killed in a military training accident when Lucas was three. The same way she did when Beth Chandler went from being Lucas's fiancée to moving in with his brother. A small part of Lucas wished his mother had thrown more of a fit. Made the happy couple miserable for a week or so. For his sake.

Then he gave himself a mental slap, put his inner four-year-old back in the closet, and followed his mother's lead. Shit happens. Move on.

Only moving on was proving harder than expected. The events of the last six weeks had put too many questions in Lucas's head. Was he really so blind? Would things be different if he'd stayed on the island instead of putting his career first? Could he have a personal life and the professional life he envisioned?

Stopping at the bottom porch step to stretch his hamstrings in the morning sunshine, Lucas assured himself that *being* partner and *having* a partner were not mutually exclusive. One he would likely have sooner than the other, but there was plenty of time to start a family after he'd achieved his career goal.

"Is that the prodigal lawyer returned to our humble island home?"

Lucas looked up to see a familiar face at the end of the drive.

"Only for a visit," Lucas said, then with a smile added, "This island isn't big enough for two lawyers."

Arthur Berkowitz, Artie to his friends, had been the only lawyer on Anchor Island since before the Dempsey family arrived two decades before. Artie's impassioned presentation on career day, during Lucas's sophomore year of high school, had set him on the path to law school.

"How have you been, sir?"

Artie waved off the moniker. "None of that *sir* stuff. We're on equal footing now, though I hear you're aiming higher than this old codger ever dreamed."

Lucas stood taller. "I have my eye on a partnership. Nothing you couldn't have achieved if circumstances had been different." In other words, if the man had practiced his trade somewhere other than this remote island.

"Maybe," Artie said with a grin, his hanging jowls, loosened by age, making his narrow face seem longer. The few wisps of gray hair covering his balding skull danced in the breeze. "But I'd have been miserable with all that ass kissing and back stabbing." He clenched his hands over a rounded stomach and rocked back on his heels. Lucas worried the shifting of all that weight might send him tipping over. "Anchor Island was always enough for me."

"To each his own," Lucas said, reluctant to defend his choices to the man he'd once considered a mentor. "I see Rufus is still hanging in there."

As if recognizing his name, the basset hound at Artie's side gave a mournful yowl.

"We're a pair, the two of us." Artie gave Rufus a pat on the head. "Two old dogs doing as little as possible."

"Not taking on a lot of cases these days?" Lucas asked.

"None at all. Retired. Rufus and I are enjoying our golden years. Taking time to smell the flowers, one might say."

Lucas had never thought much about Artie never marrying, but couldn't avoid wondering if he faced a similar future. Spending his final years with only a dog for companionship. A morbid thought.

"Wait. You're retired? Who took over the practice?"

Artie shrugged. "No one. I put out the word there'd be an opening here on the island, but there were no takers. Requires vision to recognize the benefits of a life this small. As you probably know, the word *small* doesn't enter most lawyers' vocabularies."

Lucas couldn't let that one pass. "Nothing wrong with wanting more than drawing up land deeds and writing wills."

"Nothing wrong with that at all," Artie agreed, though the glint in his eye suggested he didn't agree at all. "I was sorry to hear about your father. Is that why you're here? Hope he's going to be all right."

"Doctors expect a full recovery, but that'll take time, so I'm here to help out."

"You're here for more than the weekend?"

"Six weeks minimum," Lucas replied. "I'll be running the restaurant during the day, with Joe taking over in the evenings."

Artie's sharp eyes narrowed. "Must throw a wrench into that partnership idea. Your firm good with you picking up and leaving like that?"

A muscle ticked in Lucas's jaw. "The timing worked out. It's not a problem." Ready to end the conversation, he added, "I was heading out for a run. Better get going so I have time to shower before opening time."

"Yes. Yes. Don't let Rufus and me hold you up."

Lucas had taken three steps when Artie spoke again. "One thing before you go."

He rolled his eyes before turning back around. "Yeah. Sure."

"How many summers did you help out around the office?"

"Three before college, then another between freshman and sophomore year. Why?"

Artie took his time crossing the distance between them, his gaze on the rocks at their feet. When he'd caught up, ice blue eyes met Lucas's. "Sometimes things aren't as simple as we remember them." As if he'd just said something that made sense, the older man moved around Lucas and walked away, hound trotting along beside.

What in the hell did that mean? Before Lucas could ask, the strolling pair made a left and disappeared from sight.

∼

Sid rolled up to Dempsey's at nine on the dot. She'd offered to stop for Lucas on the way, but he'd turned her down, saying he preferred to walk. More power to him. Pushing through the unlocked doors, she found him standing by the bar scanning a menu. Assumedly to get reacquainted with the options.

Loose-fitting jeans rode low on his hips, reminding Sid of the cover model on one of the romance novels she kept hidden in her closet. Except Lucas looked better than the model. If he planned to wear those things every day, the next six weeks would be hell on her libido. The white polo shirt didn't help either. A hint of chest hair teased at the collar, while tight sleeves showed off tan, well-defined arms.

When did a workaholic find time to build that kind of muscle?

Golden-brown hair framed a face that would make a Greek god jealous. Sid didn't have to see the eyes to know specks of green and brown danced in their hazel depths. Those eyes had stolen her teenage heart long before the body caught up to its true potential.

Maybe we'll get lucky.

Those words had played through her brain all freaking night. Combined with the memory of his fingers softly twirling her hair, it's a wonder she'd gotten any sleep at all. Experience had proven that Lucas Dempsey would never be interested in a woman like Sid. His past girlfriends, at least the ones Sid knew, including Beth, shared a demure quality.

Sid was about as demure as Anchor was big.

"How's Tom?" she asked.

"Good," he said, turning over the menu. "Mom says he's driving the nurses crazy."

"Anybody else here yet?" She dropped her keys behind the bar.

He didn't look up. "Flynn's out back approving the fish. Last I checked, Chip was chopping vegetables."

The *tap tap tap* of knife hitting cutting board confirmed his words. Sid poured herself a soda and waited to see if her new coworker would put down the menu and actually talk to her. He'd ignored her long enough. If they were going to work together, that stopped now.

"Pretty sure the menu hasn't changed in five years." Leaving her glass on the bar, she started lowering the chairs.

"So I see." He finally glanced her way. "Is that what you're wearing?"

Sid looked down. "What's wrong with this?"

He tucked the menu under his arm. "Your shirt says 'Mechanics Do It With Lube.'"

His shirt should have said *Captain Obvious.* "Yeah. So?"

"So you're dealing with customers and that shirt is inappropriate. This is a family restaurant."

Sid slammed a chair onto all fours and crossed the space between them, stopping just under Lucas's nose. "Let me make this clear. I'll wear whatever the fuck I want to wear, and not you or anyone else is going to tell me I can't. I've worked in here for years and your dad has never had a problem with my wardrobe." She eyed him up and down. "At least I'm not dressed like a pansy."

He took a seat. "While I'm in charge of this business, I'll decide what is and is not appropriate. And there will be no dropping of F-bombs in front of the customers."

If he kept this up, she would have no problem pretending *not* to have feelings for him.

"You may be used to calling the shots in your other life, the boring one, but I've told you once, you're not in charge of me. We both know you need me. If I walk out of here right now, not only are you screwed, but your mother will snatch a knot in your ass as soon as she hears. So I suggest you take your *appropriate* speech and shove it."

Satisfied she'd made her point, Sid did a one-eighty and headed back to the chairs. Inappropriate. She'd show him inappropriate.

"A little old for this rebel teen act, don't you think?"

She froze, chair in midair. The man wanted to die. That was the only logical explanation. With great effort, she returned the chair gently to the table, then casually strolled back to the bar. Jaw locked, she climbed onto a stool, leaving an empty seat between them. For *his* safety.

"You've got some alpha thing going on. I get it. If playing captain gets you through the day, that's fine. If you need to do the man act to make up for shortcomings in other areas, go for it. But I've spent my entire life dealing with guys like you. And I can give just as good as I get." She leaned forward, dropping a hand onto his knee. The hazel eyes darkened, but he didn't move. Sid ignored the shot of heat that raced up her arm. "We've got six weeks. You want to make this a pissing contest, give it your best shot."

He leaned so close, she could feel his breath on her lips. "Move your hand a little higher, and you'll know there are no shortcomings here."

Sid jerked back, the heat from his body still imprinted on her hand. Her heart beat double time, and she feared he'd see how tempted she was.

"You wish, pretty boy." Desperate for distance, she all but ran to the farthest tables and started dropping chairs two at a time. How did he manage to piss her off and still make her want to jump his bones? Jerk.

The noise of tables scraping the floor mixed with the blood raging in her head meant Sid didn't hear Lucas come up behind her until he whispered against her ear. "You just lost round one. I'll expect more of a fight in round two."

Sid suppressed the urge to swing a chair in his direction. Arrogant jackass. He wanted a fight, he'd damn well get one. On her terms. By the time he'd lowered two chairs from the next table over, she had a plan.

Keeping her voice casual, she said, "Why don't you put your money where your mouth is?"

Four legs hit hardwood. "What did you have in mind?"

"Tips."

The corner of his mouth turned up in a grin that made her toes curl. "I could show you some moves, but I never mix money and sex."

"How about you stop thinking with your dick for a minute." That wiped the grin off his face. "Fifty dollars says I can earn more tips than you can. You up to the challenge?"

He leaned on the chair and rubbed his chin. "Fifty dollars and all I have to do is make more tips than you? That's too easy."

"A hundred." She could take him and earn an extra hundred for the garage fund.

"What kind of a man would take a hundred dollars from a lady?"

"You see any ladies around here, twinkletoes?"

He nodded. "Good point. Okay, I'm in. Joe and Beth will be here by six. We cut off tips at five thirty and start counting." He headed toward the kitchen. "Then you can pay up."

"Where are you going?" she asked.

"To grab one of the big pickle jars. I'm going to need it to store all my tips."

As he disappeared into the kitchen, Sid dropped another chair and mumbled, "Not if I shove that jar up your nose."

CHAPTER FOUR

Lucas prided himself on being in shape. He ran three to five miles every day. Took the stairs at work. Ate his vegetables and took his vitamins. But he'd never been as tired as he was by three o'clock that afternoon.

No wonder his dad had a heart attack. Running this bar for a day had Lucas ready to cry uncle. By the end of the week, he'd be in traction.

Sid hadn't even broken a sweat and she'd been covering a third of the floor. Much more ground than the small space behind the bar. Lucas didn't know what it was about the woman that made him say the stupid shit he had that morning. Some men might make a habit of inviting women to check out their package, but Lucas wasn't one of them.

Still, he couldn't say he regretted it. Not after seeing her reaction. Sid just begged to be teased, and heaven help him, Lucas enjoyed sparring with her. Maybe the next six weeks wouldn't be as awful as he'd first thought.

He figured she chose the station along the windows, which stayed full throughout the day thanks to a view of the water, to increase her earning potential. But traffic wasn't the key to this contest. Courtesy and charisma, two qualities Sid clearly lacked, would win him an easy victory.

Dollar bills filled Lucas's pickle jar to the halfway mark by mid-afternoon, but how much Sid had tucked in her apron was a mystery. His suggestion they count when the action slowed between lunch and the early dinner crowd resulted in her suggestion he take a flying leap.

The friendliest suggestion she'd made all day. Sid Navarro could make a sailor sound like a nun in comparison. If she hadn't been blessed with the tongue of a viper, the termagant might actually be attractive. Her dark hair was once again pulled up in a ponytail, and he'd caught that whiff of watermelon again. He'd never have pegged her for the fruity shampoo type, but that scent reminded him there was a woman beneath those shapeless clothes.

The T-shirt was obviously cut for a man, and the baggy shorts hit at knee level. The green high-top Converse should have made her look like a twelve-year-old boy, but the shapely olive-tone calves above them were unmistakably female.

The woman was a walking contradiction, leaving him torn between anger and unexpected arousal throughout the day. Pushing her buttons had quickly become addicting. Watching her every thought flit across her face, he had a feeling she didn't get flirted with often, since she had no idea how to flirt back. And though he could see she'd wanted to run every time he got close, she always held her ground and fired back.

In fact, arguing with Sid gave him the same rush as entering a courtroom. Both required a clear head and quick thinking. Both made him feel more alive. From what he'd seen so far, Sid would prove a formidable opponent.

"Jack and Coke, two sweet teas, and a Bud for table twelve. I got any appetizers up yet?" Sid asked, eyes on the stack of tickets in her hand. "Table ten is getting antsy."

"Nothing on the window right now," he replied.

Coffee-colored eyes met his. "You holding this shit up to mess with my tips?"

"Darling," he said, lifting his jar from under the counter. "As you can see, I don't need to cheat to win this little challenge."

"What I see is a lawyer talking out his ass," she mumbled, loud enough for him to hear but not the customer four stools down. "I'll expect those drinks and the appetizers ready when I come back." Sid grabbed a pitcher of tea and returned to the floor.

Talking out his ass. If she wasn't careful he'd make her wear the drinks when she came back.

"So you're the other Dempsey brother." Lucas turned toward the feminine voice carrying a hint of New England. "Not quite what I expected."

He didn't know what the slim brunette expected, but she didn't sound disappointed. He took that as a good sign. Extending a hand, he said, "Lucas Dempsey. And you are?"

"Will," she replied, tucking a strand of dark hair behind her ear as she slid her tall frame onto a bar stool.

"Not the name I'd expect with a face like that." He leaned onto the bar, ignoring the half-filled glass of tea he'd been pouring. "Tell me that's not short for Wilhelmina."

The woman gave a low chuckle and leaned in herself, bangle bracelets tapping mahogany. "Short for Willow. No one told me you were the charmer in the family. But then compared to Joe, a honey badger would seem charming."

A negative opinion of his brother. He liked her already. "Someone had to redeem the family name. What can I get you, Willow?"

"I'm headed to my next job, but I have time for a soda. Tom always adds a shot of cherry." She shifted on the bar stool. "Can you do that for me?"

"One cherry soda for the pretty lady." He was reaching for a glass when Sid slapped her tray on the bar.

"Where are my drinks?"

"You'll have them in a second. I'm helping a customer here." Lucas smiled at Willow, who was facing Sid.

"Hey," Willow said, "Beth mentioned you'd be covering here for a while. Must be better than baiting hooks all day."

"You two know each other?" Lucas asked.

"Will lives on the island," Sid said. "And she tends bar better than you do. Cut the kissy face and get me my drinks."

Lucas slid the cherry Coke to Willow, then wiped his hands on his towel to keep from wrapping them around Sid's throat. "Keep your pants on, sweet cheeks. I'm working on them."

"Order up!" came a voice through the service window.

"That's your appetizers." Lucas dropped the stuffed mushrooms and fried cheese sticks on Sid's tray. "Take those out. I'll have the drinks ready when you swing back around."

"Add two Millers and two diets for table fifteen. And don't call me sweet cheeks again unless you want to lose the ability to reproduce."

Sid stomped off and he turned back to his new friend. "She's a breath of fresh air, isn't she? Where were we?"

Willow stared back, wide-eyed. "She must really like you. Nobody would ever call Sid a name like that and live to tell the tale."

"I'm pretty sure she hates me, but I'm not taking it personally." *Trying not to anyway.* "So where do you tend bar?"

"O'Hagan's," she said, looking over her shoulder. "You two know each other well?"

"Who, me and Sid?" He shrugged. "Not really. I mean I've known her since high school, but we never ran in the same circles. How long have you been on Anchor?"

"Little less than a year." Willow took a drink, then glanced over her shoulder again. She seemed oddly nervous about something. Before he could ask, she said, "Sid's coming back."

Maybe there was something up between the two women. Sid was throwing so much animosity his way, he couldn't tell if some of the current irritation might be aimed at the tall brunette or not.

"You brewing the damn beers back there?" Sid asked. "What the hell?"

"Relax. I just have to pop the tops off the Millers and you're good to go." Lucas snagged two bottles from the next beer cooler down, then caught a look between the ladies on his way back.

"Dude," Willow was saying, "you should have told me."

"Tell you what?" Sid replied, piling the drinks on her tray. Lucas took his time with the bottle caps, pretending he wasn't listening. "I bet I could outearn him in tips so he's holding up my orders on purpose." Raising her voice, she added, "You'd suck as a PI, Dempsey. Get your ass down here and give me those beers."

"You two have a bet going?" Will asked.

Lucas put the beers on the tray. "Her idea. Fifty bucks she could earn more than I can."

"A hundred."

"Right, a hundred." Lucas shot Will his best smile. "At this rate she'll be lucky if she makes the fifty."

The look Sid sent his way should have put him on life support. "Shift's not over yet, fancy pants."

"We'll see," he said.

"I know how you can win," Will said.

Sid and Lucas gave her their full attention. Sid asked first. "You talking to me or him?"

Will snorted. "As if I'd help him." He raised a brow and she added, "You're cute and all, but she's my friend."

"I didn't realize the banshee had any friends."

"You're lucky there's a bar between us." Sid dropped an order pad into her apron pocket and leaned toward Will. "So how?"

"Easy," Will shrugged. "Take off your shirt."

"Take off my what?" Sid blinked, certain she'd heard wrong.

"I'll second that suggestion," Lucas said, his solid brows wiggling over dancing green eyes.

"Shut up, preppy."

"You're wearing a tank underneath there, right?" Will said. "I can see the white at the bottom."

Sid tugged at the hem of her tee. "I always wear a tank. So?"

Will rolled her eyes. "So take off that T-shirt that's two sizes too big and I guarantee your tips will triple."

"You're crazy. I'm not stripping just to win a bet."

"No one's suggesting you go topless." Will backed off her stool. "That night you got dressed up at O'Hagan's got me more tips in one night than I normally make in a weekend. Might as well use those curves to help yourself."

"There are curves under there?" Lucas tossed a bar rag over his shoulder. "I'll believe it when I see it."

Something took flight in Sid's gut and an unfamiliar heat shot up from her toes. She couldn't fight the blush so she reached for something familiar to cover. Anger.

"What happened to this being a family restaurant, huh? A few hours ago you were worried this shirt would offend someone. Now you want me to take it off."

"Hey," he said, throwing up his hands, "if you're ashamed of whatever you keep under those manly clothes, just keep the shirt on."

Lucas shoved a chilled glass under the beer tap but the sideways look he gave her said he knew exactly what he was doing. Damn him.

"Fine." She turned on Will. "But if this doesn't work, I'm coming after you."

"It'll work. Just don't break any noses when guys start hitting on you." Will turned to Lucas. "Thanks for the drink, Charming. I'd apologize for the killing you're about to receive, but I have a feeling you'll thank me later."

With a wink she was gone, leaving Sid to wonder what the hell that meant.

"You've got customers waiting." Lucas poured Will's soda down the sink and dropped the glass in the strainer. "If you're going to strip, get it over with and get back on the floor."

Maybe she could stuff her shirt down his throat. "I'll be right back."

Sid ducked into the kitchen and headed for the office in the back. She took three deep breaths and recalled the memory of that night at O'Hagan's when Beth had cleaned her up. Or girlified her, as Joe had deemed it. She could do this. What was the big deal?

Before losing her nerve, she ripped the black tee over her head and dropped it on the chair. Too bad the office didn't have a mirror. No way would she run to the bathroom to check her reflection. A quick glance down revealed no obvious stains, and the light pink of her bra didn't show through. Much.

Another deep breath. *Time to pull in some tips.*

Sid shot for casual as she cruised through the kitchen. As she rounded the end of the counter, she heard Chip holler and turned to see him stick his thumb in his mouth.

"You all right?"

"Uh muh," he nodded, eyes wide and cheeks red.

"Did you cut yourself?"

"Gob distwacted."

Sid nodded. "Um, okay." Tucking a stray lock behind her ear, she stepped toward the kitchen doorway, only to hear a pan drop behind her. Turning, she found Flynn staring as if he'd seen a ghost. "You didn't cut yourself too, did you?"

Flynn's Adam's apple bobbed as he grabbed a frying pan off the floor. He had to reach for it three times before catching the handle, since his eyes stayed on Sid.

"What?" she asked, throwing a hand on her hip.

"It's just . . ." Flynn shook his head and continued to stare.

"Forget it," Sid said, preferring the chaos on the floor to that in the kitchen. Maybe the guys were sneaking the liquor. She'd have to ask Patty if they did that. Didn't seem like a good idea while working around fire and sharp objects.

She exited the kitchen to find one of the other waitresses at the side of the bar sorting her tickets. Tall and blonde with the body of a devout surfer and the tan to match, Daisy stood more than a head above Sid, but then everyone beat Sid in height. Her increased attitude made up for being vertically challenged.

Sid noticed her tray was empty.

"Where are my drinks?"

"Lucas had me deliver them. Natives were getting restless." Daisy looked up. "I thought you were . . ."

"Thought I was what?"

"On a break." Daisy stuffed the tickets in her apron and pulled a tray from beneath her arm. "I'm glad Mitch isn't working today."

Mitch being Daisy's boyfriend, it seemed as if she'd have wanted him around. The waitress disappeared into the crowd without another word, leaving the mystery hanging. Sid shrugged and reached for her tray.

"Weird."

Lucas was at the other end of the bar serving customers. She went back to the floor without the satisfaction of ripping his head off for making her look bad. Natives getting restless. Whatever. Charging over to the windows, she checked on the table where Daisy had delivered the drinks.

"Sorry for the holdup, folks. Did everyone get what they wanted?"

Two women occupied the left bench while two guys in ball caps held down the right. The guy on the end wore his hat backwards and his chin looked like the home of a Chia Pet. More clean-cut, guy two looked to be hiding a unibrow under his low-pulled cap, with sunglasses perched over the bill.

They looked the type to chest bump while watching football. Both stared at Sid in silence, while the woman across from Chia smacked her neighbor, who looked up from sipping her drink. The smackee didn't look a day over nineteen. Sid would have carded her if she'd asked for anything stronger than soda.

Young thing's straw danced between cubes as she dropped her glass to the table. Chia and shades sunk into their seats like someone had let the air out of the cushions. "We've got everything we could ask for now," said one of the men. A thud came from under the table. "Ow!"

"Okay then." Either these guys were lightweights who got a buzz off half a glass, or something weird was going around this restaurant. "Ready to place your order?"

Frat boys looked smacked dumb, so she turned to the women. Chia's girl spoke up. "We're ready."

Sid waited, pen poised. Another thud and the guy closest to the window jerked upright. "We'll each have the Dempsey All American with fries on the side for her," he waved a hand toward the woman sitting across from him, "and onion rings for me."

Sid dropped her hands to her hips. "Is that your girlfriend?" she asked.

"Yes, I am," the woman answered for him.

"And he ordered for you like that? Dude. You should kick him again."

"Hey."

"I should." Another thud.

"Stop that, damn it."

Sid tsked. "Not the way to talk to a lady." She turned to the other man. "I bet you can do better. What will it be, scruffy?"

He scooted his legs outside the booth before ordering. "Meagan will have the grilled chicken salad with dressing on the side and I'll take the cheeseburger." Girlfriend lifted a brow and he added, "Please."

"That's the way to do it. Two All Americans, fries and onion rings, grilled chicken salad, dressing on the side." She lifted her pen. "What kind of dressing?"

"Ranch."

"Got it." Sid pointed the pen at Scruffy. "And you're the cheeseburger. Fries good with that?"

"Yes, ma'am."

"Then we're all set." Collecting the menus, Sid leaned close to the brunette. "Just my observation, but you two could do better."

The woman's blue eyes widened, then she grinned.

Before the first customers had rolled in, Daisy told Sid that if the female customers were happy, then everybody's happy. Since the frat boys didn't look like big tippers, this table seemed like the right place to test that strategy.

"I'll put the orders in, then come check on you for refills." Sid tucked the menus under her arm and moved to the next table over. This one held a family of four—mom, dad, boy, and girl—but the mom and girl had disappeared. "How we doing over here? Are the ladies going to need refills?"

A towheaded boy, maybe six years old, looked up from the Matchbox car he'd been pushing around his plate. When he caught sight of Sid, the car zoomed off the table. "You look like the ladies on daddy's secret calendar."

Daddy choked on his tongue and covered the little guy's mouth. Thanks to a receding hairline, the blush covered his entire head. "Yes, we'll take drinks all around if you don't mind."

"Don't mind at all." Sid winked at the little boy. "That's not a dog calendar, is it?"

Munchkin shook his head.

"Good. Be right back with the drinks."

Weaving through the tables, she reached the bar and found Lucas back at her end filling a beer from the tap. "You shouldn't have sent Daisy out with those drinks. I wasn't gone that long."

Lucas looked up and froze, the beer still pouring.

"Not you, too," she said. "Did someone spray brain fog in here while I was back in the office?"

"You took your shirt off." The beer flowed.

"That *is* why I went back there."

Beer reached the top of the glass and spilled over, drenching his hand. "Shit." Lucas cut off the tap and set the glass in the sink. Pulling the rag off his shoulder, he wiped his hands. "You look . . . different."

Sid looked down. Nothing looked different from that angle. "Did I grow a third eye?"

"No, but you grew something." Lucas huffed, pacing the two feet to the back counter, then back to the bar. "That's what you hide under those T-shirts?"

"You act like I'm wearing a sidearm. They're tits, Dempsey. Every woman has them."

"Not like those they don't."

Daisy stepped up next to Sid. "Look," Sid said. She stood close to the other waitress for comparison, ignoring the fact the blonde's boobs were at her eye level. "She has them too. In fact," she waved an arm in the air, "this place is crawling with the things."

"I hope we're talking about eyebrows," said Daisy, "or this would be weird."

Sid snagged the pitchers of sweet tea and soda. "We're talking about boobs. Dempsey here's never seen any before."

"I've seen plenty," he argued, but Sid kept walking.

CHAPTER FIVE

S id considered pouring the pitchers over her own head. The heat in Lucas's eyes had loosened up her gut and sent currents shooting through her limbs. Felt like when she used a drill too long and the vibrations skittered along her skin even after she'd turned it off.

The night Beth had dolled her up, Sid had felt like a girl for the first time in years. Maybe ever. But the look she'd just gotten from Lucas made her feel like a woman. Something new and freaky and unexpected. In a good way. Kind of.

"Who needed the refills?" she asked, returning to the little boy's table. The mother and daughter had returned. The dad kept his eyes on his plate.

"I'll take one, but no more for the kids, thanks," said the mom.

"She's our calendar girl," the little boy said, smiling to reveal a gaping hole where a tooth used to be. "Ain't she, Dad?"

"Our what?" the mother asked.

"Nothing, dear." The dad wrapped an arm around the boy's head, tucking him into his side. The move looked more like an attempt to suffocate the kidlet than hug him. "Could we get the check, please?"

"But mom said we could have cherry pie for dessert and we haven't even ordered that yet." The girl looked slightly older than her brother and sported the same toothless grin. Sid wondered if they'd knocked them out for each other the way Randy had once knocked hers out during a wrestling match.

He'd panicked at the sight of blood, giving Sid the chance to pin him the required three seconds and claim victory.

"One piece of pie for each?" she asked the mom.

Headband askew on her short brown hair, the woman looked from one child to the other. "One piece and they can split it."

"Aw, Mom," echoed in stereo.

"One piece of cherry with two forks on the way." Sid glanced over to the dad, who looked ready to bolt. "And I'll bring the check."

Spotting new customers filing into an empty booth in her section, Sid decided to get their drink orders before hitting the kitchen for the pie. Though she'd never admit it, she kind of liked being called a calendar girl.

～

Lucas had never been punched before, but seeing Sid standing there looking like a goddess in white cotton and hints of pink lace knocked the wind out of him. The one or two times he'd seen her smile had sent him back a step, but the full blast of that body about put him on his ass.

How the hell could anyone hide all that? From the smooth, olive shoulders to the trim waist and sultry curve of her hips. And the breasts were perfection, especially in that lacy number clearly visible beneath the white cotton of the tank. The designer of that garment deserved an award.

And that begged another question. What was Sid doing wearing a girlie number like that?

Lucas decided there needed to be a law against Sid Navarro ever wearing anything baggy. Ever. Maybe he could file the papers to add a statute to the island bylaws. Gather a petition if necessary. Every male on Anchor would sign.

For the two hours following what he now thought of as the big reveal, Sid barked out drink orders and he filled them. No casual banter. No snide insults. No harmless teasing. Something had changed between them. As if a switch were thrown and a cloud of sexual tension fogged up his brain.

He'd like to think the same cloud fogged Sid's brain, but then he hadn't taken anything off (something he'd be willing to correct) and her face gave nothing away. The woman was operating like a robot. No facial expression, unless you counted that crease between her brows and stubborn set of her chin to be a facial expression.

"Looks like the place is still standing. That's a good sign," said Joe, joining Lucas behind the bar. "Everything go okay?"

Lucas was tempted to say no, then demand to know why Joe hadn't warned him about Sid and her best-kept secret. Or secrets, in this case. But then Joe wouldn't notice a glacier unless it landed on his boat. He never did have much of a radar for hot women. Until Lucas had put his fiancée in Joe's path. Then the radar zoomed right in.

"What'd you think, that I'd ruin the business in one day?"

"Forget I asked." Joe dropped his keys in a drawer below the register. "Let me grab some rags, then I'll take over so you can count your drawer."

A simple "thanks" should have been his response. Instead Lucas said, "You do that." Six weeks of acting like a douche was not in his plans, but he needed another day or two to adjust his attitude. He'd prefer to make the adjustment himself rather than force Joe to take matters into his own hands.

Lucas had been ready for a brawl six weeks ago, but that night he'd been running on anger and hurt. Both emotions remained, but neither would be quelled with his fists. The fact Joe worked out with a punching bag on a regular basis put the odds squarely in his brother's favor anyway. Lucas preferred litigation over pugilism.

"I'm heading to the office to count my tips," Sid said, dropping her tray with the other spares under the bar. "I'll take your jar with me so you can't add to it while I'm gone."

"You don't trust me?" Lucas asked, struggling to keep his eyes above her neck.

"You're a lawyer."

"And you're a mechanic."

"So what?"

"So mechanics are notorious for telling people they need shit fixed when they don't." The line between Sid's eyes deepened at his words. "If we're going by occupation, you're more likely to cheat."

"You piece of sh—"

"Hey guys," Beth said, stepping between them. "How did it go today?"

Lucas raised his brows at Sid, giving her the chance to answer first.

"Fine," Sid said, making it sound like a totally different four-letter word.

Beth glanced his way as if waiting for his agreement. He nodded. Whatever war waged between him and Sid was their own business.

"Good." Beth returned her eyes to Sid and must have noticed the steam coming out of her ears. "Are you sure? This feels a little . . . tense."

"I'm not tense. Are you tense, Sid?" He'd probably regret pushing her, but Lucas couldn't help himself. Sid was gorgeous with a smile, but sexier than hell when pissed off. Right now, she looked hot enough to burn the place down.

God knew his own smoke alarms were going off.

"You're picking up on pretty boy's nerves is all." Sid removed her pocketed apron, careful not to spill the contents. "We have a little bet going that I could outearn him in tips. He's about to lose, which has his fragile ego all atwitter."

She had him atwitter all right. But not his ego. "I suggest we have Beth count the money. Not that we don't trust each other or anything." Lucas leaned on the bar. "But an unbiased third party never hurts."

Through pinched lips, Sid agreed. "Everything I made is in here," she said, handing the apron to Beth. "I'll get Annie caught up on my stations while you count."

≈

Ten minutes later, Beth strolled out of the office carrying two ziplock bags full of money. One looked more full than the other, but Sid couldn't be sure whose was whose.

"This one goes to Sid," Beth announced, dropping the bags before their respective owners and looking up at Lucas. "She outearned you by more than a hundred dollars."

"There's no way."

Sweet victory. Sid considered being gracious about the win, but where was the fun in that? "Pay up, sucker," she said, a satisfied grin on her lips, hand out expectantly.

He crossed his arms, emphasizing those damn muscles. Keeping hazel eyes locked on Sid, he asked Beth, "How much do I have in there?"

Beth pulled a piece of paper from her pocket. "One hundred thirty-eight dollars and twenty-three cents."

Without a word, he hoisted the bag off the bar and hurled it at Sid's head. She caught it three inches from her nose. "You expect me to count out the hundred myself?"

"Nope," he said, spinning his register keys on one finger. "Take it all. Consider it a bonus for our first day together."

Another one-forty on top of her earnings on the day would add a nice chunk to the garage fund. But instead of feeling satisfied about taking his money, she felt guilty. Why couldn't he have been smug or demanded a recount? Instead, he'd been the gracious one.

Such a jerk.

"If you're going to be that way, you can keep it." Sid threw the bag back, but he returned it as if they were playing a game of hot potato. She kept the game going, throwing it back, harder this time. "I said forget it."

The bag headed for her forehead. "You won fair and square," he said.

She returned it. "We weren't playing for all or nothing."

He sent it back. "What's forty dollars either way? Just take it."

Forty dollars meant half a day closer to her garage but hell if she'd let him know that. She sent the bag sailing through the air again, but this time Joe caught it.

"That's enough," Joe said, then looked at Beth. "Open Sid's bag." Beth did so and they all stood motionless as Joe emptied Lucas's tips in with hers. "Now," he said, shoving the bag into Sid's hand. "Take the damn money and get the hell out of here. Both of you. We have a restaurant to run."

Joe stormed off, leaving the three of them in stunned silence. Then Beth turned to Sid and whispered too quietly for Lucas to hear, "He's going to make such a good dad."

Sid turned raised brows on Beth. Had she missed a memo?

"Someday!" Beth exclaimed. "I mean someday. Not anytime soon. Sheesh. Don't even joke about stuff like that."

"Stuff like what?" Lucas asked.

"Nothing," Sid said. She didn't have to be a psychiatrist to know the subject of Joe and Beth having kids would not sit well with Lucas. At least not yet.

"Guess I'd better go." Sid tucked her tips and winnings under an arm, then grabbed her own keys. The thought of Lucas walking home intensified the guilt she already felt for taking his money. Not that the man needed more money. He drove a BMW for Christ's sake. But still. "You want a ride?"

Lucas didn't answer right away. His eyes locked on her face for several seconds, then dropped to the floor as if he were contemplating a difficult puzzle.

Sid held her breath, wondering why she'd offered when the man seemed determined to keep her pissed off at all times. Admitting she wanted to be near him regardless was out of the question.

His eyes met hers again. "I'll pass, thanks."

A sound rejection. Twice in twenty-four hours. Lesson learned.

Lucas nodded a silent good-bye and walked away without looking back. As Sid took the same path, Beth whispered two words. "Be patient." Sid ignored her.

∼

Being around Joe and Beth should have been the toughest part about this extended visit to his island home. If anyone had asked him a week ago, Lucas would have said so without hesitation. Now he was starting to wonder.

From the moment he'd looked up from the bar to find a goddess with attitude ready to do battle, the only thing he could think about was how hot Sid would be in bed. No trouble figuring out which head that thought came from, which is why the upstairs brain needed to take over.

Sleeping with Sid would be bad. Okay, that wasn't true. Sleeping with Sid would be amazing, and likely test his endurance and blood pressure. Getting involved with Sid would be the bad part. Sid belonged to Anchor, and one look in those melted caramel eyes told him she was the noncasual type. Her reaction to both his brief brush of her hair during the ride from the hospital and his offhanded flirting that morning revealed an innocent vulnerability he hadn't expected.

She may act tough, but Lucas was certain Sid didn't play games or take sex lightly. Two qualities he found refreshing, considering the people with whom he associated on a regular basis were almost always working an angle and willing to play whatever role necessary to get what they wanted.

Bottom line, Sid Navarro was his temporary coworker and nothing more, regardless of how tempting she might be. With that settled, Lucas rounded the corner onto Old Beach Road feeling as if he'd just solved a difficult life problem and come to a wise decision.

Clearing a set of trees, he spotted Artie sitting on a bench in the shade.

"How was the first day at the new office?" the older man asked.

"Tiring," he said, stepping into the trees. "We have to stop meeting like this, Artie."

"Take a load off." Artie tapped the seat beside him. "And you found me this time." Rufus barked as if backing up his owner.

"Right. Is this what you do in retirement?" Lucas asked, taking the offered seat. "Wander around and occasionally occupy shade-covered benches?"

"Just about." Artie flashed the smile of the unencumbered and Lucas felt a twinge of jealousy. Which made no sense at all since doing nothing had never appealed to Lucas before.

"Don't you miss it?" he asked, enjoying the relief of getting off his feet.

"What, the law?" Artie shook his head, his wattle swaying with the movement. "Nah. Feeling needed. That I miss." Rufus plopped his head onto Artie's knee and the man gave him a loving pat. "You feel needed up there in Richmond?" he asked, the question taking Lucas by surprise.

His first reaction, to say yes, was drowned by a voice whispering *They barely notice you're gone,* making him rethink his answer. Every case he worked included an entire team of lawyers. He flattered himself thinking he was the best of the pack, but no one had even called for input since his leave started.

That didn't mean anything. Maybe they'd been told not to bother him.

"I do a good job."

Artie chuckled. "That's not what I asked."

Lucas shrugged, uncomfortable with the topic. "Every defendant needs a lawyer, right? So I'm needed."

"They don't necessarily need a lawyer, they're just entitled to one. And I've never figured you for the type to be one of many."

"I'm making something of myself up there. My name will be on the door someday. Someday soon," he added.

"Ah, yes. But one name among many."

"It's been a long day." Lucas rose from the bench, ignoring the protest from his feet. "I'd better get going. I need to get to the hospital before visiting hours are over."

"By all means, don't let me hold you up. Tell Tom we're all thinking about him." Artie leaned an arm across the back of the bench, shifting his center bulk. "About the feet? Epsom salts and hot water. Takes the sting out."

Lucas nodded and continued on his way.

One of many.

That just meant he'd risen over many to get to the top. Nothing wrong with that, he told himself, ignoring the doubts his former mentor had just planted.

CHAPTER SIX

Sid parked her truck outside the abandoned brick building at eight the next morning. Old Man Fisher's Cadillac blocked the garage door so she knew he was inside. The codger had been giving her grief about not having the down payment ready, but this time she had better news.

The funds weren't in place—yet—but if she pulled in the same tips for the next six weeks as she had the day before, the goal would be hit by Labor Day, one month before Fisher's latest deadline.

He'd been pushing back the deadline since the spring, always with the demand that this was the last time. They both knew no one else was interested in this piece of property. Too close to the water. Too far from the main strip. Too old to be of interest to tourists, and too run down for anyone to see its true potential.

But Sid could see it. Her dream would come to life inside these old bricks. All she needed was Fisher to be a little more patient, and the tips to keep rolling in.

"About time you got here. I've been standing around for thirty minutes."

Sid sighed. These meetings were always a test. If she were her usual, go-fuck-yourself self, Fisher would have turned her down without a second thought. The property had been empty for five years and she knew he'd leave it empty for five more just to spite her if she called him on his bullshit.

"You said eight o'clock. I'm right on time." Not giving him a chance to argue, Sid charged through the faded front door into the dank interior. Hot air encased her like a wet blanket as she checked for damage from the last rainfall. All cobwebs remained in place. No puddles beneath the windows.

Storm weathered, like she knew it would. The building had been standing for nearly eighty years, through countless hurricanes and storms, and would endure another eighty years to come. With her name on the door.

"You got the money together yet?" Fisher brushed a sleeve against the doorjamb, then pulled back as if frightened of a little dirt. "Or did you bring me out here for nothing?"

"Good news on that front," Sid said.

"Better be," said Fisher, his furrowed brow sending wrinkles into his receding hairline like waves chasing the sand.

Sid was too happy to be put off by the attitude. "You gave me until October first, but thanks to a new opportunity, I should have the full down payment by Labor Day. That's almost a month early."

"Who said October first?" Fisher pushed his glasses up his bulbous nose and stuck out his bottom lip. Why did everything have to be an argument?

"You did. The last time we talked. And it doesn't matter because I'm going to have the money the first week of September."

Pulling a handkerchief from the pocket of his gray polyester pants, Fisher mopped his forehead. "I don't remember anything about October."

"Are you listening to me?" Sid asked, struggling to control her temper. "I'm going to have the money."

"You've been saying that since the first of the year. I'll believe it when I see it." Exiting the building, he added, "But don't expect me to wait forever. I've got others looking at this place too."

Sid had been dealing with Fisher long enough to recognize a bluff when she saw one. "Six weeks, Mr. Fisher. Six weeks and this will be a done deal." She trailed behind him, using the sleeve of her West Marine T-shirt to catch the sweat running down her cheek. "I'll have the money and you won't have to deal with this place anymore."

"Like I said," he opened his car door, "I'll believe it when I have the check in my hand. And don't go assuming I can't find another buyer."

Sid grabbed the door handle as Fisher plunked onto the leather seat. "Mr. Fisher." She waited until he met her gaze. "Six weeks. I swear. Just give me six weeks."

The man smacked his chops like a cow chewing cud, then conceded. "I've waited this long, haven't I? I make no promises, that's all I'll say." With that, he tugged the door from her grasp and started the engine.

Doubt crept into her brain as Sid watched him drive away. No one else had even glanced at this property in years. Fisher had to be bluffing. If there'd been another offer on the table, he'd have told her right then to forget about it. But he hadn't.

Turning back to the garage, she pictured how the building would look when she was done with it. New paint around the windows. Pressure-washed red bricks gleaming in the sun. A new garage door with the words Navarro Boat Repair & Restoration in bold black letters.

Six weeks. That's all she needed.

~

For the first time in three years, Lucas skipped his morning run. His body refused to get out of bed, and since he needed his body to perform the exercise, the run was a no-go. As it was, he had to negotiate a deal to make his body move in time for a shower before work. Where he'd find a rocking Key lime pie, Lucas didn't know. But his body took the bribe, which put him at the restaurant less than five minutes before Sid.

Sporting her now familiar ponytail, Sid charged through the door the way a boxer enters the ring. She seemed to wake up every day ready to take on the world. But there were moments, when she didn't think anyone was watching, that she dropped her guard. In those brief lapses, Lucas caught a glimpse of the woman behind the act.

The snarl would slide into a sexy grin. The brows relaxed and the normally challenging eyes softened. Lightened. Her body shifted to a casual stance, one hip kicked out giving the impression of soft curves beneath loose-fitting denim.

Lucas made a note to add an amendment to the new bylaw. Sid not only was not permitted to wear oversized shirts, she must wear form-fitting jeans or nothing at all.

The thought of nothing at all threatened to drain the blood from his brain, and a new fantasy developed in his mind. Ebony curls dropping onto olive shoulders. Full breasts covered in lace peeking through a satin robe.

"You smoke something before coming in?"

Lucas shook the erotic scene from his mind. Why the hell was he fantasizing over something he'd never get near? Stupid ass. He went for a blank expression, but knew it was a long shot.

"I'm fine. Why?" He busied himself wiping down the clean bar.

"Because your eyes glazed over and you got a dopey grin on your face." Sid lowered the last chair, then took a seat on a bar stool. "Same challenge as yesterday?"

"I don't think so."

"Why?" She actually looked petulant. His chest tightened, as did something lower.

"Your tips are your tips and my tips are mine." No way would he give her another reason to skim down to a tank top. His lower half didn't like the decision, but his brain was still in charge. For now. "You need a challenge, find a new one."

Sid huffed, turned her back to the bar, and glanced around the room. Then she spun back. "Pool."

"What about it?" Lucas asked, stacking beer glasses.

"Bet I can take you before it's time to open."

Despite himself, Lucas was tempted. He'd grown up in that poolroom, had snookered his fair share of money from the regulars over the years. Probably wasn't fair to take her on, but then she hadn't played fair the day before.

And playing pool wouldn't involve taking off articles of clothing. Unless they played strip pool. Then they could find out how much weight those tables could hold.

A glass slipped from his hand, nearly sending a row to the floor.

"You need help back there?"

The glasses saved, Lucas mentally scolded himself. There would be no strip pool or climbing on pool tables with Sid Navarro. Not today. Not ever.

"So what do you say?" His current temptation hopped off her stool. "I'll rack 'em. How much you want to play for?"

Lucas dropped his rag on the bar and headed for the poolroom. He could win back the money she'd taken from him yesterday, but that would be cruel. "Twenty-five."

"I was thinking fifty," she said, swiping a cue off the wall. "You got some quarters?"

He slid three coins in the slots. The rumble of balls rolling out of the table echoed in the empty room. Seemed weird playing in silence. "Hey," he said. When Sid turned he tossed two more quarters her way. She caught both. "Put something on the jukebox. I'll rack 'em."

"I can do that." Sid crossed to the jukebox in the corner. "Is it fifty then?"

"Twenty-five."

"Fine," she conceded with little enthusiasm. He heard two buttons being pressed, then a smooth male voice filled the room.

"Is that that Bubble guy?" Lucas asked.

"It's pronounced *Boo-blay*. And yeah. I like this song."

The song choice took him by surprise. He figured Sid for Metallica maybe. Old standards, never. "I know how to say it. I was just teasing. Mr. Bublé isn't what I expected from you." Lucas stepped back from the table. "Let's get this going. You break."

"What did you expect?" Sid asked, before striking the cue ball and dropping four balls into various pockets. "Three stripes and a solid. I'll take stripes."

"Of course you will," he said, settling on a stool. "I figured you for hard rock. Something loud and dark."

The ten ball dropped into a side pocket. The cue ball rolled up behind the fifteen.

Sid moved around for her next shot, putting herself between Lucas and the table. Chalking her stick, she shot him a look over her shoulder. "I can go that route, when I'm in the mood."

Replacing the chalk on the side, she bent over, giving him a clear view of prime posterior real estate. His brain nearly melted. The fifteen banked off the right rail, then dropped into the far corner pocket. She was down to two balls and he'd yet to take a shot.

Though losing didn't matter much so long as he could keep watching her. She moved with complete confidence. An air that made her seem taller. More potent. More desirable.

She must have every man on the island after her. A thought that made Lucas want to barricade the door, though he warred with the question of which side he'd be on.

She bent over again and the fourteen flew up the table, clipping the side of the pocket and remaining on the felt. "Damn it."

He took several seconds to realize it was his turn. "About time," Lucas said, his voice steadier than the rest of him. "Three in the side." The ball dropped and he moved to the next one. "One in the corner." A little bottom-right English and the ball dropped, sending the cue ball right where he'd intended. This game needed to end before he got any more ideas about his pint-sized opponent.

"I thought you'd be rusty," Sid said, leaning on her cue, a hand on her hip. "Why didn't you go for more money?"

"You may not think you're a lady, but I do. I told you yesterday, a gentleman doesn't take money from a lady."

"At this rate, you'll take twenty-five dollars."

"Five-six combination." He dropped the balls as called, but the cue got away from him. "I had to agree to something to shut you up. And you owe me for yesterday."

"Really?" The spitting Sid returned, as he knew she would. Keeping her angry meant keeping her at a distance. "I don't owe you shit from yesterday. I won that challenge fair and square."

Lucas sized up his next shot. He couldn't get the two in the corner without glancing the eight, which could send it into the side. The four wasn't any better. He'd have to float the cue down the table, away from her remaining balls.

"You won yesterday by using what I estimate to be two D cups, which I don't have. That qualifies as an unfair advantage." He looked her way and let his eyes linger somewhere just below her chin. "Not that I'm complaining."

A subtle shade of red crawled up her neck. He'd already vowed not to go there, so why was he being a jackass? To make up for the comment, he sailed the cue ball past the two, leaving her a perfect position on the eleven. "Your shot."

With stiff movements, Sid took her place behind the cue and dropped the eleven in the side. But she'd left herself a difficult shot on the fourteen. Lucas slid up next to her and bent over to see the line. "Go high left on the cue and you can make it."

Liquid caramel eyes locked on his, that now familiar line forming between her brows. She looked to the ball across the table, then back to Lucas. "High left?"

"High left."

He gave her room, moving out of her peripheral vision to avoid being a distraction. She suffered no lack of determination or skill. It seemed whatever Sid Navarro attempted, she did well. His new-found admiration had more to do with the person he was coming to know than the killer body she inhabited.

The fourteen careened across the table, dropping cleanly into the pocket. Sid gave a triumphant "Yes!" then turned for a high five. He complied, but something told him to hold on. They stood there next to the pool table, hand in hand, eyes locked. Sid licked her lips and Lucas nearly gave into the urge.

Instead he dropped her hand and sauntered to the other side of the table. "It's not over yet. You still have to make the eight ball."

Sid continued to look dazed for several seconds. Lucas gave her time to recover, since he needed a moment himself. This was only their second day together and he was already struggling to keep his hands off her. A complication he did not need.

"Right," she finally said, her voice low and unsure. She stared at the table while chalking her stick, presumably figuring out her shot, though Lucas saw her eyes dart in his direction more than once.

"I'd go for the side," he said, anxious to finish the game. He didn't give a shit about the money. He'd pay twenty-five hundred to break the spell she was weaving around him.

With a nod, Sid bent to take the shot. Lucas had replaced his cue on the wall before the ball dropped. "We need to open in five. I'll hand over your winnings this afternoon." Before she could respond, Lucas headed back to the bar.

CHAPTER SEVEN

What the hell had just happened? One minute they were bickering and trash talking like normal, then Lucas got all weird again. First, he'd insulted her, which would normally have pissed Sid off, but the way he'd looked at her, as if he wanted to pick her up and carry her off somewhere, screwed with her wiring and anger was trumped by lust.

Sid had wanted Lucas to notice her for years, but never believed he ever would. Maybe she'd been wrong. Just imagining the things *he* might be imagining sent heat to the tips of her ears. But if he was interested, why did he keep backing off?

Maybe he was just a sore loser. Except without his help, she never would have won. She'd underestimated his skill going in. If he'd gotten another turn, the game would have been over in seconds. Instead, he'd helped her win. A fact she'd never admit aloud, but true all the same.

This was why Sid didn't spend time with a lot of people. She sucked at figuring them out. Joe was a simple guy. He didn't say much, but when he did, the words were straightforward, easy to understand. No hidden meanings. No games.

When Lucas talked, he might as well have been speaking another language for all she understood him.

"Sid?" said Annie, dashing into the poolroom, short black hair dancing around her face.

"Yeah?"

"Lucas said to come get you. We're opening the doors."

Only then did Sid realize she was still holding the cue stick, standing next to the pool table like an idiot. "I'll be right out."

The rest of the day was a blur. Saturdays were always the busiest, especially the lunch crowd. Dempsey's was known throughout the Outer Banks for the best fish and chips in the mid-Atlantic, but the burgers ran a close second in popularity. Both featured special recipes concocted by Patty in the early days of the restaurant.

By the end of the day, Sid wanted only two things: a cold beer and a hot bath.

"Tough day?" Beth asked, coming up beside Sid as she counted her tips at the end of the bar.

"Why do you ask?"

"Because your ponytail is falling off the back of your head, and there's enough ketchup on your shirt to fill a couple bottles."

Sid looked down. "Gross." She grabbed a napkin and rubbed, but the red sauce had dried long ago. "It's not coming off."

Beth laughed. "Nearly every time I see you, you're covered in either fish slime or grease. But ketchup bothers you?"

"Shut up, Curly." Sid gave up on the condiment and yelled to Lucas, "Cash me out. I've got a hundred fifty in ones."

With the ring of a bell, Lucas opened the register and exchanged the money. "There you go." He turned to Beth. "Where's Joe?"

"In the bathroom. He should be right out." Tying an apron around her hips, Beth looked from Sid to Lucas, then asked, "No bets today?"

Sid had forgotten about the pool game. She considered telling Lucas to forget the twenty-five, then recalled her run-in with Old Man Fisher. Every little bit got her closer to that garage.

"Not on the tips," Lucas said, before Sid could answer. "But Sid smoked me in pool this morning. I still owe her twenty-five dollars."

"Forget it," Sid said, determined to be the bigger person this time. She'd made nearly as much in tips today as she had the day before. What was twenty-five more dollars?

"Nope, I always pay my debts." Lucas pulled a wallet from his back pocket and pushed the money her way. "Now we're even."

"How are you even?" Beth asked. "You've had two bets in two days and she's beat you both times."

"True." Lucas leveled hazel eyes Sid's way. "How about that ride?"

"Ride?"

"Home," he said. "Is the offer still open?"

She'd sworn the night before never to offer again, but Lucas didn't know that. And telling him he'd hurt her pride by turning her down twice would only make her sound pathetic. In truth, there was no reason to refuse. Except that being near him made her feel like she'd sucked in too many exhaust fumes, and trying to figure him out was like trying to read the directions on a new lift kit. In Japanese.

"No problem." Right. No problem. This playing it cool thing was going to put her in the loony bin.

In that moment, Joe strolled out of the kitchen. "You got a minute?" he asked Lucas.

"Sid was just about to drive me home."

"I can wait," Sid said, knowing Joe wouldn't ask unless he had something to say that needed saying. Far be it for her to cause a problem.

Lucas didn't look happy, but he followed Joe back into the kitchen.

"What's that about?" Sid asked Beth once the men were out of earshot.

"I'm not sure," Beth answered, chewing her bottom lip.

Since Joe and Beth seemed to share the same brain, Sid couldn't believe Beth didn't know what Joe had up his sleeve. "You think this could get ugly?"

"No," Beth said, fidgeting with her apron strings. "Joe wouldn't start something here, right? Of course not." She threw a bar rag over her shoulder. "I'd better cover these customers until they come back. You good? You look a little tired."

"Is that your way of saying I look like shit?"

Beth rolled her eyes as she filled a glass with ice. "Forget I asked, cranky ass. And if you want to get anywhere, you'll be a little nicer to Lucas."

"Who says I want to get anywhere?" Sid wanted to get somewhere with Lucas, but with her limited experience and his taste for fancy chicks, she'd need a road map and a body double.

"Listen to your fairy godmother for once and just try to be nice. Maybe you'll grow on him." Beth filled the glass with soda and grabbed another. With a smirk, she added, "Like a fungus."

Sid rolled her eyes. "Tell Lucas I'm waiting outside."

~

Lucas warred between curiosity and annoyance as he followed Joe into the back office. Curiosity won out, until worry kicked in. "Is this about Dad? Did something happen at the hospital? He was fine when I talked to Mom this morning."

"No, Dad's doing good, far as I know," Joe said, taking the chair behind the desk. Of course.

Lucas suppressed the eye roll. "Then what's this about?"

Joe exhaled while rubbing the back of his neck. He looked . . . uncomfortable.

"Was there a problem with the restaurant last night?" Lucas asked. "Everything was fine when I left, and my drawer came up perfect."

"This has nothing to do with the restaurant. I'm not sure how to say this."

Lucas took the chair on the other side of the desk and crossed an ankle over his knee. "You've never had any problem saying exactly what you think. I don't see why now should be any different."

"Right." But Joe stared at the desk as if the answer might be written there. "I know shit is still awkward between us. I want that to change."

Joe talking about his feelings? Lucas hadn't seen that coming.

"I do too, but it's going to take time. It's only been six weeks."

"I know." Joe sat up, leaning his elbows on the desk. "That's not very long."

"Depends on what you're talking about. Six weeks for Dad to recover from this heart attack is feeling like forever. When it's my future suddenly becoming your future, six weeks feels like six hours."

"Then why did you send me up to Richmond?" Joe asked, meeting Lucas's eyes for the first time since they'd entered the office. "You wanted me and Beth to be happy. Nobody set out to hurt you."

"Yeah, I know." Lucas ran a hand through his hair. "I'm mostly mad at myself for blowing it, though Beth tells me there was nothing to blow in the long run. It's not easy to hear your fiancée would have left you whether she fell for your brother or not."

Though he'd had this kind of conversation with Beth back when it all happened, Lucas had never called up Joe to hammer things out. He'd been more interested in hammering his brother into the ground at the time. Maybe they should have done this sooner.

"She's happy here," Joe said. "We're both happy. We owe that to you."

"Glad I could be of service." As soon as the words were out, Lucas regretted them. "Sorry. Bruised ego. Leads to a lot of scorch-and-burn comments like that."

"No problem." Joe picked up a pen and starting tapping it against the desk. "That's why this part is so hard."

"What part?" Lucas tried to imagine what could possibly make things worse.

Then Joe pulled a small black box from his pants pocket. A ring box. Holy shit.

"Is that—"

"My mom's ring. Dad gave it to me the day before we moved Beth's stuff down here." Joe spun the box between his fingers. "I think he expected me to propose before we shacked up."

The air in the room felt thicker and nonexistent at the same time. A knot formed in Lucas's stomach as if he'd just swallowed the paperweight on his desk back in Richmond. In the office where he should be right now. Where he'd be if his brother hadn't screwed up his life and turned him into an unfocused idiot.

"So you're going to—"

"Yeah. But I wanted to tell you first."

"Why?" Lucas fought to keep his voice even. Unable to sit, he began pacing the small space. "You want my permission? My advice on how to do it?" Slamming his palms on the desk, he asked, "What the fuck do you want from me?"

Joe didn't flinch. He just looked up from the ring box. "I don't expect anything from you. But I figured I owe you the respect of letting you know before I did it. That's all."

Lucas had known this was for real. That Beth and Joe loved each other. That she loved his brother in a way she'd never loved him. But somewhere in the back of his mind, he'd wanted them to fail. He'd wanted this to be temporary, for Beth and Joe to break up.

What a selfish son of a bitch he'd turned out to be. He cared about these two people. How could he want them to suffer? To soothe his fragile ego or appease some arrogant need for revenge? What the hell kind of person would think like that?

"I guess that's it." Joe slipped the box back into his pocket. "Maybe I'll wait awhile. Give it more time."

"Don't do that," Lucas said.

"What?"

"If you want to wait to make sure you two are ready, then do it. But if you're waiting for me, don't bother."

"I see," Joe said, his shoulders dropping.

"No, I don't mean it that way." Lucas paced the room twice more, then sat down. "I'm not really mad at you. Hell, I'm not even sure if I'm mad." He left the chair again. "Change that. I'm mad. But some days it's with you and Beth, and some days it's with this damn island, but most days I'm pissed at myself."

Joe rose from his chair and grabbed a couple bar rags off the shelf by the door. "I can't change what went down. I wouldn't if I could, though I do wish it had happened differently."

Off course he wouldn't. He'd come out the winner once again.

Instead of voicing the callous thought, Lucas nodded and remained silent. Joe was trying to be considerate. Maybe if he'd done that two months ago . . .

"I'd better get out there. You want to take my Jeep?" Joe asked, holding out his keys. "I can ride home with Beth. I meant to offer last night."

That's when Lucas remembered Sid was waiting for him. "No, Sid's taking me home."

Joe put the keys back in his pocket. "Right." He started to leave the office, then turned back. "About Sid."

Lucas tensed. "What about her?"

"Just . . . be careful."

"Why? Are you claiming her too?"

Joe leaned against the door frame. "I'll give you a pass on that one. For now."

He'd been out of line and he knew it. Damn temper. "Then why do I need to be careful around Sid?" Lucas asked, trying to change the tone between them. "Is she as violent as she seems?"

"No," Joe said, without hesitation. "She's not nearly as tough as she acts, but if you tell her I said that, I'll kick your ass."

Lucas couldn't help but smile as Joe walked away, marveling at the power Sid Navarro seemed to wield over everyone on the island.

~

"Why'd you take me up on the ride this time?" Sid asked. They'd driven less than half a mile in silence. After his talk with Joe, Lucas was hoping the silence would hold.

"Honestly?"

Sid looked over. "Why would I ask a question and then want you to lie?"

"Right." This woman was entirely too literal. "I'm tired."

Her eyes returned to the road and she nodded. "I can relate. I've helped out on weekends but that was nothing compared to the last two days. How the fuck do your parents do this?"

Lucas didn't consider himself a prude, but the vulgar language from the delicate looking, if not sounding, package to his left took him off balance.

"Do you always talk like that?"

"Like what?"

"Dropping the F-bomb like that?"

The truck sped up and then zipped around a tourist on a bicycle. "Why? Do I offend your delicate sensibilities?"

Was she ever not defensive? "I'm not offended. Just curious." Soaring oaks flowed past his window, their heavy limbs trailing the roof of the truck cab. He'd missed those old trees, though he hadn't realized it until just now.

Sid was quiet for nearly a minute, then she said, "I grew up with men. I work with men. I guess I talk like a man." The statements were made with no apology or regret, but he noticed her white-knuckled grip on the wheel. She wasn't comfortable with this line of questioning, but she wasn't fighting him either.

"Do you *want* to talk like a man? And for the record, not every man talks like that."

"You saying you don't curse?"

"I curse. But you can't throw profanity around a courtroom so you learn to keep it in check." His first year out of law school, Lucas had made the mistake of dropping a four-letter word in court and nearly found himself in judges' chambers. He never did it again.

Sid's grip on the wheel loosened. "That makes sense." She fell silent again and Lucas returned to watching the old oaks mingle with a cedar here and there.

"No," she said, sometime later.

"No, what?"

Caramel eyes darted his way, then back to the road. "I don't want to talk like a man."

He didn't know what to say to that so he changed the subject. "Where can I get good, homemade sweets around here?"

If the change of topic threw her off, Sid didn't show it. "I know just the place." The wheel jerked left, sending the truck in a tight U-turn in the middle of the street.

Lucas braced one arm on the door and another on the ceiling above him. "What the hell are you doing?" Besides trying to kill him. Maybe this is what Joe was talking about.

"Getting you sweets."

"This road makes a circle around the damn island. Why the fuck couldn't we go around?"

Sid tsked. "Such ugly language."

"I'm less restrained when I'm about to be thrown out of a moving vehicle."

"If I wanted you out of the truck, I'd have shoved your door open before making the turn."

Jokes. Now she decided to be funny.

"Where are you taking me?" he asked, straightening in his seat, but keeping a hand on the door handle. Just in case. "It better be worth the whiplash."

Their eyes met and she gave him a wink. "Trust me."

"After that stunt? I don't think so." Though the wink was actually kind of cute. And the relaxed smile that went with it. When Sid dropped the ass-kicker routine, he thought she might be fun to hang out with. Too bad she didn't drop the act often.

CHAPTER EIGHT

Minutes later, Sid parked the truck in front of a tiny white building with baby blue shutters. The entrance sat off to the right, while brightly colored rockers occupied the left end of the covered porch. From the eaves hung a sign reading SWEET OPAL'S BAKERY & CONFECTIONS.

"I don't remember this place," Lucas said as he climbed from the cab. The mouthwatering scent in the air made him forget his near brush with death.

"Hasn't been here long, but if you came home more often, you'd know there are lots of new businesses on the island."

The scent grew stronger as he followed Sid up two steps onto the porch. This had to be what heaven smelled like.

"I don't care about other businesses right now," Lucas said. A teenager exited the building carrying something that resembled a tart. He nearly followed her to the parking lot. "I'm too busy smelling this one."

"You always did have a sweet tooth," Sid said, gaining his attention again.

"How do you know that?"

She pushed through the door, setting off chimes to mark their entrance. "I've known you since high school.

One year at Joe's birthday party you nearly punched him when you thought he'd spit on the cake while blowing out the candles."

He didn't remember her being there. "Mom worked on that cake all day. Would have been rude to spit on it." And a waste of a perfectly good cake.

"Right." Sid's throaty laugh hit Lucas somewhere below the belt. Had to be the sugary wonder floating in the air.

Sliding up to the counter, Lucas spotted the very food he'd been craving since waking up that morning. "Is that Key lime pie?" he asked, pointing to a meringue-covered confection on the top shelf of the display case.

"Best on the Eastern Seaboard." Sid stuck two fingers in her mouth and let out a whistle that threatened to split his eardrums. "We need some service out here!" she yelled.

A heavyset woman with bright blue eyes, white hair, and wearing a pink apron that read "Be nice and I'll let you lick the beaters" stepped through the doorway. She looked pissed. If Sid got them kicked out before he got his pie, he'd never forgive her.

He whispered to Sid. "Ruin this for me and I'll key your truck."

As if he hadn't spoken, and the apron lady didn't look mad enough to ban them both for life, Sid said, "Roll your ass out here, woman. We're paying customers."

Lucas closed his eyes and said good-bye to his Key lime dream. When he opened them again, the older woman was charging around the end of the counter.

When she reached Sid, her arms went wide. "Where have you been for the last few days, darling? I was getting worried."

Sid stepped into the bear hug like she'd been doing it her whole life. He hadn't seen her touch anyone in the two and a half days he'd spent with her. When he'd touched one strand of hair that night in the truck, she'd turned into an ice queen.

He could not figure her out.

Once the hug ended, Sid stepped back. "I'm covering over at Dempsey's since Tom had the heart attack."

The woman's blue eyes filled with concern. "I heard about that. Is he okay? Such a lovely man. And Patty too. They've been so good to me."

The praise didn't surprise Lucas. His parents had been ambassadors for the island almost since the day they arrived. "Dad is doing well, thanks." When the woman turned to him as if just noticing his presence, he stretched out a hand. "Lucas Dempsey. Helping out with the business while Dad recovers."

"Opal," the older woman said, taking his hand. "Are you that fancy lawyer everyone is always talking about?"

Lucas looked down to his beer-stained khakis and worn tennis shoes. "I don't know about fancy, but yes, I'm the lawyer."

She switched focus back to Sid. "You never told me what a cutie he is. Hubba, hubba."

No one had ever used such terms in reference to him, at least not in his presence. Lucas felt the blush rise and also felt like an idiot.

Taking Sid's hands, Opal pulled her around the counter. "I made your favorite cupcakes today. Put one aside in the hopes you might stop by." Addressing Lucas, she asked, "And what can I get for you, sweet cheeks?"

He'd called Sid that name a day ago and she'd threatened his manhood. Now he knew why. "A piece of Key lime pie, please."

Opal's eyes danced. "Good choice." Then she disappeared into the kitchen.

Nodding toward the seating area behind him, Sid grinned. "Grab us a table, sweet cheeks." She escaped into the kitchen before he could think of a good comeback, though truth be told, he had that one coming.

～

Seeing Lucas red-faced and uncomfortable was adequate retribution for him questioning Sid's language during the ride over. He hadn't really judged her on it. Hadn't called her a name or talked down to her. His question sounded more like curiosity than condemnation.

Beth, who liked to call herself Sid's fairy godmother, had been trying to clean up her language almost since they'd met. Curly, as Sid preferred to call her, gave orders like *be nice* and *smile more* and *keep the cursing to a minimum.*

Sid ignored all orders, though she'd been trying the *be nice* stuff on Old Man Fisher with little success. That man needed an enema and a happy pill before he'd soften up. She'd even smiled at him once, even put her heart in it. But still. Nothing.

So what if she cursed like the proverbial sailor? For as much time as she spent on the water, she might as well be one. None of the guys at the dock seemed to mind. Randy made her keep it down at the gym, but only so she wouldn't offend the skinny female tourists as they fast-walked the treadmills. Heaven forbid they overindulge on vacation and go home three pounds heavier.

One might say the thought was hypocritical since Sid ran every morning and lifted weights several times a week. But she ran because she enjoyed it, and lifting engines required muscle. Muscle required weights.

Carrying the Key lime pie Opal had sent out for Lucas felt like lifting weights. He'd never be able to eat the entire piece.

"About time you came back," Lucas said. "I was three seconds away from ripping into the sugar packets."

"Opal couldn't decide how big a piece to cut. As you can see, she went with one as big as the damn ferry."

Lucas's eyes widened as she set the plate on the table. "Is that a piece or half a pie?"

Sid set her own cupcake down and took a seat. "Opal's pie pans could double as hubcaps for my truck. That's a piece."

Still eyeing the Key lime, Lucas lifted a fork, looking unsure how to proceed. With anything Opal made, the best plan was to go in close to the point. Even then, the height of the creation made getting the bite in cleanly damn near impossible.

He moved the fork to one side, changed his mind, and switched to the other side.

"Just stick the fork in it, Dempsey. It's not going to fight back."

"You're right." His fork sliced through the meringue, pierced the Key lime, and scooped up a chunk of crust. "Here we go." Somehow he managed to get the entire bite in his mouth on the first try, though a hint of meringue lingered on his upper lip.

Without thinking, Sid reached out and wiped it off with the tip of her finger. Lucas caught her wrist, sending heat sizzling along her skin, and stared with one brow raised.

"That's my meringue."

Sid stuttered. "I was . . . It was . . . You had . . ." She might have regrouped and finished a sentence but his next move struck her mute.

Lucas licked her finger clean, holding it in his mouth longer than necessary for such a small amount of cream. Sid's brain shut down while the rest of her came alive. Her skin tightened. Her legs loosened. Her toes curled.

With a satisfied smack of his lips, Lucas relinquished her finger, but continued to hold her wrist. His eyes met hers and the usual light hazel shade turned to liquid green. Like damp moss in the sunlight.

"Mmmmmm," he said, "so good."

Sid jerked her hand away and slipped it under the table. Her body's reaction to his seemingly innocent flirtation would prove much more difficult to hide. Looking down, she noticed her nipples showing through her T-shirt. With a quick tug she undid the knot holding it tight in the back, loosening the material enough to fall away from her body.

Thankfully, Lucas was too busy staring at his pie to notice.

They ate their desserts in silence from that point on, Lucas's attention centered on his plate. Who'd have thought a woman could feel jealous of a slice of pie? If Lucas ever reacted to her the way he was drooling over Opal's Killer Key Lime, Sid would die a happy woman.

Such a stupid thought. Lucas would never drool over, melt for, nor lust over her. He'd nearly sucked all her brain cells out the tip of her finger, then returned to his food as if they'd been discussing the weather. All the more reason to keep her hopeless fantasies to herself.

∾

Lucas had to keep his head down the rest of their meal so Sid wouldn't see how much he wanted her. The taste of her on his tongue had been better than the Key lime pie, and that pie might have been the best thing he'd ever tasted in his life. When she dropped him off at his parents' house, there'd been no offer of a ride for the following morning. Maybe he'd freaked her out. Or grossed her out.

If a brush of the neck made her bristle, sucking on her finger definitely crossed a line. But she hadn't pulled away, and the heat he felt beneath his hand on her wrist wasn't from tension.

At least not the unwelcome kind.

Not working together for two days helped create plenty of distance. Joe's charters had canceled for Sunday and Monday, so they'd switched things up. Joe ran the bar with Sid during the day, and Lucas covered nights with Beth, which went smoother than expected. The awkwardness was starting to fade, and he knew they'd be friends eventually. Beth was a difficult person not to like.

He'd been surprised to see her working the floor as if she'd been waiting tables her whole life. Beth reminded him she'd worked her way through law school as a waitress. Something she claimed she'd told him *while* they were dating. He had no memory of the conversation, and since he doubted Beth would lie, the truth of his own douchery felt like one more smack in the face.

When had he become such a self-centered jerk?

He and Sid were back together on Tuesday, but something had definitely changed.

"Rum and Coke, two diets, and a sweet tea." Sid barked off the order the same way she'd done every order of the day. Eyes down and back straight. Then she returned to the floor with the appetizers he'd placed on a new tray for her.

They couldn't spend the next five weeks like this. He couldn't anyway. In some masochistic way, Lucas enjoyed Sid's jabs and steady flow of imaginative yet insulting names for him. And he had to give her credit. In front of customers, she kept the profanity to a minimum.

Lucas filled the drink order and considered how to approach Sid for a peace treaty. They needed to find some level ground where they could work together without all this tension. Maybe even be friends. Though he'd never had a female friend who could likely hold her own in a bar fight and still look sexy while throwing a punch.

"Table nine is getting rowdy," Sid said, slapping her empty tray on the bar. "Make sure there's a fresh pot of coffee brewing."

He nodded toward the back corner. "Frat boys giving you trouble?"

"Nah. Red hatters."

"Red what?"

"Red hatters," Sid said again, shooting him that "duh" look of hers. "Little old ladies who wear red hats and purple clothes everywhere they go."

Lucas covered the snort with a cough. "Are you telling me you can't handle a bunch of old ladies?"

Sid swiped the now drink-covered tray and balanced it on her shoulder. "You know all those rum and Cokes and whiskey sours you've been making?"

No way. "The hatter ladies?"

"Yep. Have that pot of coffee ready when I come back."

Surely they could handle a few old women who couldn't hold their liquor. Lucas stepped through the kitchen door, tossed the cold coffee, and put a new pot on to brew. Then he returned to the bar and surveyed the room.

Weekdays weren't as busy as weekends. Most seats at the bar were empty, as was the majority of Daisy's section. Sid carried the bulk of the load, but he could see several of her customers getting ready to leave. A glance at the clock showed Beth and Joe were due in less than an hour.

"Show 'em how to do it, Flo!" shouted a high-pitched Southern voice over the crowd. Lucas swung around the end of the bar looking for the source. Rounding the divider that split the dining room in half, he saw a floppy red hat bouncing over a swaying purple body.

The woman seemed to be doing some imitation of riding a horse. That's what he *hoped* she was imitating anyway.

"Hello there, ladies," Lucas said, slipping on his best gain-the-witness's-trust smile. "You all seem to be having a lot of fun."

"Well, hello to you, sugar breeches," said the woman sitting next to the dancer. "You're just in time. Flo here needs a partner."

Before he could register that comment, a woman he assumed to be Flo sashayed up behind him and slapped her hands on his hips. Removing her hands, he spun around to find tiny round glasses perched on the end of a button nose, and watery green eyes twinkling under bushy eyebrows.

"Come on, handsome. Shake your groove thing." Flo then proceeded to bend at the waist and do what Lucas believed was called a booty pop.

Afraid she might break a hip, he pulled out a chair and slid it behind her until she was sitting. Then he scooted the geriatric dancer up to the table. "Appreciate the offer, ladies, but we need to tone things down just a little bit."

The first woman spoke up again. "Relax, honey. We're just having fun." Reaching for her drink, she added, "Don't get your panties in a wad."

Maybe this was Sid's grandmother and she hadn't bothered to tell him. And maybe she'd had enough to drink.

"Nothing wrong with a little fun, but we have to be considerate of the other customers." Lucas reached for an empty glass. "Why don't we bring out some coffee?"

The elder version of Sid popped out of her seat and poked him in the chest. "Look, sonny. We're old enough to drink whatever we want, and no one is going to tell us when we've had enough."

"You tell 'em, Maggie!" cheered a woman on the other side of the table.

Maggie poked him again. "Now send over that little waitress of ours. We're ready for another round. And it ain't going to be coffee."

Handling a gang of angry bikers would be easier than this. Lucas opened his mouth to speak, but that little waitress of theirs joined the fray and spoke first.

"Is this man bothering you, ladies?"

She had to be kidding.

"He's cramping our style is what he's doing," Flo said, wiggling in her chair.

Sid raised a brow in Lucas's direction, as if *he* were the problem.

"I'm trying to keep order here."

"This isn't a courtroom, Dempsey," she whispered. Then louder so the group could hear, "He's just a natural born flirt. We never can keep him away from a table full of hot women."

That got cheers from the geriatric set. The dirty looks coming his way stopped, but the looks that replaced them made him feel dirty.

Sid tapped him on the arm. "Take your time heading back to the bar so these ladies get a good show for their trouble."

A woman next to Maggie, who looked to be pushing the century mark if she hadn't hit it already, said, "I'd better put on my glasses."

Lucas knew not to argue in front of customers, no matter what. So he did as ordered and tried not to feel like a side of beef on display as he crossed the room. Sid had it coming for this one. Distance shmistance. He'd get her back.

CHAPTER NINE

Sid figured if the old ladies could enjoy the show, so could she. Tray pressed against her chest, she watched the play of Lucas's firm ass beneath his Dockers until the derriere disappeared around the bar. How did he manage to look that good in such sissified pants?

"You've got a hot one there, honey child," said the woman she'd overheard called Maggie. "I bet he's a killer in the sack."

Sid's turn to blush. "He's not my boyfriend." She unclenched the tray and cleared three empty plates off the table. "We just work together."

"Couldn't prove it by the way he's been watching you."

"What?" Sid nearly dropped the plates on the floor.

"That boy has been undressing you with his eyes ever since we sat down at this table. And I'd wager since long before that."

Sid grabbed a chair from the next table over, which was thankfully empty, and sat down next to Maggie. "He has?" She glanced over her shoulder toward the bar. Lucas had his head down and was filling a glass. "How can you tell?"

Maggie chuckled and leaned back in her chair. With sharp eyes, the older woman sized Sid up from head to toe, making her squirm. "Flo," Maggie said, keeping her eyes on Sid. "This little thing doesn't know her own power."

"With that centerfold body?" Flo said. "I don't believe it."

Centerfold? Sid? Maybe it *was* time to cut these ladies off.

Flo leaned so close, Sid could smell the whiskey on her breath. "Every woman has *the power*, but you've got more than most. You could have any man in this room with one crook of a finger."

"Bullshit," Sid said, bolting from the chair and adding three empty glasses to her tray. "You ladies have had way too much to drink."

Maggie nudged the ancient woman next to her. "Tell her, Frannie."

The octogenarian looked nearly asleep, but perked up at the sound of her name. "What?"

Maggie raised her voice. "What do you think of this one?" she asked, motioning toward Sid.

Frannie put on the glasses she'd removed once Lucas's derriere had gone out of range, and squinted through lenses that made her eyeballs look three times their size. Now Sid knew what those chicks on magazine covers felt like. Who would volunteer for this kind of scrutiny?

"Little short, but those tits are perfect. Curves in all the right places." Frannie nodded in what Sid assumed to be some kind of approval. "Hef'd like her. She's got enough vavavoom to light up Atlantic City."

This woman was on something way stronger than alcohol.

"See there?" Maggie said, looking pleased with herself. "Frannie worked for Hugh back in the sixties. If she says you've got it, you've got it."

She might have something, but not what Maggie was insinuating.

"Look, ladies, I appreciate the effort. But that man," she motioned toward the bar, "has known me since I was fourteen years old, and until five days ago, barely acknowledged my existence. Whatever I've got, he's not buying it."

"Darling," Maggie drawled. "That boy is buying, investing, and dreaming about what he could do with the inventory. You just have to let him know the store is open for business."

Sid gnawed her bottom lip, and looked back to Lucas again. What if these ladies were right? What if she could have him, even for a few weeks?

Snagging the last two empty glasses from the table, Sid avoided Maggie's direct gaze. "I'll think about it."

And she thought about nothing else until the moment she joined Will at Opal's for their Tuesday night treat, a standing appointment instituted when Beth had moved to the island. Curly had wanted the three of them to get to know each other, something about her not having had a lot of female friends, but tonight was a duo since Beth was working at Dempsey's.

"What's up with you?" Will asked, sliding Sid's favorite cupcake and a sweet tea across the table.

"Nothing," Sid lied, dropping onto the metal seat. "Why?"

"Because you have that look you get."

"What look?" She kept her head down, hoping Will would drop the interrogation.

"The one you get when you're debating something." Will unfolded a napkin and draped it over her lap. "You had that same look the night Beth suggested we have these little meet-ups, and again when you wanted that new sanding thingy but couldn't decide if it was worth the money."

"The orbital sander."

"Yeah, that thing," Will said. "Spill it."

This is why Sid had never minded her own lack of female companionship. Damn nosy wenches. She debated how much to tell. For a bartender who doubled as a barista and worked at nearly every business on the island, Will didn't gossip much. And she seemed comfortable in her own skin. Maybe talking to another woman, one less than sixty years her senior, would help.

"Do you think I'm hot?"

"Whoa," Will said. "Didn't see that coming. I know I haven't dated much since I got here but I don't—"

"Knock it off. You know that's not what I mean."

"Right," Will chuckled, then cut into her usual, rhubarb pie. "You're probably the hottest chick on this island, but you know that."

"Not really."

Will froze, fork in midair. "You own a mirror, right?"

Sid shifted in her chair and pulled the wrapper away from her cupcake. "Curly asked me that same thing once. I don't see what that has to do with anything."

"A lot. What do you *see* in the mirror?"

"I don't know," Sid shrugged. "Brown eyes. Round face. Normal nose. Brown hair. What am I supposed to see?"

Will set down her fork. "You remember that night at O'Hagan's? What did you see that night?"

"I was smokin' that night," Sid said, sliding a fork through the cupcake. "But that was the dress and makeup and whatever Curly had done to my hair. A bunch of artificial stuff."

"Are those boobs artificial?" Will asked.

Sid tilted her head and raised one brow. That didn't deserve an answer.

"I'm just saying. It's what was under the dress and makeup that had all those guys drooling and emptying their wallets to buy your drinks."

She had felt pretty good that night. Maybe there was something to what the old ladies said. "Remember when you came into Dempsey's the other day? When you met Joe's brother for the first time?"

"You mean when it was obvious you have a thing for him? Sure."

Her fork slipped. "How could you tell?"

Will swirled her straw. "For one thing, he called you sweet cheeks and you didn't slug him." Leaning her elbows on the table, she pushed her pie to the middle. "But mostly it was on your face. You were trying to look all bad ass, like usual, but when you thought he'd been flirting with me, I saw the hurt in your eyes." She shook her head. "That's how I knew."

Silence fell over the table as Sid moved a bite of the cupcake around her plate. Even Opal's chocolate buttercream couldn't coax her past this feeling. Confusion mixed with fear mixed with hope.

"It started in high school," she said, keeping her eyes on the dessert. "Dad died when I was fourteen and Randy brought me here. He didn't own the businesses yet, but knew this would be a safe place to raise a teenager. Safer than Miami."

"So that's where you're from? Miami?"

"Yeah." Thinking of Miami brought memories and images, good times and bad. She didn't want to think about those right now. "Anyway, I saw Lucas the first day of my freshman year. He was a sophomore and smart and gorgeous. Even then he had that hint of polish. Like he belonged in a display case, not buried in a heap of sand where no one could appreciate him."

Sid looked up to see Will nodding. "I can see that. He is pretty." She smiled with understanding. "Go on."

"Of course I never had the guts to talk to him. These boobs everyone keeps yapping about hadn't shown up at that point. But when they did, junior year, shit got crazy."

"What do you mean?" Will asked, leaning forward again.

"I wasn't invisible anymore, and at first I liked the attention. But one guy coaxed me out to the football field during a dance. I was so stupid." Sid shook her head at the memory, then crossed her arms until she was practically hugging herself. "I thought he just wanted to talk and hang out, but he wanted more. We were too far away for anyone to hear me yell, but I kept fighting."

Cold washed over her and her heart rate sped up. Stupid reaction to have more than ten years later. This is why Sid never talked about that night.

Will reached out and laid a hand on her arm. "Did he . . . ?"

"No," Sid said, shaking her head. "Lucas showed up. He never threw a punch, but he didn't have to. The kid acted like it was no big deal and headed back to the gym. I was so embarrassed, I ran to my truck and drove home like a maniac."

"Had Lucas followed you two? How did he know you were out there?"

Sid shrugged. "I don't know. I didn't stick around to ask. He'd looked really concerned, like he cared, and tried to offer me a ride home." She looked up and met Will's eyes. "But I ran."

"Honey," Will said. "Did you ever tell anyone?"

"Nah." She forced herself to take a bite. The sugary confection helped to block the taste of humiliation on her tongue.

They ate in silence, Sid figuring she'd said enough, and Will presumably processing what she'd just heard. Once she'd finished her pie, Will pushed the plate aside and sat back with her lemonade.

"He was your knight in shining armor. He slayed the dragon, which still counts, even if your dragon was a seventeen-year-old jackass."

Sid snorted, picturing Lucas on a white steed, lance in hand, and another of her romance covers came to mind.

"We need to do something about this," Will said, propping one foot beneath her and leaning on the table. "We have to let him know how you feel."

"No," Sid said, any sense of the power to which Maggie had referred long gone. "That is not going to happen."

"Oh, come on. This is your shot."

"You've seen the type of girl Lucas likes. Do you see a single similarity between me and Curly?"

Will pursed her lips to one side. "Well, you're both beautiful. But personality-wise, not so much."

"Exactly." Sid scooped up her last bite of cupcake. "He likes dainty and sweet. The girl next door."

"And you're more the boy next door trapped in a porn star's body."

Sid threw her napkin at Will. "Har har har. Besides, he's only here for five more weeks."

"So?" Will asked. "Give him a reason not to leave."

Another snort. Sid had never seen a man more determined than Lucas Dempsey to get *off* Anchor Island. There was nothing she or anyone could do that would make him stay.

"Then have a fling. Maybe he's not all that and a box of bonbons." Will threw the napkin back. "Try him out. Take him for a test-drive. Make the man see Jesus, then leave him wanting more while you get him out of your system."

The idea had merit. Not that Sid had ever made a man see Jesus. In her limited experience, she was pretty sure sex with her had never been a religious experience for anyone. Forgettable, yes. Spirit moving, no.

"I don't know."

"And you won't know until you try." Will lowered her leg and collected the dishes. "You turn on the charm and that man doesn't stand a chance. Remember, the bigger they are, the harder they fall." With a wicked grin she added, "You might as well be under him when he goes."

～

Less than a week. That's how long it took Sid Navarro to drive him up a wall. When not insulting him or making him look like a talentless chump, she was setting him on fire with a body that could fuel a man's fantasies for decades. Half the time he wanted to throttle her, and the other he longed to drag her into the back room and have wild sex on the office desk.

The woman was a menace. Challenging him at every turn. Turning him on without any effort whatsoever. And somewhere in the back of his mind, he liked it. Another indication he'd gone completely freaking whacko.

"Look up, son, before you hurt yourself," came a voice from Lucas's left. His eyes shot up in time to see the tree less than a foot in front of him.

That damn woman.

He glanced over and spotted Artie sitting on a bench next to a mountain of a man. Lucas sighed and moved around to the front of the bench.

"Thanks for that," he said, gesturing toward the tree. "I was distracted."

"I'd say you were. What's got your tail in a twist?" Artie asked. Before Lucas could answer, the old lawyer added, "You remember Randy Navarro?"

"Sure." Lucas extended a hand and took the opportunity to avoid Artie's first question. "How's it going?"

Randy took the offered hand with an easier grip than expected for a guy with arms the size of Lucas's thighs. "It's good," he said with a genuine smile. "I hear you're working with my sister?"

So much for avoiding the subject. "Yeah. She's helping out while Dad recovers."

"That heart attack stuff is no joke," Randy said. "Our dad had the same thing, but didn't make it. I was relieved when I heard Tom had pulled through."

Sid had never mentioned her dad died of a heart attack. "We were relieved too. He's coming home tomorrow, but recovery will take another five weeks or so. You run a gym, right?"

"I do," Randy said with a nod. "Island Fitness. You looking for a place to work out?"

"I've been keeping up my running, but missing the free weights I have at home," Lucas said. "You offer any kind of temporary membership?"

"We could work something out. Where are you running?"

Strange question on an island so small. Lucas shrugged. "Around the village is about the only option, isn't it?"

Randy shook his head. "Sid runs along the beach next to Highway 12. You should run up there with her."

"Sid runs?" He was learning all kinds of things about his little coworker today.

"Every morning like clockwork." Randy pointed east. "Show up at mile marker ten at seven fifteen in the morning and you'll catch her. No sense in running alone if you don't have to."

Running with Sid gave Lucas an idea. Maybe it was time for another one of their challenges. Only this time, he'd be the one to come out on top.

CHAPTER TEN

At seven the next morning, Sid stood on the sand next to Highway 12, performing her usual warm-up stretches. Thankfully, tourists who typically visited the island didn't start their sunbathing this early, which meant a clear beach for ten miles.

She could do five miles up and back before the first umbrella pierced the sand.

Sid was pulling her left heel up to her ass when someone jogged by her, throwing sand against her knees. The runner turned around a few feet away and yelled, "Come on, short shit. Try to keep up."

Oh, it was *on*.

She dug her feet into the sand until she'd caught up to Lucas. He was setting a slow pace that would take her twice as long to make her ten miles.

"What are you doing here?" she asked between huffs.

"I'd think that's obvious. I'm running."

Smart ass. She chose to remain silent. They ran for another ten yards before he spoke again.

"You ready for our next challenge?"

She dodged a piece of driftwood, then glanced his way. "What challenge?"

He turned around and started jogging backwards. "We could go for a distance race, but this strip is too short for that."

The full strip would be twenty miles up and back. What kind of marathons did this freak run?

"I'm here to exercise," she said, annoyed that he'd invaded her private time, and forgetting any talk from the night before of making him see his maker. "Shut up and run or find another beach."

Sid pulled away, leaving him jogging backward behind her. Seconds later he was beside her again. They continued on in silence another fifty yards. She couldn't help but notice Lucas was barely breathing heavy. Jerk.

She picked up the pace. He did the same. Another fifty yards and she kicked it up a notch. He stayed even, but to her satisfaction was huffing more than before. They held steady another fifty yards before he started to pull ahead.

Not about to be beat, Sid caught up, then took the lead again. He devoured the ground between them, pushing her harder. They were both in a steady sprint when Sid found another gear and started pulling away. He didn't catch up immediately this time and she felt a wave of triumph.

Until she felt strong arms wrap around her middle and yank her off the ground. In her surprise, Sid kicked out, tangling their legs and she could feel them both going down. Lucas spun her around and the next thing she knew, her back hit the ground. Hard.

Half a second later, Lucas landed half on top of her, but managed to send most of his weight to the side, assumedly to keep from crushing her beneath him.

Will's words echoed in her brain.

Might as well be underneath him when he goes.

What the hell had just happened? Sid would have leapt off the sand except the ground had knocked the wind out of her, making it difficult to breathe, let alone move. And then there was the issue of the large, virile, sexy man on top of her. Lifting her lids for the first time since coming to an abrupt stop, Sid looked up into searching hazel eyes, half covered by a wet lock of dark hair dangling over his brow.

"Are you all right?" he asked, concern etched in his voice. "I didn't mean to hurt you."

Though her brain was screaming, Sid's mouth had stopped working. Which was good since her brain was screaming things like *Kiss him!* and *Good God, this feels good.*

Her ponytail must have come loose because a long strand of hair covered the right side of her face. Lucas swept it back, tucking it behind her ear. His eyes met hers and time stopped. She licked her lips, causing his eyes to drop to her mouth.

One warm fingertip slid across her bottom lip and she considered tasting him the way he'd tasted her at Opal's. Too bad they didn't have any meringue with them. Tracing the outline of her face, Lucas said two words.

"So beautiful."

A tear threatened in the corner of her eye, and her heart beat so fast she thought she might be the next to have a heart attack. Surely Lucas could hear it. Or feel it, he was so close. His face drew down, then tilted to the left, but he pulled back before their lips could touch.

He leaned in again, this time tilting to the right. With no idea what to do next, Sid held her breath, praying she wouldn't screw this up. His breath brushed her lips a split second before the wave slammed over them.

~

Lucas's throat and eyes burned from the salt water, which was cold enough to quell the effect Sid splayed beneath him was having on his anatomy. When he could finally see again, the sight before him took his breath nearly as quickly as the wave.

A goddess had risen from the sea, her white cotton tee molded to a perfect body, revealing firm breasts that heaved up and down as she struggled to catch her breath. Wet hair draped across one shoulder while tiny drops of water clung to the tips of her long, dark lashes.

If sirens did exist, Lucas was looking at one.

And then she did something unexpected. Sid started to laugh. She laughed so hard, she snorted, which threatened to ruin the goddess thing. Until she leaned back on her elbows and threw her head back. The occasional snort could be overlooked with a body like that.

Considering what he'd been about to do, and how his body did not appreciate the interruption, Lucas didn't see the humor in the situation.

"Why are you laughing?" Maybe the force of the water had knocked her senseless.

Sid took in a full breath, pointed at him, then fell over with laughter again.

Lucas ran a hand through his hair, checking to see if something had attached itself to his person. No clinging crabs in sight. "Have you lost your mind?" he asked, sitting up and noticing he'd be extracting sand from between the boys for quite a while. Damn it.

Laughter abating, Sid sat up and crossed her legs while shoving the hair away from her face. Caramel eyes danced as she glanced his way. "You were going to kiss me."

That's what she found so damn funny? He'd show her a joke.

"No, I wasn't."

The shit-eating grin disappeared, and her face sobered immediately. "Yes, you were."

"Was not." He rolled to his feet. "Don't flatter yourself."

He'd taken two steps when he heard the growl. She was on him before he took another, charging around to block his path. "Don't flatter *yourself*, dickhead. I didn't say I wanted you to kiss me, I said you were going to try it. You're lucky that wave hit or I'd have kneed you in the nuts."

"Bullshit," Lucas said, forgetting he'd been toying with her. "You were the one all soft and sexy, laying in the sand, staring up at me with those doe eyes and licking your lips. You wanted that kiss just as much as I did."

Sid froze, arms dropping to her sides. For once, she kept her mouth shut. If he'd known talking kissing was how to shut her up, he might have tried the tactic long before now.

Her eyes dropped and she dug a toe in the sand. When she looked up again, the goddess was back. "So you *were* going to kiss me?"

He tucked his hands under his pits to keep from pulling her against him. Looking out over the water, he said, "Yeah. I guess I was." Which would have been a stupid thing to do.

That wave had been sent by sailors past to save him from the call of the siren.

The siren stepped closer. "Do you still want to?"

Lucas did the wrong thing. He looked her in the eye. Those watery candy depths nearly brought him to his knees. How could a woman with a body built for sin look so damn innocent?

Somehow he found the strength to look away. As he moved around her to head back down the beach, he said, "Sorry I knocked you down like that. I'd better go."

"What?" Sid stomped through the sand beside him. "You can't just leave."

"I have to." If he didn't get away from her now, they'd both regret it. "Get back to your run. I'll leave you alone."

She moved in front of him, her turn to jog backwards. "But what if I don't want you to leave me alone?"

"Trust me. You do."

He tried to pick up the pace to get around her but she cut him off. "No, really, I don't."

Stopping, Lucas rubbed a hand across his forehead. This little visit home was temporary. Every instinct in his body told him Sid was not the temporary kind of girl. Regardless of what might be hidden, or not so hidden, under her clothes, her reactions gave her away.

Sid Navarro was not the casual type. And he was in no condition to do anything but casual. Especially when not casual meant being tied to Anchor Island.

"We can't," he said. Not his most eloquent argument but thinking wasn't easy with her standing there looking like the winner of a wet T-shirt contest. The blood kept draining from his brain.

"We can't what? Kiss?" she asked. "I think we should try."

Wait. Was this the same woman who'd sooner spit on him than kiss him?

"Since when?" he asked, curious to know what had caused this sudden change.

"Well . . ." she sputtered, waving her hands and pointing to the spot where they'd fallen. "You started this. You should finish what you started."

He wasn't the only one coming up with shitty arguments.

"You don't even like me," he accused. And if she did she had a funny way of showing it.

"Ha!" she squeaked. "I never said that."

Lucas charged down the beach again. "The way you act, you don't have to say it."

"Then make me like you," she said, stopping him in his tracks.

Oh, so that was it. He knew what she was doing. Another one of her damn challenges. A challenge is what had gotten him into this godforsaken situation to begin with. He wasn't going to fall for it this time.

"You don't think I could do it?" he asked, calling her bluff.

Sid crossed her arms, which thrust her breasts toward her chin. Lucas's mouth went dry.

"I have my doubts." She tapped a toe. "You're not exactly my type. Too prissy. Too pretty. Too . . . what's the word? Metrosexual?"

"Metro what? Did you just call me prissy?" Lucas bridged the distance between them in two strides. "I'll show you prissy."

~

Sid never saw the kiss coming. With little effort, Lucas swept her off her feet and slammed his mouth against hers. Stunned by the sudden contact, her brain took several seconds to realize what was happening. But once it did, instinct took over.

Her legs wound around his waist as Sid latched onto broad shoulders, determined to give as good as she was getting. Which was really freaking good. Lucas tasted of mint and heat. His lips were hot and wet and threatened to turn her brain to mush. The power humming beneath her fingertips was more arousing than any joy ride she'd ever taken.

Talk about horsepower.

Even their kiss was a competition. Sid didn't give two shits whether she won or lost, so long as Lucas kept his lips on hers. The muscles in his shoulders bunched and flexed every time he pulled her closer. Higher. Tighter.

Sid shoved her hands into his damp hair, tightening her legs around Lucas's narrow hips. Solid abs pressed against her core, drawing a sound from her throat Sid had never made before. Her breasts ached, pressed against his broad chest.

As much as she loved the feeling of soaring off the ground, she wished he'd put her down somewhere so their hands could be free to explore. But then he thrust his tongue deeper and any thought of logistics disappeared.

If she'd known calling Lucas prissy would garner this kind of reaction, she would have done it years ago. Just when she thought her body couldn't get any hotter, Lucas slid his hands down to her ass and she bucked like a speedboat bouncing over a rolling wave.

As if desperate to hold on, her hands fisted in his hair as she scattered tiny bites along his bottom lip. The reality of kissing Lucas was better than all her fantasies combined. He tasted better. Smelled better. And good God did he feel better. Without thinking, Sid said the words running through her mind.

"I want you so bad," came out on a harsh breath.

His response was as unexpected as the kiss had been. With a growl, Lucas dropped her to her feet and backed away as if she were a live wire. And she felt like one, too.

Lucas bent, dropping his hands to his knees. He didn't look happy and he didn't speak. Sid waited half a minute but couldn't take the silence.

"Are you all right?"

"Other than Mother Nature trying to kick my ass and you trying to fry my brain, I'm doing great."

Her trying to do what?

"That shouldn't have happened," he said, panting. "We shouldn't be doing this."

Sid fought between breaking his nose and breaking into a run. But she wasn't sixteen this time. And there was no reason they shouldn't be doing what they were just doing.

"Why shouldn't we be doing this? What the hell is your problem?"

"I crossed a line. It won't happen again."

Sid's hands balled into fists. "What line? Stop acting like we did something wrong, damn it. That was the best kiss I've ever had, and you're ruining it."

"I'm trying not to ruin you!" he yelled, standing tall again. Tall and hot with his hair a mess from where she'd been grabbing it seconds before.

She couldn't go back now. Couldn't finally get a taste of him and then have it taken away. "I'm not some storybook virgin here. In case you didn't notice, I wasn't exactly fighting you off."

"You should have been." Since when did guys argue with women not to have sex with them? And no matter what he claimed, that's where they were headed with that kiss. Maybe what the other guys had said was true. Maybe she really did suck at this.

"Did I do something wrong?" she asked, clutching the sides of her running shorts.

Lucas ran a hand through his hair and began to pace. "You didn't do anything wrong. I'm the one making a mess of this." Stopping, he gripped the top of her arms until she met his eyes. "I'm sorry."

"For what?" Dark curls swirled around her face. "I was bad at it, wasn't I?" Shoving off his hands, she kicked the sand. "Goddamn it, I knew it."

"You knew what?"

"That I can't do this. I can't even kiss a guy right."

"You can't . . . What are you talking about?" But before he finished the question, Sid ran down the beach toward her truck. She needed to get away.

"Sid!" he called, chasing behind her. "Where are you going?" She reached her truck and was halfway in the cab before he caught up. His left arm blocked her from closing the door. "You did nothing wrong back there."

"Let me go." She pulled the door but he held it open.

"Not until you listen to me." He trapped her on the seat, her knees pressed against his chest. "There was nothing wrong with how you kissed me. That's the problem."

"How is that a problem?" She wrapped her hand around the wheel and bit her lip to keep it from quivering. "You're not making any sense."

Lucas ran a hand over his face. "Sid, another few seconds and we both would have been back on the beach getting sand in places neither of us would enjoy. Not that I wouldn't have enjoyed how we got it there."

"So I'm such a good kisser you were ready to have sex, but that's a bad thing." This never happened in her fantasies. He was supposed to be ripping her clothes off, not ordering her to keep them on. "What am I missing here?"

"My time on Anchor is temporary," he said, as if that were supposed to be a news flash.

Sid rolled her eyes. "What does that have to do with anything?"

He brushed the hair from her face. "Anything we started now would have to be casual and temporary. And you're neither of those things."

"I am so," she said, with a kick to his ribs. She could do casual. "Try me."

Not the two words he expected if the look on his face was any indication. She could see it in his eyes. Temptation warred with whatever fucked-up gentlemanly delusions were going around that damn head of his.

"No," he said, moving away from the truck.

She hit the ground behind him. "No? Just like that? Why do you get to decide? I get a vote, and I say yes."

"No," he said again, stopping when she pulled on his arm. "I won't start something I can't finish." His voice dropped to nearly a whisper as he wiped sand from her cheek with his thumb. "I've screwed up enough lives lately. I won't screw up yours, too."

His touch was so gentle and the regret in his eyes so real, Sid didn't have the heart to keep arguing. Instead, she watched him walk away. He could have his upstanding ways today. But she'd change his mind. One way or another, Lucas Dempsey would have a spiritual moment in the bed of Sid Navarro. He could bet on that.

CHAPTER ELEVEN

By the time Lucas reached the house, he'd berated himself for being an idiot, vowed never to touch Sid Navarro again, and prayed his father would recover faster than expected. The last reminded him of his parents' imminent arrival. At least he hadn't had time to mess up the house, though there were dishes in the sink he needed to load into the dishwasher.

He'd driven his mom's minivan up to the beach and the ride back felt like torture. Between fighting a hard-on, thanks to Sid's scent and taste lingering in his brain, and the sand shot up his shorts by what he now thought of as the sanity-restoring wave, sitting comfortably in a bucket seat was not happening.

Cutting the engine, Lucas climbed from the van with one goal in mind: a long, cold shower followed by a hot, rich cup of coffee. Thank God his mother kept the good stuff on hand. As he approached the porch, he spotted a man and woman occupying his mother's Adirondack chairs. The faces looked vaguely familiar so he knew they had to be islanders.

"Lucas Dempsey, I need to hire you," said the man sitting to the left of the front door. Lucas stopped at the bottom step to buy time. Putting a name to the faces took a second.

"Mr. and Mrs. Ledbetter?"

"Mr. and Ms.," corrected the woman. "I'm not married to this SOB anymore."

Lucas didn't have an answer for that. Ms. Ledbetter didn't sound like she needed condolences, but offering congratulations seemed rude since the SOB in question was present.

"What is this about?" he asked. Based on the greeting, this wasn't a social call.

"Gladys cut my tree and I'm going to sue her for it." Franklin Ledbetter crossed his arms but remained seated. No neck could be seen between his large, bald head and thick, rounded shoulders. Bushy black brows anchored his forehead like one long hedgerow, and his bottom lip protruded in a pout that should only appear on someone four years old or younger.

Gladys occupied the chair on the other side of the front door. Flat brown hair, parted down the middle, flowed over her shoulders while blue eyes carried a look of amusement. If the threat of being sued by the man four feet to her right was keeping her up nights, she hid it well.

"I only cut the branches on my side of the tree. I was perfectly within my rights."

Unless they had joint custody of a tree, this made no sense. Lucas took a step up, making the sand in his shorts slip higher between two parts of his anatomy that had experienced enough strain for one day.

Then Mr. Ledbetter's words of greeting sunk in. "Did you say you want to hire me?"

"That's right." The older man pointed to his left. "I told her I'd cut that tree when I got around to it and she went and did it on her own."

"Please," Gladys said. "I've heard 'when I get around to it' for thirty-five years and you haven't ever gotten around to anything in your life except a fishing pole and a beer."

"You see what I'm dealing with here?" He went into full pout again. From the look of his gut and the tackle box next to his chair, Lucas didn't doubt Gladys spoke the truth.

"I'm afraid I'm not for hire, Mr. Ledbetter. Now if you'll excuse me." Lucas reached the top step but Frank blocked his way to the door. For a man who resembled a Weeble Wobble, he moved quick. The smell of not-so-fresh fish filled the air. Lucas tried not to breathe in.

"Artie said you could help us. Said a lawyer up in Virginia could practice anywhere. You're here, so you need to practice with me."

The only thing Lucas would be practicing with Franklin Ledbetter would be his patience. And what the hell was Artie doing sending islanders to his door?

"Mr. Ledbetter, I'm on this island to run my family restaurant. Though Mr. Berkowitz is correct about my ability to practice here, that is not my intention or inclination. I'm afraid you'll have to find yourself another lawyer."

As Lucas swung open the screen door, Frank stomped his foot. "You have a civic duty here."

He considered ignoring that statement, but worried the man would follow him into the house, assaulting the interior with his putrid odors. Lucas turned to Gladys. "Did you cut down his tree?"

"No, I did not." Gladys smiled up at him. "I trimmed the branches on my side of the yard because they were getting too close to the house. It's hurricane season and I'm not having my windows knocked out because his lazy butt won't get out a ladder."

Her side of the yard? "Didn't you say you're not married to him anymore?"

"That's right."

"Then how do you share a tree?"

"She won't stay married to me," Frank interjected, "but she moved next door so she can still torture me 'til my dying day."

Gladys had no rebuttal. She simply continued to smile. Perhaps she wasn't the innocent in this situation after all.

Turning to Frank, Lucas asked, "Did she only cut the branches on her side?"

"Maybe." Shoving his hands in his pockets, the pouter avoided eye contact.

"Mr. Ledbetter, I need the truth."

"Fine. Yeah, she only did her side."

"Then there's no suit." Lucas slipped through the door, pulling and locking the screen behind him. Turning back to the pair, he added, "Case dismissed!" and shut the inside door.

~

Sid charged into Hava Java coffee shop on a mission. According to Will, and drunk old ladies in red hats, she possessed the weapons needed to seduce Lucas Dempsey. Now someone just had to show her how to use them. Will had been free with the advice to this point, so she seemed the natural place to turn.

After Lucas had left her standing on the beach, angry, aroused, and covered in sand, Sid raced home for a quick shower so she could stop at the coffee shop before reporting to the restaurant. Best to go in with a plan in place. Especially now that the game had changed.

What she hadn't counted on was catching Beth at the coffee shop as well. Since Curly had been Lucas's fiancée, she'd clearly been in his bed. Something Sid didn't like to think about. The words *sloppy seconds* came to mind, but were instantly rejected since she'd wanted Lucas long before Beth ever met him.

Every woman had her own way of rationalizing what she didn't like to deal with.

Sid had to make a decision. She could duck out before Curly saw her and talk to Will another time, which would mean facing Lucas without a plan, not something she wanted to do. Or she could somehow let Will know they needed to talk alone and together shoo Miss Annoyingly-Happy-In-Love on her way.

She chose shooing. Beth finished placing her order, then moved to the end of the counter, noticing Sid as she did so. "Morning, Sid. You look more awake than usual."

"A cold dip in the ocean will do that to you. Is that Dozer out there?" Sid asked, pointing out the front window. As Beth turned to look, Sid mouthed "We need to talk" to Will. Then she nodded toward Beth and mouthed "without her."

"Um . . ." Will murmured, sliding a brown cup under the metal nozzle on the espresso machine. "Sid, you mind if

I make Beth's drink before taking your order? I think she's in a hurry."

"What?" Beth said, turning back to the counter. "I don't see Dozer out there. And who says I'm in a hurry?"

"Sorry," Sid said, lifting a CD off the counter and reading the cover intently. "Must have been another dog."

"You have to open the store in ten minutes," Will said, passing the cup to Beth. "Don't want to be late."

Beth glanced up to the clock over Will's shoulder. "I have half an hour."

"Clock is slow," Will said without hesitation. Sid had to give her credit for the impressive display of deception.

"It is?" Beth looked at the clock again. "Well crap. I'd better go." She dropped a hand on Sid's arm. "Tom is coming home from the hospital today and he's insisted Patty take him by the restaurant on the way in. I tried to tell Lucas this morning, but he wasn't at the house. Have you seen him?"

Sid had deception skills of her own. "Nope."

"Weird," Beth said. "He must have been out running. Anyway, I've got to go. Thanks for the heads-up on the clock, Will."

As Beth disappeared through the door, Will turned on Sid. "Why'd you make me lie to her like that?"

"I didn't tell you to lie. You did that all on your own. You got a break coming?"

Will yelled to a tall, long-haired kid wiping down tables, "I'm taking a break! I'll clean up the patio in a few minutes." To Sid she said, "You want your coffee before we sit down?"

"I already had my morning jolt today. Think I'll skip it."

Will's brows shot up. "Do tell." They moved to an empty table near the windows. "Did you say you took a dip in the ocean?"

"Not on purpose. Lucas showed up on the beach this morning."

"Where you run? Did he know you'd be there?"

Sid snatched a napkin from the dispenser and began tearing off little pieces. "I don't know. Seemed like it. He wanted to race or something. I think he was tired of losing all of those challenges."

"What challenges? And do you always shred things like that?" Will asked, gesturing toward the growing mound of white paper.

"Bad habit." Sid slid the pile aside. "Anyway, we were racing and I was winning and he swept me off the ground. I don't think he meant for it to happen, but we both hit the beach and the next thing I knew, he was moving in for a kiss."

"Ha!" Will exclaimed. "You move fast."

"Calm your ass down. I wasn't moving at all. I froze and then the wave hit and I nearly drowned."

"Damn. So what happened next?"

Sid went back to tearing the napkin. "I laughed."

"You what?"

"I don't know what happened. I was under him and then I was coughing up salt water and then I was laughing. It's as if my brain got overloaded or something."

"Hmmm . . ." Will tapped a nail on the table. "That's probably not the reaction he expected."

"None of it was what I expected. But then he tried to play it off like he wasn't going to kiss me and I pushed and called him prissy and he snapped."

Will straightened. "He snapped?"

"Yeah. Picked me up and kissed the shit out of me."

Will cringed. "Not the most romantic description I've ever heard. So this is good, right? This is what we talked about."

"Except Lucas turned all noble and pushed me away. Said something about me not being the casual sex type." Sid ground her teeth. "It's not like I'm walking around with a veil or something. What's he mean, not the casual type?"

No answer came. Sid met Will's eyes and the woman shrugged. "He's got a point."

"What do you mean he's got a point?" Sid slapped a hand on the table, sending tiny pieces of napkin flying in the air. "I'm just as casual as the next chick."

"You're cleaning that up," Will said, unaffected by Sid's outburst. "I've been on this island nearly a year and never even seen you go out on a date. When was the last time you had a boyfriend?"

Sid didn't like this line of questioning. "A while. What's that have to do with anything?"

"How many boyfriends have you had?" The woman would not let up.

Behind her hand, Sid mumbled, "Two." Will held her hand behind her ear as if to say *speak up* and Sid clarified. "Two, okay? And the last one was five years ago. So I'm not good at the dating thing. That makes this the perfect situation. I don't want to date Lucas, I want to fuck his brains out for a few weeks."

Will shook her head. "You do have a way with words. But you've wanted *this* guy for more than a decade. You think a few weeks will be enough?"

117

Damn it. This had been Will's idea. "You're the one who said I should rock his world and get him out of my system."

"True," she admitted. "That might have been bad advice."

"I'm telling you, I can do casual. I'm not ready to settle down. I like my space. My independence. I've got plans, and they do not include having a man underfoot all the time."

Will gathered the scattered paper. "You're sure? If this turns into something, you won't have any problem watching him drive away?"

Sid pictured the scene. The silver BMW fading up Highway 12. Her chest tightened.

"I can handle it."

Will didn't look convinced, but she caved. "Okay then. How can I help?"

~

Sid had never worn a shirt this tight in her life. And she did not want to know why Will kept a change of clothes and all basic necessities packed in her VW van. The bartender came by her moniker honestly, being as willowy as the tree that bore her name. And she was a B cup at best, which meant her shirt stretched across Sid's double Ds was like wearing a neon sign over her head.

Look, everyone, I have giant knockers flashing in bright letters.

At least the plain tee was olive green instead of orange or pink. Will might wear an arm full of bangles but she liked to pair them with army boots, which sounded strange but somehow worked on the lanky brunette.

The shorts were another matter all together. Will had cut the things so short, the white material of the pockets stuck out below the tattered denim. Sid wore bathing suits that didn't show this much of her ass.

According to Will, the best way to barrel through a man's morals was to make him too horny to hitch a ride on the high road. Which made it sound a lot like Sid was taking the low road, but if that low road led to sex with Lucas, she'd follow it to the end.

With part A of the plan in place, that being the new wardrobe, the time had come to initiate part B, which sounded way harder than a change of clothes. Pretend nothing had happened.

With a deep breath and a final tug on the T-shirt, Sid waltzed through the doors of Dempsey's Bar & Grill attempting to look cool and unaffected. No kiss on the beach. No scaling Lucas like a drowning woman desperate for higher ground. And definitely no argument about who was or was not going to have sex.

The mission—to drive Lucas crazy with indifference.

"Sweet Cheez-Its, Mary, and Charlie, what are you wearing?" Georgette stared at Sid, wide eyed. "Did your dryer shrink all your clothes or something?"

Sid's confidence waned. Maybe this was too much. But there was no going back now.

She held her head high. "I'm behind on laundry." Right. That didn't sound pathetic at all.

"Sure you are," Georgette said. "Is this getup for Manny's benefit? He was over at the house watching baseball with Milo last night and must have asked about you three times."

Shit. Sid forgot about Manny. Another transplant from Florida, Manuel Sullivan worked at Anchor Adventures, Randy's watersports business, along with Georgette's husband, Milo. In contrast to the olive skin and dark hair of his Cuban mother, Manny possessed the bright blue eyes and endless charm of his Irish father.

Every young and not-so-young female on the island sighed as he walked past, and Sid could appreciate the pretty face, but the kid did nothing for her otherwise. Technically, he wasn't a kid, being only three years younger than Sid's twenty-eight, but Manny looked barely old enough to shave, which gave him the appearance of a naughty schoolboy most of the time.

Every Wednesday, Manny picked up lunch for the Adventures crew, and spent each brief visit trying to catch Sid's attention. Will hadn't mentioned making Lucas jealous, but when she thought about it, going into battle required being flexible. Adaptable. Maybe Manny could work in her favor.

Before Sid could correct Georgette on her assumption, Lucas appeared from the kitchen buttoning the cuff on his tailored shirt, which emphasized his broad shoulders perfectly. He glanced in her direction as he rounded the end of the bar. A second later, he walked into an empty bar stool.

"Damn it," he barked, righting the stool before he and it hit the floor.

"Something wrong there, skipper?" Sid asked. The immediate sign part A of the plan was working bolstered her confidence.

"No." Lucas slid the stool against the bar. "That's . . . You . . ." He made befuddled look sexy and Sid's blood began to hum. Like the purr of a powerful engine.

"I what?" Sid asked, hands on her hips, flashing what she hoped was an innocent face.

Lucas shook his head slowly. "Nothing."

Sid smiled. A half smile, half grimace was Lucas's response. As he moved about, righting already straight chairs around the tables, his eyes returned to her over and over.

"Oh, I see," Georgette said. Sid jumped, having forgotten the other waitress was there.

"You see what?"

"I don't blame you, girlfriend." The woman hugged her serving tray to her chest. "If I didn't have Milo . . ." She gave Lucas an appreciative once-over. Sid managed not to punch her in the throat, but just barely.

"But you do have Milo, so back off."

Georgette didn't look worried. "Don't get your panties in a bunch. There isn't a woman on this island who could compete with that body of yours. Just be careful." She pointed toward Lucas. "A girl could lose more than her inhibitions with a man like him. I understand the temptation to play with his kind of fire, but don't let yourself get too close. That singe can leave a permanent mark."

While Sid tried to decipher Georgette's cryptic message, the restaurant doors swung open. Tom Dempsey stopped just inside the entrance.

Looking Sid up and down, he said, "Patty. I'm going to need one of those heart pills."

CHAPTER TWELVE

L ucas saw his mom and dad enter the restaurant, then noticed his dad's face when he caught sight of Sid. Nothing like testing the old ticker right out of the gate. She was definitely testing Lucas's. Based on his body's reaction to the new getup, all systems were up and running.

"Hey there, Dad. How are you feeling?" He knew they'd be home today, but didn't know they'd make a stop at the restaurant. Tom moved with slow deliberation, his left arm held tight against his side. His pale face carried a pinched expression.

"I feel like shit," Tom said, clearly shooting for honesty. Lucas couldn't blame him, considering what he'd been through.

"He insisted we stop here on the way to the house," Patty said, leading Tom to the bar and guiding him onto a stool. "The doctor said no stress and limited physical exertion for at least the rest of the week." Turning to Sid, she said, "More outfits like that and we'll have to install a defibrillator."

Sid crossed her arms as if trying to hide, but that only made matters worse. "I didn't—"

"We've been competing to see who can earn the most tips," Lucas said, coming to Sid's rescue. "She's been kicking my ass." After hugging his mother, he moved behind the bar. "You need some water, Dad?"

"I'd rather have a beer, but doubt your mother will allow it," Tom grumbled. "Make it an iced tea."

"Unsweet," Patty said.

"Coming right up." Lucas snagged a glass from behind the bar, filled it with ice, then topped it off from a pitcher to his right. "I bet the nurses were happy to see you go."

"Ha!" Patty said. "He'd charmed every last one of them. Even Bruce. But your father wasn't too keen on Nurse Bruce giving him a sponge bath."

Tom grumbled again. "That was not going to happen."

Patty laughed, then turned to Sid, who stood a few feet behind the older couple. "I hear you and Lucas have been lighting things up around here," she said.

Sid sputtered and Lucas rode to the rescue again. "We're getting along just fine. Sid has a way with the customers you wouldn't expect from someone used to bait, tackle, and tool boxes." He smiled when her expression turned to defiance. That was his girl.

"I have to make up for Lucas's lack of service skills." She shot him an evil glare. "Just yesterday he offended an innocent group of little old ladies."

"Those women were drunk and disturbing the other customers. They'd have been dancing on the tables if they could have gotten their walkers up there."

Sid plopped onto the stool next to Tom. "Only Miss Frannie had a walker. And they were just having a good time." She rested her arms on the bar. "I liked them."

"Why doesn't that surprise me?" he said, sliding a glass of sweet tea to his mother. Sid would be one of those old ladies someday. Drinking, swearing, and challenging everyone around her. Part of him thought she'd look cute with glasses on the end of her nose, shaking her geriatric moneymaker.

"You two sound like an old married couple," Tom said, chuckling into his tea. After taking a drink, he addressed Lucas. "What do you think of the place?"

Lucas blinked, unprepared for the question. "What do you mean? The restaurant?"

"Yeah," Tom said, leaning forward, then flinching back. "Damn stitches."

"You need to be home lying down," Patty scolded.

Tom bristled. "I've been cooped up in that hospital for a week. I'll climb back into a bed when I'm ready." Lucas had never heard his dad snap like that, and fully expected his mom to snap back. Instead, she rubbed his arm and held her tongue.

Strange.

"Yes, the restaurant," Tom said, picking up the conversation again. "You've been gone long enough to see it with fresh eyes. What do you think of it?"

Lucas looked around, taking in the neon signs and empty tables. Upon agreeing to run the place, he'd thought of the job as filling drinks and keeping the staff going. He hadn't even considered analyzing the actual business.

With a shrug, he said, "I think it runs like a well-oiled machine. The staff is capable. Customers haven't complained about the food or service since I've been here."

"The drinks have come out a little slow," Sid said, shooting him a challenging look, daring him to fire back.

"That's something I have to give you credit for, Dad," he said, keeping his eyes on Sid an extra second before turning to his father. "I can see now why you had the heart attack. A long day in court is nothing to working behind this bar. I think you need help."

"You volunteering again?" A corner of Tom's mouth curled up, but something in his eyes said he wasn't kidding.

Lucas broke eye contact, grabbed a rag, and started wiping down the bar. "Not this time. You'd better get home before the crowd rolls in and you try to weasel your way back here. I'd hate to see Mom drag you out by your ear."

"He's right," Patty said. "If you don't want to lie down we'll set you up on the porch. I'm sure once the locals find out you're home, they'll be coming around to console and commiserate."

Sid hopped off her stool. "Let me help you to the car."

Tom moved slowly to his feet, then wrapped an arm around Sid's shoulders, dwarfing the tiny woman beneath his six foot five frame. Lucas thought she might buckle under the weight, but Sid moved with little effort beside his weakened father. A man he'd thought of as a superhero once upon a time.

No one liked to think about the mortality of their parents, including Lucas, so he pushed reality to the back of his mind. "Mom," he said, sliding up beside her once his dad was out of earshot. "I've never seen Dad talk to you like that. Are you okay?"

Patty sighed. "I'm fine. It's a side effect of the heart attack and surgery. The doctor warned me he'd be a bear for a while. Feeling weak and vulnerable isn't easy for any man, but especially not your father."

Lucas gave her a hug. "Everything is going to be okay," he said, not sure if the words were for her benefit or his own.

"Yes, it will." Patty gave him an extra squeeze before pulling away. "He's my life, you know. I'm not sure what I'd do without him." Tears floated in her eyes and Lucas's heart clenched. Just thinking about life without his dad made his mind revolt. There was still too much ahead—weddings and grandchildren and holiday gatherings—that Tom needed to be a part of.

"That man will outlive us all," he said. "In a few months he'll be behind this bar barking orders and keeping the tourists in check."

"But maybe he shouldn't be." The words were spoken so softly, Lucas almost didn't hear them. "I know he loves this place, but I can't let it be the death of him."

Lucas slid a finger beneath her chin, forcing her to meet his gaze. "We won't let that happen. Let's just get him healthy for now and cross that bridge when it comes."

His mom gave his hand a squeeze. "You being here means the world to him. I can't thank you enough for that."

"Make me your roast and potatoes with homemade slaw, and we'll call it even." Lucas dropped a kiss on his mom's forehead. "Then I'll whip up my latest specialty—chicken marsala. I found an amazing recipe, then gave it a kick to make it even better."

"I guess that's one good thing about you being away from home. You have to feed yourself. Joe's version of cooking is ordering a pizza." Patty walked with Lucas to the door. "About Sid's outfit? Is that for your benefit?"

"Not going there, Mom." He tried to shuffle her out.

"You could do a lot worse," she said, stopping just inside the door. "She's rough around the edges, but you could use a woman like Sid. You've gotten too polished up there in the city."

"If you keep this up, I can be on the next ferry out."

"Fine. Fine. But that girl has had a thing for—" Just then, the front door flew open, cutting Patty off and sending her headfirst into Lucas's chest.

"What the . . ." Sid came around the door and spotted them. "Sorry, Mrs. D. I didn't know you were there."

Lucas righted his mom. "I've got one parent down, let's not take out the other, huh?"

"I'm fine," Patty said. "We shouldn't have stopped so close to the door like that." Patty lifted her hand to Lucas's face, pulling him down to drop a kiss on his cheek. Then she tapped his chest and smiled. "You'll figure it out. You're a smart boy." With that, she left the building.

"What are you supposed to figure out?" Sid asked as the door closed behind Patty.

"I have no idea."

∿

By noon, Sid began to question the effectiveness of the plan. Lucas's eyes remained on her face whenever he deigned to look her way, which wasn't often, and she'd done so many laps around the dining room, her inner thighs were starting to chafe. Cutting the squats down to once a week might not have been the best idea.

They hadn't talked about the kiss on the beach, Sid's blatant invitation to sex, or Lucas's reluctant yet firm refusal. In fact, the man seemed to be using the same tactic she was, pretending nothing had happened.

Fine. If he could blow it off, then so could she.

What she couldn't seem to blow off was Lot. For a seventeen-year-old, the boy had enough pickup lines to fill a *How Not To Pick Up Women* manual. Each less creative and original than the one before, they'd made her laugh at the start of the day. After a couple hours, she wanted to deck him.

"I've got a fifteen minute break," Lot whispered. "What do you say we sneak out back and you make a man out of me?" Did the boy stay up nights thinking of this shit?

"If you keep it up, Lot, I'm going to make a girl out of you."

"So that's a maybe?"

Sid shook her head and walked away. Too bad school didn't start for another month.

"I've got three drafts, one diet, and an order of onion rings," she said, sliding the drinks from her previous order onto her tray. "Add a cup of ranch dressing with the rings."

"Coming right up." Lucas called her food order through the window to the kitchen, then moved three chilled glasses to the taps. "How did you think Dad looked this morning?"

Loading the tray onto her shoulder, Sid answered, "Like he had a heart attack a week ago. What did you think he'd look like?"

Lucas lifted one shoulder as a glass filled with beer. "I don't know. I guess I hadn't thought about it."

He looked worried so she said, "My dad had the same thing, only he never made it out of the hospital. Tom looks weak right now, but the fact he's walking around shows he's stronger than you think."

"Your dad died of a heart attack?" Lucas asked.

"Yeah," she said, the sudden turn of conversation bringing the threat of tears. "I'd better deliver these drinks."

When Sid returned for her next order, four large white bags sat on the stainless steel shelf, each marked with the letters *AA*. Manny.

"There's my girl. How you doin', Sid?"

She took a deep breath before turning around. "I'm good, Manny. How are things in Adventure Land?"

Instead of answering, Manny did his best impression of a drowning fish. Georgette floated past him and said, "Breathe, Manny."

"*Oye mamacita, que buena estás.*" He followed that statement with, "I'll take lunch duty for the rest of the summer if you keep dressing like that."

Before Sid could respond, Lucas stepped in front of her, cutting off her view of anything but his back and broad shoulders. "Can I help you?" he asked, sounding less than cordial. In fact, he sounded pissed.

"I was talking to Sid," she heard Manny say. "Who are you?"

For half a second, Sid considered taking out one of Lucas's knees for acting like a macho ass, but then she realized he was acting like a macho ass on her behalf. She was no expert, but his stance and tone indicated a bout of jealousy.

"I'm Lucas Dempsey. Who are you?"

"Oh, hey bro. Randy told me about you." Sid leaned to her left to see Manny extend his hand. "Manuel Sullivan. I work for Sid's brother."

Lucas took the offered hand, but his body remained tense, continuing to block Sid from the rest of the room. "You here to pick up the food?"

"That and to see Sid."

Over the tough guy act, Sid stepped around Lucas. "I thought you two forgot I was here." She threw a harassed look over her shoulder and stepped closer to Manny. Time to show Lucas she had other options. "You still need your oil changed? We could do it after work today."

"Can't unless you've got a garage," Manny said. "Hurricane Ingrid took a turn our way. They think she'll turn back out, but the rain should be here this afternoon and probably won't stop until the weekend." Moving into her space, he added, "We could do something else instead." His eyes dropped several inches below her chin, evoking a growl from Lucas.

Turned out pretty boy had an alpha side after all. Though she should have learned that lesson on the beach. Now to keep the ruse going without encouraging Manny.

"She can't," Lucas said, taking the next move out of her hands.

Manny moved his gaze from Sid to Lucas. "That's up to Sid."

"Sid is busy tonight."

"I am?"

"You are." Lucas shot her a look that clearly said *Do not argue.* She considered it, then opted to quit while she was ahead.

"Right." Sid turned back to Manny. "Sorry, I forgot. Lucas and I have this . . . " she hesitated, "thing."

The three stood awkwardly for several seconds, Lucas trying to bore a hole through Manny's chest with his eyes, Manny looking less than convinced about Sid's explanation, and Sid not sure what to do next. Manny was a good guy. She didn't want to hurt him.

"Would you excuse us for a minute?" she said to Manny, then without giving him a chance to answer, turned to Lucas. "I need to see you in the kitchen."

"I'm good. Just bring him the food."

"Dempsey," Sid barked, tiring of the macho act. "Kitchen. Now."

Once certain Lucas was following, Sid charged back to the office. "You want to catch me up here?"

"On what?" Lucas asked, fumbling through the mail as if nothing weird had happened. As if *he* hadn't just announced they had a date.

"We have plans?"

"Oh, that." He dropped the mail back on the blotter. "I just said that to get rid of lover boy out there."

Instant dislike of the other guy. Good sign.

"What if I didn't want to get rid of him? And don't call Manny that. He's not so bad."

Lucas crossed his arms. "You seeing that kid?"

"He's not a kid."

"He looks barely old enough to shave."

"For your information, Manny is only four years younger than you are."

One brow shot up. "You haven't answered my question. Is he your boyfriend?"

No sense in lying. "No, he's not. And you should know I'm not the kind of girl who would offer sex to you if I was seeing someone else. But what do you care anyway? If I remember correctly, you don't want me."

His arms dropped and he moved closer. "I never said I didn't want you."

"You said no." A girl didn't forget throwing herself at a man, only to watch him walk away.

"That's not the same thing."

So much for men being simple creatures. "What was all that growling out there?"

"I didn't like what he said to you." The arms crossed again.

"The part about doing something else tonight?" That *had* taken her by surprise. Manny had never come on that strong before. The damn outfit was working on everyone but its intended target.

Lucas paced the four feet to the door and back. Running a hand through his hair, he said, "No. The part in Spanish."

"You speak Spanish?" she asked, mystified.

"My first job out of law school was immigration work."

Sid had to admit, she was curious. "What did Manny say?"

"You don't know?" His eyes went wide.

Sid shrugged. "It's been fourteen years. Randy rarely speaks it and I've forgotten the little I knew as a kid. So tell me what he said."

Lucas mumbled, "He said you're fine."

"I'm fine?" Sid tried to imagine how that could be offensive. "That's it?"

"It's not what he said, it's how he said it." Another hand through the hair. "I need to get back out there. No one's behind the bar."

"Wait a minute." She stopped him with a hand on his arm. "What are we doing tonight?"

"We're not doing anything."

"Oh, yes we are. I told Manny we were doing something, and you're not going to make a liar out of me."

"He'll never know."

She tapped her chin. "Needs to be something we can do in the rain if the storm is moving in."

"Rain or shine, we don't have plans." He looked ready to throttle her, but Sid pushed forward.

"Don't even think about standing me up."

Lucas threw his hands in the air and looked up as if seeking divine intervention. "What did I do to deserve this woman?"

"I don't know," Sid answered for whomever Lucas sought in the ceiling. "But it must have been damn good. Since you're skittish, I better pick you up."

"You are not picking me up." Lucas pushed up his sleeves.

"You can drive then. Don't get so hostile. I'm at the end of Tuttle's Lane." Sid moved past Lucas, then stopped at the door. "Be there at seven and don't be late."

Sid headed for the dining room without giving Lucas the chance to refuse. From the office his voice boomed, "Fine. But you better be ready."

CHAPTER THIRTEEN

All right. Tell me what the heck's going on." Beth stomped to the counter, curls bouncing and eyes snapping. Will had never seen her usually even-tempered friend this worked up.

"Aren't you supposed to be running the store?" Will asked, looking to the clock to see if she'd lost track of the afternoon.

"Don't start with the clock crap again. I've been off all day thanks to that little stunt you pulled." Beth threw a stirrer at Will. "Why did you get rid of me this morning? And don't tell me that's not what happened."

Will knew when to come clean. She called out, "Brad, I'm going out to lower the umbrellas before the rain starts." Stepping out from behind the counter, she said to Beth, "Come on. I'll explain outside."

The air had turned cool with the impending hurricane. Will rubbed her arms, turning to face Beth. "Sid wanted to talk about something, but didn't feel comfortable doing so with you around."

"Why? What did I do?"

"You slept with Lucas." Not the best approach, but Will didn't like being the go-between in this. "Now Sid is trying to sleep with him, and she thinks talking about that with you would be weird."

Beth blinked. "I think I need to sit down."

Will pulled out a chair at the nearest table and motioned for Beth to do the same. "For the record, I told her she shouldn't keep you out of this."

"Does Lucas know?" Beth asked.

"That you slept with him? Um . . . I'd think so."

"Stop that. You know what I mean."

Will answered honestly. "I don't know. I mean, I know she offered him sex and he turned her down."

"Whoa." Beth held up a hand. "You're going to have to start this from the beginning."

"Right." Will conveyed the details she knew about Sid and Lucas's kiss on the beach, and the subsequent sex offer and refusal. How any man could turn Sid down was a mystery to her, but Lucas seemed to have a valid reason. Which Will couldn't fault the man for.

"He does have a point about the casual thing," Beth said, once the story was out. "Has Sid ever even been in a relationship?"

"She's not a virgin, based on what little she's told me. But she's not exactly the queen of girl talk, you know." Not that Will wanted to have slumber parties and discuss menstrual cycles, but Sid was more likely to talk head gaskets and crank bait.

"Did you know she reads romance novels?" Beth whispered, as if conveying national secrets.

"No shit. Really?" Sid didn't look to have a romantic bone in her body. Even when she talked about kissing Lucas, there was nothing sappy or swoony about it. "I had no idea."

"I don't think anyone does," Beth said. "In fact, she threatened that if I told the guys about it, she'd kill me. Only she phrased it in a more Sid-like way."

Sid did have a creative way with violent description. "Good thing I'm not one of the guys."

"That's her problem. She's been one of the guys for too long." Beth leaned back in her chair. "I was amazed the first time I saw her. She was playing pool with a bunch of the islanders, and they were smacking her on the back and acting like there wasn't a centerfold bending over the table. Men can be so clueless."

"Lucas doesn't strike me as the clueless type, but he's definitely playing the gentleman." Will had noticed how Lucas's eyes followed Sid around the room, so she knew there was interest. Even when he'd been flirting with Will, his heart wasn't in it.

"I'm not sure what's going on with him. He's pragmatic and the most ambitious man I've ever met, but what Joe and I did to him left a mark." Beth looked off in the distance. "I wouldn't change how things are now, but I wish he hadn't been the one to get hurt. Even with that, he's the one who sent Joe to get me."

"You never told me that." Will hadn't been friends with Sid and Beth back when the whole fiancée exchange had happened. They'd met, as Will had been the one to serve them drinks the night the ladies got tanked on tequila, but their little threesome was more recent.

"I was leaving for Boston. I didn't want to work in law anymore and even if I had, I never could have stayed at the firm. Seeing Lucas would have been like seeing Joe and not being able to talk to him, or touch him." She shrugged.

"Anyway, Lucas called Joe and told him I was leaving. Said to get his ass up to Richmond or he'd lose me forever."

"Wow. That was big of him."

Beth laughed. "That's Lucas. There's a suppressed superhero behind those Dockers and button-up shirts. Fighting for justice and setting the world aright."

"So if he thinks having a fling with Sid, then leaving her a few weeks later would break her heart, he won't do it." Will hadn't encountered many men of Lucas's caliber. Shame there wasn't a third brother for her.

She nearly slapped that thought out of her head. Will would never drop her guard for a man again. No matter how decent he appeared to be.

The women sat in silence for a long moment, then Beth asked, "What are we going to do?"

"Hell if I know," Will said. She'd been pondering the situation all day, but kept coming to the same conclusion. "She wants him and is determined she can love him and leave him with no problem. Who are we to say she can't?"

Beth caught Will's eye. "Her friends. Don't we owe it to her to protect her?"

Will knew better than anyone how little your friends could protect you. "Sometimes you have to let friends figure things out on their own. I think this is one of those times."

~

Lucas pulled in behind Sid's truck at 6:55, still with no idea what the hell he was doing there. Nearly twelve hours before, he'd told her they couldn't start anything. And now he was picking her up for a date. The only place he could think

137

to take her in the rain was the marina restaurant. Dinner at Dempsey's was out of the question.

Too many people to whom he'd have to explain. Besides, they'd never hear each other over the noise. At the marina, they could have a nice meal, just two adults sitting down to eat, then he'd take her home and this farce of a date would be over.

He considered honking, but his mother's voice in his ear saying *I taught you better manners than that* had him climbing from the car. At least he didn't have to use his mother's minivan. Now that his parents were home, Lucas could once again enjoy the smooth ride of German engineering.

The rain had eased to a drizzle so he pulled the collar up on his sport jacket and made a break for the porch. The inside door was open so he knocked on the metal screen.

"Come on in," yelled a voice from somewhere inside. "I'm almost done."

Torn between irritation that she wasn't ready and the lack of a proper greeting at the door, Lucas stepped inside and stopped to take in his surroundings. The interior before him could have been a magazine shoot for the perfect beach cottage. White paneling, well-worn aqua blue area rug, seashell-covered picture frames. Even the coffee table looked to be made out of salvaged wood from an old pier.

Two accent pillows on the couch. A multicolored throw draped naturally over the back of the sofa, and the arrangement of frames on the wall was artful chaos. Somehow it worked.

He'd expected something resembling a frat house. What he'd walked into was spotless without feeling sterile, welcoming, and purely feminine. Sid was clearly no frat boy.

Something he should have remembered from their encounter on the beach.

"I just have to feed the cat, then I'll be ready to go," Sid said, entering the room while putting her hair up in a ponytail. She'd thankfully returned to her normal style of dress with jeans and an oversized gray shirt. Though not her usual tee with some obscene message. This one had a wide neckline that fell off one shoulder, revealing olive skin and what looked to be a black tank underneath.

Two questions hit Lucas at the same time. Why didn't she ever wear her hair down? And Sid had a cat? He went with the second since having her hair down would undoubtedly have him longing to touch it all night.

"I didn't peg you for the cat type."

"I'm not. Curly made me take her." Sid padded across the floor in white socks and snagged a pair of black boots off the floor beside the couch. "You can come all the way in, you know. I promise not to jump your bones and tie you to my bedpost."

Lucas ignored the ping of disappointment. "How did she make you take a cat?"

"Curly has her ways."

He followed her into the kitchen and spotted a smudge of gray fur hovering under a kitchen chair. At first it looked like a dried hair ball, then it moved. "That tiny ball of fur is your cat?"

"Yep." Turning with a can of cat food in her hand, Sid put the can opener to work. "Lucas, meet Drillbit. Drillbit, this is Lucas. Shake hands and come out fighting."

Lucas bent down to get a closer look. Big blue eyes blinked up at him. Upon closer inspection, he could see dark stripes throughout the light gray hair and a solid white chest with white on the tips of its feet. He didn't go for pets much, but this one was cute.

"What kind of a name is Drillbit?"

"Stand around long enough and you'll see." Sid scooped the food into a small pink bowl, then moved to the sink to rinse off the spoon.

Before she'd turned off the water, something sharp pierced Lucas's leg. "What the . . ." The innocent-looking blue eyes stared up at him again, but this time the rest of the animal was attached to his thigh. And climbing dangerously close to an important area of his anatomy.

He grabbed the cat around the middle. She was so small his fingers overlapped under the belly. He pulled but she held tight. "Can you get this thing off?"

Sid turned around. "Shit." Before she could intervene, the demon spawn let go of his leg and wrapped around his hand.

"Motherfucker, this thing is possessed."

"Such language, Counselor."

He could see Sid was suppressing a laugh and shot her an evil look. "I should have known any pet of yours would have claws and not be afraid to use them."

"Keep it up and you can get her off all by yourself. But I'll warn you, she'll shred that fancy jacket before you know what hit you."

Sid lifted the feline by the scruff of her neck, supporting her with a hand beneath her bottom, and the kitten let go. Lucas's hand was covered in scratches, two of them bleeding.

"You need a 'beware of cat' sign on the door." He rinsed his hand in the sink as Sid cooed to the lioness-in-training. "Aren't you worried she'll latch onto your face?"

"We have an understanding." Sid nuzzled the kitten's tummy in a completely un-Sid-like way. "It's funny, actually. Someone dropped her at Joe's and Curly was afraid Dozer would eat her." Sid spoke to the fur ball in a baby talk voice. "You'd have ripped that slobbery mutt to pieces, huh? That's my girl."

Lucas turned off the water and stood with his dripping hands over the sink, staring in disbelief. "Who are you and what have you done with Sid?"

She flipped him the bird.

"Ah, there you are." After drying his hands on a towel hanging over the sink, Lucas noticed the cuts were still bleeding. Feeding the menace to Dozer sounded like a damn good idea. "I'm going to need a Band-Aid. Has that thing had its shots?"

"She's like seven weeks old or something. Of course she hasn't had her shots." Sid pulled a box of bandages from the drawer behind her and threw them his way. "Doctor yourself up, then we'll go. And don't be such a whiner."

"You're going to have to help me."

Sid turned, eyebrows up. "Excuse me? Do I look like a nurse?"

"No," he said, "but you'd look really hot in the uniform." She blushed, as he knew she would. A compliment was the only way to shut the woman up. "I'm buying you dinner; the least you can do is put a Band-Aid on me."

"You're buying me dinner?" Sid asked, opening the small white box.

"I made you lie by insinuating we had a date, so now I'm fulfilling my obligation by taking you out to dinner." Best to set the boundaries up front. "Quick meal at the marina, on me, then we're done."

Sid ripped the bandage open. "No."

"No, what? Are you refusing to go out with me?" About time Sid came to her senses.

"No on the 'then we're done' part." Raising the Band-Aid, she stopped. "We should put something on that first. Hold on." A tube came from the same drawer where the bandages had been. "Hold still."

Sid held his hand steady, calloused fingers pressed gently against his palm. In the same way he imagined she'd change a spark plug, she squeezed antibacterial cream onto the tiny wound, then placed the Band-Aid over it, making sure the ends were secure.

"There." When she looked up, he felt her breath against his chin. Chocolate eyes went wide, then her lids lowered, long dark lashes resting softly against her cheek. She wore not a speck of makeup and he found the lack of affectation attractive. Sid didn't need anything artificial to look beautiful.

She just was.

Sid licked her lips and Lucas cleared his throat. "We'd better get going."

Maybe the rain had picked up. He could use the cold shower.

∼

They'd arrived at the restaurant by the time Sid's heart rate returned to normal. Which wasn't that long since her house was about a minute from the marina. Though with Lucas at the wheel it was more like two minutes. The man drove like he couldn't reach the gas pedal. Frannie the Red Hatter could have outrun him. On her walker.

By the end of the main course, they'd exhausted such scintillating topics as the weather, Joe's business, the necessary evil of tourists, and the passable taste of the wine. Sid sucked at small talk, but she was doing her best. Lucas didn't look miserable, which she took as a good sign.

When the waiter breezed past, Lucas waved him down.

"What are you doing?" Sid asked.

"Asking for the check. Why?"

Sid huffed. "We haven't had dessert yet."

Lucas looked pained. "You've had half a basket of rolls, a baked potato, the largest steak they serve, and eaten my broccoli as well as your own."

"You said you didn't want it." Wasn't as if she'd swiped it from his fork.

"I didn't want it. But how could you have room for dessert?"

What kind of a question was that? "There's always room for dessert. Especially here."

The waiter had finished taking the order from a couple three tables down and now stood over Sid and Lucas. "Can I get you folks anything else?"

"I guess so," Lucas said. "We'll need to see a dessert menu."

"Forget the menu, Goober. Bring one To Die For and one cheesecake."

"Coming right up."

Lucas leaned over the table and whispered, "Did you just call him Goober?"

Another waiter passed their table carrying a large plate of scallops. The scent made Sid's mouth water. She'd have to talk Lucas into another date so she could order those. Her budget didn't allow dinner at the marina anytime she wanted.

"Of course. Why?"

He whispered louder. "A bit insulting, don't you think?"

Sid propped her elbows on the table. "That's his name. We went to high school together. Don't you remember him?"

Lucas jerked back, his gaze shooting toward where the waiter had disappeared into the kitchen. A second later his eyes opened wide. "That's Goober McGruber?"

"The one and only. How could you forget that red hair?" Sid straightened her napkin. "Though I guess there's less of it now."

"Huh." He shook his head. "Doesn't anyone get off this island?"

Sid prickled. "There's nothing wrong with this island. If you spent more time here you'd know that."

Lucas snorted. "I grew up here, Sid. There's nothing on this island."

He had no idea how close he was to getting a bruised shin. "Then what are we sitting in? Where have we been working every day for the last week? And where did you get the best Key lime pie of your life?"

"I didn't mean—"

"And what about your family? And my family, small as it may be. We have lives here, and friends, and it's pretty shitty of you to dismiss us all as nothing."

Goober returned with their desserts, but looked apologetic for interrupting what was clearly a heated discussion.

"The cheesecake goes to asshole over there," Sid said, too frustrated with Lucas's attitude to curb her speech. Curly would have scolded her for that one.

Lucas slid his empty plate to the edge of the table to make room for the new course, but remained silent. Sid did the same, allowing Goober to set down the new plate and pick up the empty ones.

"Will there be anything else? Coffee?"

"This is good, thanks." Lucas smiled at Goober, then once he walked away, stared at Sid.

After several seconds, she cracked. "What?"

"I'm sorry."

CHAPTER FOURTEEN

She looked for mocking in his hazel eyes but only found contrition. "Good."

"Let me rephrase."

Her eyes rolled so hard she nearly went dizzy.

"There is nothing *to do* on this island," he corrected.

Sid slid a bite of her chocolate cake layered with chocolate mousse sitting on a crunchy chocolate cookie base—hence the name "To Die For"—into her mouth, and contemplated her reply as the sweetness soothed the bitterness brought on by the man across the table.

"You know, preppy," she said, sliding another piece onto her fork, "for such a smart guy, you don't know much of anything."

Lucas coughed, nearly choking on his cheesecake. After wiping his mouth with his napkin, he said, "Excuse me?"

Another warm dose of chocolate heaven delayed her response. "By my calculations, you've been off this island, for the most part, for eleven years now." It was eleven years, one month, and four days, but who was counting?

He leaned to the side, draping an arm over the back of his chair. "And?"

"A lot has changed around here."

The man had the nerve to bust out laughing. Rearranging his napkin on his lap, he retrieved his fork, but before taking a bite, he pointed the utensil at Sid. "You're funny. Nothing ever changes on this island. The natives still talk the way their ancestors did two hundred years ago—like they grew up in New England in the seventeen hundreds. They still tell the same stories, sitting in the same old rocking chairs, because making life sound interesting is the only way to keep the reality of how uninteresting it really is from putting everyone into a depression."

Lucas shoveled a large bite of cheesecake into his blowhole as if that would add punctuation to the load of crap he'd just spewed.

Sid shook her head. "You're wrong. And I'm going to prove it."

"How?" Lucas mumbled around his cheesecake.

"I'm telling your mother you talked with your mouth full." He smacked his free hand on the table, but she ignored him. "I bet I can show you a good time on this island. Several good times. And I don't just mean sex, though that's still on the table. For now."

She dug into her cake again, enjoying watching Lucas gasp for air. Cheesecake must have gone down the wrong pipe. Once he appeared to be out of danger, she continued.

"We'll start tonight. After dinner we're going to the movies."

The dessert down, Lucas leaned back and motioned for the waiter again. "There is no movie theater on Anchor Island." He pulled a wallet from his inside coat pocket and drew out a gold credit card. Fancy ass.

"See? You're wrong again." Sid reached over and grabbed Lucas's left wrist to see his watch. "Movie starts in twenty-five minutes. We're good to go."

Goober set the check on the table, then looked to Sid. "You want a to-go box for that, Sid?"

"I'll have it done before you finish running pretty boy here's credit card."

Lucas sighed and slid the card into the guest check holder without saying a word. Goober deserved credit for remaining professional and ignoring his customers' strange behavior. They would certainly be the winning odd couple of the night.

"Are you going to insist on playing out this charade? You and I both know there is no movie theater anywhere on this island."

"Dude," Sid said, slicing what was left of her cake into three large pieces. "When are you going to learn I don't bluff? I wasn't bluffing this morning. And I'm not bluffing now. I'll prove to you there's plenty of fun to be had on this island. With and without our clothes on."

~

Lucas had no intention of having sex with Sid Navarro, no matter how often she insisted they would. Sex with Sid would only lead to unwanted complications. He was going back to Richmond. He would straighten out his career, and he would make partner.

And yet, he really wanted to have sex with Sid.

If someone had told him he'd be attracted to a hard-headed, dirty-mouthed, mentally unstable woman with a competitive streak and a body built for sin, he never would have believed them. Lucas liked good girls. He always had. Not that Sid was necessarily a bad girl. She just played one in his dreams.

Bottom line, Sid was not his type. He liked the girl next door. The woman who could throw a dinner party, schmooze with politicians, and go shopping with the other partners' wives. Not that he had antiquated ideals about the fairer sex. Though maybe referring to them as the fairer sex didn't make him sound all that progressive either.

Regardless, women could do it all and they had the right to do as much or as little as they wanted. He wasn't out to set societal standards for all womankind. He just wanted a certain type of woman, preferably one who wouldn't pretend to be one thing, turn into something else, then leave him for his brother.

"Turn left up here, where those cars are parked." Sid had been giving him directions since they'd left the restaurant. He hadn't bothered to argue with her statement about them having sex. He'd made his stance clear that morning and would not be swayed.

At least not from the neck up. From the neck down was a different story.

Once he'd parked the car and cut the engine, Lucas recognized the building before him. "This is Arthur Berkowitz's law office. What are we doing here?"

"Wrong again, Dempsey. This *was* Arthur Berkowitz's law office." She flopped a hand toward the building like a game show model showing off the next item up for bid. "Now it's Artie B's Island Theater."

He leaned forward and looked up. Sure enough, those four words flashed on a gaudy red and blue neon sign hanging from the roof peak. "You have got to be kidding me." Artie had said there were no takers for the practice, but a movie theater?

"I need a bathroom stop and time to get popcorn so hurry up." Sid dashed out of the car and jogged through the drizzle to stand under the rusty awning covering the front door.

She might be the least pretentious woman he'd ever met. Whatever tactics she planned to use to lure him into bed, sophistication and charm would not be among them.

Lucas hurried through the rain, locking the car on his way, then shuffled Sid through the door. A bell rang over their heads, causing him to look up. That same bell had been there during the summers he worked for Artie.

Further proof nothing ever changed on this island.

The reception window—still in the same place—slid open as they approached. "Well if it isn't Lucas Dempsey, prodigal lawyer. Come to check out the old digs?"

"Something like that." Movie posters lined walls that once held Artie's framed college degrees—one from Georgetown, the other from Duke. Spending the majority of his career on Anchor Island had been a waste of both in Lucas's opinion.

"Good to see you getting out and enjoying the island a bit. I remember you were always griping as a teen that there was nothing to do. Plenty to do around here these days." Artie beamed through the window opening, as if he'd heard the conversation they'd had at the restaurant.

"What's playing tonight, Artie?" Sid asked, pulling cash from her front pocket.

"I'll get the tickets," Lucas said.

"You paid for dinner. I'll get the tickets." She laid ten dollars on the counter.

"Tonight we're showing one of my favorites. *The Fugitive*." Artie slid the ten back Sid's way. "The tickets are on the house. Thanks to you two I don't have to run the movie for an empty theater. Hard to bring folks out on a rainy Wednesday night."

Sid tried to argue, but Artie disappeared from the window and reappeared through the doorway to their left. "Come get yourself some popcorn and then take your seats. Show starts in five minutes." He pulled the door wide, showing them into a large room full of couches of varying shapes and sizes. "Maybe we'll get some other stragglers before then."

Sid shot Lucas a challenging look as she spoke to Artie. "We don't mind watching the movie alone."

Sitting in a darkened room, on a couch, alone with Sid. His brain said not a good idea, but other parts of his anatomy were all for it.

"What kind of theater has couches instead of chairs?" Lucas asked. Theaters had seats. Individual, hard, uncomfortable seats. With protective and immovable arms between them.

"The welcoming kind," Artie said, an innocent grin splitting his chubby face.

"You go grab our . . . uh . . . couch, Sid. I want to talk to Artie for a second." Time to discuss the Ledbetter fiasco and nip this legal advice crap in the bud.

"Extra butter on your popcorn?" she asked, walking backward toward a large red popcorn machine.

"Yeah, thanks." Turning to Artie he said, "I don't appreciate you sending the Ledbetters to see me this morning."

Had it really only been this morning? From his inadvisable encounter with Sid on the beach to now felt more like a week had gone by.

"Aw," Artie said, waving Lucas's words away. "They just needed a mediator to help 'em work out that tree issue. I'm out of the business now, but I knew you could handle it."

"Artie." Lucas ran a hand through his hair, struggling to remain patient with his former boss. "I am on this island for one reason: to run my family's restaurant while my dad recovers. I am not here to practice law, mediate tree issues, or take over your practice. And don't think I don't know that's what you're up to."

The lawyer cum theater owner looked wounded, revealing acting skills that would have been priceless when applied in a courtroom. "I object to your accusation."

Clearly you could take the man out of the lawyering but not the lawyering out of the man.

"Object all you like, but I'm on to you, Arthur Berkowitz." Lucas pointed a finger at the opposing counselor's chest. "Don't send anyone else to see me about a legal matter. I practice in Richmond, not here."

"But your license to practice in Virginia is good here too," Artie pointed out, unfazed by Lucas's stern tone. The man was being obtuse on purpose.

"Irrelevant. Let it go, Artie. I'm not moving back here."

But if I did, I could have Sid.

That disturbing thought took him by such surprise, Lucas actually stepped back, bumping into the fake fern behind him. Where in the hell did his brain get off throwing that kind of bullshit into the ether? And no he could not have Sid. He didn't even want Sid. The woman would have him jumping off a pier into shark-infested waters within hours.

"You all right there, Lucas? You look like you're having a stroke."

Lucas wasn't sure what the symptoms of a stroke might be, but if sudden loss of sanity was one, he could definitely be in trouble.

Shaking his head as if to eject the crazy thoughts out his ears, Lucas stepped forward again. "I'm fine. Sugar rush from the cheesecake I had at the marina."

Right. Sugar was doing this to his system. He looked to his left and spotted Sid leaning over the back of a cushy, red leather sofa, watching him with a look that made him feel like *he* should have been on the dessert menu. Damn woman.

"Just remember what I said, Artie." He walked into the theater, tempted to claim a couch of his own. But that would reveal a weakness that Sid would no doubt pounce on until she had him moaning against that hot little body of hers.

Be strong, Dempsey. That way madness lies.

∼

When Lucas finally joined her on the red sofa, Sid had no idea what to do next. She'd been talking big all night. Talking big had been her specialty for years. And in most cases, she could back it up with action. But in this moment, she was totally out of her element.

Sid had never seduced anyone. In fact, she could count her sexual encounters on one hand and still have three fingers left over. The dating pool wasn't deep on Anchor. Most of the males on the island saw Sid as one of the guys, which never bothered her. Much. Unless they made some joke about her liking other women. She'd punched men for lesser transgressions.

As for the tourists, they hit on her often enough, but a fling with a stranger didn't appeal. Which she supposed made Lucas and Will correct on the casual thing. So Sid didn't change bed partners like changing her socks. She didn't have sex just for the sake of having it. So what?

A fling with Lucas would be different. For one thing, he wasn't a stranger. And though he'd never again live on the island, he had ties here. He'd be back. Seeing him once or a twice a year would suck, but that had always sucked. She'd survived this long. She'd survive again.

And as Will put it, he'd be out of her system. She could get on with her life without this unrequited thing hanging over her head.

"Where do we get the drinks?" Lucas asked, setting his bag of popcorn on the table in front of the couch. Artie had collected every unwanted couch and coffee table he could find on the island to furnish the place. Gave a nice home theater vibe. Sid hoped it would lead Lucas to forget they were in a public place.

"There's a fridge back that way, near the bathrooms." Sid pointed toward a hallway to their right. "Just leave a dollar in the honor box next to it. I'll take a bottle of water." Her stomach tended to make strange noises when she drank soda late at night. Would not be good trying to get cozy with Lucas in the dark only to have him think an alien might burst through her belly button.

With a nod, her date—which was more fun to say than she'd admit—headed for the hallway. Just as he disappeared around the corner, a shrill voice echoed from the back of the room.

"Sidney Navarro? Is that you?"

Shit damn fuck. Not Crystal Casternack. Not tonight.

"Aw, are you here by yourself?" The slender blonde gave a knowing smile to her minions, Heather Ledbetter, who had the misfortune of looking just like her dad, and Lissa Whitmore, the most clueless twit to ever graduate from Anchor High.

Why couldn't Lucas's prom date have put on a hundred pounds and grown a mole? On her chin? That sprouted long black hairs?

"Now that we're here, you can pretend you came with friends."

Sid would rather drop a couch on Crystal's head. No jury would convict her. "I'm not alone, Casterhack, but thanks."

Prom queen's jaw tensed. "That's Caster*nack*."

"Right. My bad." Sid hunkered down deeper into the couch, thinking of all the ways she could turn Crystal and her chicklets into fish bait. No one would ever find the bodies.

A second later, the dimmed sconces on the walls went out and the sixty-inch flat screen at the front of the room came to life. Halfway through the first trailer, Lucas returned to the couch, nearly tripping over the coffee table and landing on the cushion beside her with an oomph.

"Holy shit. Why didn't you warn me how dark this place would get?"

Shushing noises came from the couch beside them. Thanks to Artie's penchant for a totally black theater, Lucas's identity remained a mystery to the three bimbettes.

"Who is that?" Leaning forward, Lucas tried to see who was beside them. Of course the screen went bright white in that moment, increasing visibility.

"Lucas Dempsey, is that you?"

Sid gritted her teeth until her jaw ached. She longed to make Crystal's jaw ache.

"This is Lucas. Who are you?"

"It's Crystal, silly?" Blondie said, as if they'd been chatting on the phone just last week. Sid snagged her water from Lucas and resisted the urge to accidentally douse the next couch with it.

"Crystal?" Lucas's seeming confusion won bonus points from Sid. With fewer than ten people in his graduating class, how hard could it be to remember the chick he took to prom? He had to be playing stupid.

"Casternack!" Without an invitation, the blonde pranced over, inserting herself between Sid and Lucas. "I haven't seen you in forever. You look great."

Sid leaned around the interloper to see one perfectly manicured nail on Lucas's knee. Oh, hell no.

"Excuse me," Sid said, tapping Crystal on the shoulder with much less force than she could have. The blonde turned around, rubbing the spot where Sid had poked. "Lucas and I are here to watch the movie. Get your skinny ass back on your own couch."

Crystal's head spun toward Lucas, back to Sid, then back to Lucas. Maybe the thing would spin right off and improve everyone's night.

"You two are together?" Without waiting for an answer, she went on. "Is someone paying you to take her out?" she asked Lucas.

Sid reached out to grab a handful of hair, but Lucas caught her wrist before contact. "I stopped taking payment for dates after the prom," he said, sounding more put out than Sid expected. And what did that last crack mean? Had someone *paid* him to take Crystal to the prom?

This night was looking up.

Crystal leapt to her feet. "I see you're still the pompous ass you always were. Thinking you're better than the rest of us."

"And you're still as hateful and self-centered as I remember. Now if you could honor Sid's more than polite request and return your . . ." He looked to Sid. "How did you put it?"

"Skinny ass," she said, smiling as the warm spot in her chest spread to her knees.

"Right." Back to Crystal he said, "Your skinny ass back to your own couch."

By this point he'd gone from holding Sid's wrist in midair to holding her hand on the couch between them. Sid felt like giggling. Something she never, ever did.

Crystal huffed. Stomped. Squealed. And finally returned to her couch. The minions were whispering reassurances, but Sid couldn't have cared less. She looked over to find Lucas smiling at her, still holding her hand, slumped down in the overstuffed red leather sofa.

Best. Date. Ever.

CHAPTER FIFTEEN

Lucas knew he should feel bad, but Crystal Casternack had made his life miserable in high school, stalking him in the halls, telling everyone they were getting married and she'd be the pampered wife of a powerful lawyer. They'd never even gone out on a date. He'd only taken her to prom because Crystal's mom kept calling his mom about it. Desperate to end the torture, Tom gave him a hundred bucks to bite the bullet and take one for the team, as he'd put it.

As a result, Lucas's prom had sucked. Not that guys cared much about that stuff, and with only four girls total in his graduating class, there wasn't a large number of other dates to choose from. All the others were spoken for by the time he asked Crystal.

But none of that was cause for him to be so rude to her all these years later. The way she'd talked about Sid was what sent him over the edge. As if any man would have to be paid to go out with Sid Navarro. Grant it, she could be brash at times. Okay, all the time. But she had her moments. Like when she smiled the way she had after he sent Crystal stomping back to her friends.

She'd looked happy, surprised, and grateful with that one adoring look. The adoring part made him nervous. The way she'd sprinkled the sex comments into their dinner conversation, he'd begun to believe maybe a casual fling could work. Then he saw that look. But she hadn't clung to him through the movie. Didn't protest when he let her hand go to open his drink, then didn't take it back again.

No pressure. No sign she was going all gooey on him. Then again, Sid was likely incapable of going gooey over anything. Maybe he'd just imagined the look.

They'd enjoyed the movie in silence, then waited until Crystal and her friends had gone before moving toward the exit. Other than telling Artie good night, neither had spoken since before the movie started.

"Thank you," Sid said, staring out the passenger window into the falling rain, her expression unreadable.

"You're welcome," he said, out of reflex. After a moment of silence he asked, "For what?"

Sid turned his way, brown eyes serious. "You didn't tell Casterhack in there that this isn't a real date."

Lucas shrugged one shoulder. "We went to dinner and a movie, right?"

"Yeah. But not because you wanted to go."

"Says who?"

"Said you." She went back to staring out the window. This was a side of Sid he wasn't sure how to handle.

"This may not have been my idea, but I had fun. Great food. The most comfortable theater seat I've ever experienced." He elbowed her softly. "And the company wasn't bad either. I mean, you have your moments."

Like this one. The spitting, cursing, challenging Sid he knew what to do with. Softer Sid was an enigma wrapped in a centerfold threatening his peace of mind.

"Careful, you might woo me with your romantic words." She grinned his way, the vulnerable look gone. "Did someone really pay you to take her to the prom?"

He cringed. "You caught that, huh?"

"I'm quick like that."

Crystal had suffered enough for one night. "Let's hold that story for another day."

"Fine. Keep your secrets." Sid grew quiet again, which made Lucas nervous.

Quiet meant she could be plotting something diabolical. "You okay over there?"

"Just thinking." Before he could toss off a witty retort to that she said, "No cracks, preppy. I was thinking since you were a good sport tonight, I should cut you a break and not bother you anymore."

Not what he expected. And surprisingly not what he wanted. "So you're forfeiting the challenge?"

She turned to face him while leaning back against the door. "What challenge? We didn't make a bet tonight."

"Yes, we did. You said you could show me a good time on this island." He might live to regret his next statement, but in spite of his better judgment, Lucas wanted to spend more time with her. "You've got five weeks to do it."

Narrowed eyes pinned him in place. He said the one thing he knew would push her to agree. "Unless you want to give up now. I wouldn't blame you."

"You're going down, Dempsey. I hope you're up to the challenge."

Such a predictable woman. "Bring it on, Navarro. Bring. It. On."

～

Still floating on the high of her date, Sid took a full minute to wake up enough the next morning to register the deluge of water pounding against her cottage. A brush of heavy rain from a far-off-the-coast hurricane was typical for Anchor, but the amount of standing water in her backyard was not. Maybe Ingrid was getting closer than they'd expected.

Sid switched on the radio in her bathroom, which was always tuned to WANK radio, the voice of Anchor Island. The call letters were unfortunate, but fitting.

"It's not looking good, folks. All tourists should leave the island today. Ingrid is expected to be a cat two when she slides by less than seventy-five miles off shore." Hermie Dash, an Anchor native and avid storm watcher, sounded almost gleeful as he reported the update. "The brunt should be here around three a.m. tomorrow morning if she holds the current course."

"Hundred mile per hour winds," she said aloud. "Shit."

Sid checked the landline and got a dial tone. At least they hadn't lost service yet. A quick punch of two buttons and the tone turned to a ring.

"Did you hear?" Beth asked, forgoing the typical greeting.

"Just now. Is Joe getting the boat up?"

"Left fifteen minutes ago. I'm lining up help to board up the art store, and the volunteer fire squad should be working on Tom and Patty's house before noon. They'll need a hand up at the restaurant."

The last thing Tom needed on his second day home was a damn hurricane. He needed no stress, not a bitch of a storm threatening his home and business. "Mr. D's not going, is he?"

"He's trying, but Patty will duct tape him to the floor before she'll let that happen."

"I'll help her," Sid said. "Lucas headed in then?"

"I think so." The line went quiet and Sid feared Beth knew about her non-date turned pseudo-date with Lucas. "Sid, I'm scared. I've never been through a hurricane before."

Remembering her first experience the year after moving to the island, Sid understood Beth's fear. But she'd dealt with Mother Nature often enough since then to know they were in no severe danger from a category two storm.

"No worries, Curly. These things are a nonevent around here." Not exactly true, but Beth didn't need the truth in that moment. "I'll pack up my tools and be at the restaurant in thirty minutes."

"But what about your place? You're right on the water. Won't that be worse?"

Her pier faced more danger than her house, but Sid knew how to prepare. "We've got more than twelve hours. Plenty of time to board up the place once Dempsey's is secure."

Forty minutes later, Sid pulled up before the restaurant and hauled her drill and tool belt out with her. The extra ten minutes had been spent debating what to wear so as not to look too butch in front of Lucas. While checking her ass in the mirror, realization dawned. She was not one of *those* chicks, and to hell if Lucas would turn her into one.

The scene on the porch was chaos. Boards were being brought from the back storage room, but no one seemed to know where to put them. Lucas was nowhere to be found.

"What are you guys doing, trying to recreate some Stooges skit?" Four men froze in place, staring wide eyed in her direction. How the hell men ever managed to rule the world, Sid did not know. "Put the boards down where you are."

Two large sheets of plywood hit the decking with no hesitation. "Vinnie and Chip," she barked, "put your board against the railing here." Sid pointed to her right and the men followed the order. "Now you two," she said to Mitch and Lot. "Slide yours in place in front of it."

As soon as the boards were stacked, Lucas came around the corner with his head down and a plastic container in his hands. "I can't believe these things are still in the same box." Looking up, he spotted Sid standing on the top step.

Her heart did some crazy flutter thing so she worked harder to school her features.

"What are you doing here?"

"I work here." If he made a crack about men and tools and women and kitchens, she'd deck him. Date or no date.

His eyes dropped to the drill in her hand. "Good. You have tools." He handed her the box. "See if you've got a bit that will work for these." The flutter turned into a full-on somersault. Turning to the silent crew, he said, "There are six more sheets of plywood inside. We'll bring them all out and stack them, then start putting them up."

It took the guys five minutes to carry out the rest of the boards. During that time Sid found two bits that would work on the two-inch screws. Passing one off to Lucas, she asked, "You know how to use a drill?"

Lucas pursed his lips. "How would you feel if I asked you that question?"

Point taken. "Sorry," she mumbled. Sid didn't apologize often so the word didn't come naturally. "I suggest we work in teams." Glancing toward the guys dropping the last sheet on the stack, she said, "I'll take Vinnie and Chip. You can have Mitch and Lot."

"Why do I get Mitch and Lot?"

"Because if I take Lot, we're going to be a man down after I drill a two-inch screw through his forehead."

"Good point." Lucas nodded. Turning to the crew, he said, "Mitch and Lot, you're with me. We'll start at the left down here. Vinnie and Chip, you go with Sid around to the other end. We'll meet in the middle and have this done in no time."

The words were clearly an order, but delivered in a way that sounded more like a suggestion. Interesting technique. None of the men questioned the plan, each following their respective leader. Sid hadn't expected resistance, except maybe from Lucas. But he'd treated her as an equal.

There went that fluttery thing again.

Thanks to the wind, the job took a good thirty minutes. Every time they lifted a board off the floor, it threatened to blow out of their grip. Vinnie bitched about his delicate hands getting blisters, as only one side of the plywood was treated, but Chip kept his mouth shut and picked up the slack.

Once all was secure, the guys headed out to help other friends and board up their own homes. Sid turned to Lucas. "We might as well head over to your place. Beth said the fire crew was going to do your parents' house, but we can get a head start on the bottom and let them use the ladders to do the second floor."

"Works for me." He picked up the drill and tool belt from where he'd dropped them by the steps. The combination of khakis, polo shirt, and a tool belt hit harder than expected.

The man was sex on a stick. And he was staring at her as she went loopy picturing him in nothing but the tool belt.

"You okay?" he asked. "You look like you're going to pass out or something."

"I'm fine," she lied. "So I'll see you over there?"

"Right behind you, boss."

Sid drove away from Dempsey's grinning like an idiot, but she didn't care. Curly was right. Being nice worked. Not that she'd ever tell Curly that.

∼

By six o'clock that evening, Lucas was tired, soaked, sore, and starving. They'd boarded up his parents' house, Joe's place, and then helped with the fitness center, which had the window wall from hell. The plywood sheets required four guys just to hold them and even then the damn things nearly broke their wrists when the wind caught them.

"I may never be able to lift my arms again." On his back on a weight bench, Lucas turned his head to the left. "What are the chances you'd lift my beer so I can get a drink?"

Sid snorted. "No chance at all."

And she'd been so nice all afternoon. He should have known it couldn't last. "You're not going to carry me home on this bench either, are you? I'll have to sleep here then. It's not like anyone will be going out in a hurricane to bench-press dumbbells."

"There's no kitchen here and once the power goes out you'll be screwed. Go home, Dempsey." Sid rolled off the balance ball she'd been using as a chair and tossed her empty beer bottle in the trash. "I've got to go put the boards up at my place."

"What?" he said, sitting up faster than his body liked. A pain shot through his ribs. "Why didn't you say something sooner?"

Sid shrugged. "We were busy doing all these other places."

Lucas pushed off the bench, taking two tries to reach his feet. "I'm coming with you."

"Are you kidding?" Sid poked him with one finger and he swayed. "You're spent, dude. I can handle it."

"There's no way I'm letting you do that alone. Not when you're right on the water and by now the winds have to be pushing sixty out there." Damn stubborn woman. "Let's go before we lose what light is left."

"But—"

"Don't argue with me," he yelled over his shoulder, pulling his keys from his pocket as he stomped to the door. What was wrong with her? Did she have no sense of self-preservation? She'd spent all day helping everyone else, and never asked for a hand in return. Well, she was getting one.

The waves crashed against the pier as Lucas pulled into Sid's driveway. At least there were no trees around to crash through her roof. He waited for her to pull in on his left before hopping out and ducking under the opening garage door. Sid must have pushed the button as she pulled in.

The garage was cave-like and dark, so Lucas stayed near the entrance until the door was open far enough to illuminate his surroundings. Through the dusty beams from Sid's headlights, he saw wall-to-wall workbenches, each covered in more tools and junk than the one before. A cacophony of metal chaos.

The lights went out and Sid ran through the door with her head down, stopping just before crashing into his stomach like a missile. "Son of a bitch," she said, shaking off water like a wet Lab coming out of the surf. "This is going to suck."

"Then let's get moving." At least it wasn't pouring as hard as it would be later. "Where do you keep the boards?"

"In the shed out back," she yelled, the wind making it difficult to hear. "I'll let the drill charge while we pull them out."

His first thought was where in the world would she charge anything in that mess, but Sid walked straight to a workbench, slammed the drill onto a base, then turned his way. "Let's go."

He followed her back out into the storm, giant drops pinging off his face like they'd been shot from a BB gun. Joe had shot him with a BB once, so he knew exactly how it felt. As Sid worked the key into the lock of the shed, he tried to buffer her from the wind. Her hood blew down and dark hair whipped around her face.

When the shed door slid open, Sid pointed toward four boards along the right wall standing behind a riding mower. Verbal communication would have to wait until they were out of the elements. Together they removed the boards, laying each piece flat on the ground under whatever window of the house it was meant to cover. Information Sid had long ago spray-painted on each piece. A quick trip back for the drill and hardware, then they went to work.

The two windows in the back were the most difficult, as that side faced the water and was getting the wind full on. The two in front went on with little trouble, then Sid and Lucas were once again standing in the garage, both creating a puddle on the concrete floor.

As Sid pulled the wet hoodie over her head, the blue Evinrude T-shirt underneath rode up high enough for him to catch a glimpse of a delicate white bra with purple and green stars. Never in a million years . . .

"You can hang your jacket over there," she yelled, flopping her sweatshirt on top of a bench and reaching for a switch on the wall. She flipped it, but nothing happened. "Shit. Power's out already."

"What now?" he asked, knowing he should drive home while he still had the chance, but reluctant to leave until certain Sid would be okay.

"Generator."

"Where?"

"In the corner, but the gas cans are in the freaking shed."

CHAPTER SIXTEEN

Not the answer he wanted to hear. "I'll get them," he said. "Go dry off."

"You can't carry all four cans. And there's no way we'll get back out there once Ingrid gets closer." Sid headed for the open garage door. "We'll go together." She stopped just inside, glanced up at the darkening sky, then back his way. "You don't melt, do you?" Her words were accompanied by a full-fledged smile. The one that put him on his proverbial ass every time she flashed it.

He joined her at the door. "You ready?" She nodded, then, eyes locked, they each took a deep breath. "Run!" he yelled, diving into the storm.

A blanket of water covered them instantly, icy drops rolling down his back and filling his shoes. That drive home was going to be damned uncomfortable. Sid kept pace, slipping on some wet grass, but Lucas reached out and kept her upright. They reached the shed side by side, Lucas pulling the door open and shoving Sid inside.

With mere inches of open floor space, they stood for a long moment, pressed together and breathing hard. Sid looked up, her head tilted back due to their vast difference in height. He had her by at least a foot. Somehow he always forgot that until moments like this one.

One drop slid down Sid's nose, landing on her full upper lip, where she licked it off. His body responded as if he'd been hit head on by a train. Leaning forward, he regained control inches from her mouth.

"Where are they?" he growled, tension and heat rolling through his body despite the cold material clinging to his skin. He half expected steam to fill the air around them.

Sid shoved wet strands of black hair off her forehead and glanced around. Stepping onto the riding mower she said, "Over here."

The packed shed prevented Lucas from moving beyond where he stood. "Hand them over."

Two red, five-gallon cans appeared over the mower as if they weighed five ounces instead of thirty pounds each. He dropped them at his feet, then reached back for the next ones. By the time the last two hit the floor, Sid had scaled the John Deere and was once again pressed against his side.

The sound of the rain driving against the shed roof made it impossible to hear, so he motioned toward the door and she nodded in response. Lifting two cans, Sid ran out first, with Lucas close behind. They didn't make it ten feet before tiny balls of ice filled the air, pelting them like golf balls on a driving range.

He heard a scream seconds before the cans hit the ground and Sid's ass followed suit. The back porch was less than twenty feet away so Lucas made a hard right, dropped his two on the deck, then slid them toward the door. When he turned back, Sid was sitting with her arms over her head, trying to protect herself from the pounding hail.

She shouldn't be out here, damn it. Shredding the ground between them, Lucas swept Sid off the ground, cradling her against his chest to offer what little protection he could.

"Wait," she screamed. "We need the gas!"

He bent at the knees so she could reach the two cans, then once she had a solid grip, broke into a run again. He'd wonder later where he found the strength to pull off the Herculean task, but in that moment he'd have carried the damn shed if it meant getting Sid safe inside.

Ducking into the garage, he tossed Sid to her feet and turned to close the door behind them. As he slid the latch home, Lucas heard Sid dragging the generator into the middle of the floor.

"Forget it," he barked, grabbing her arm and dragging her to the inside door.

"But we need—"

"Dry first." Pushing her into the kitchen, he bent to loosen his shoelaces, kicking the Nikes off next to the entry rug, then ripping off his socks and dropping them inside. "You got towels around here?" he asked, looking up to find Sid staring at him.

He couldn't see more than her outline in the darkness, but her stance expressed loud and clear what his body had been telling him for days. They stood there, in Sid's pristine kitchen, panting and dripping in silence for what felt like an eternity before Sid launched herself against him.

~

Their lips met as if their lives depended on it. She clung to his wet body, vibrating with the tension coursing between them. Sid had always wanted to jump Lucas's bones, but never more than in this moment. All day he'd been teasing her with that tool belt hanging low over his perfect ass. She'd wanted him so bad she could taste it. And now she could taste him.

Fuck Death By Chocolate. Sid wanted to die devouring every last bite of Lucas Dempsey. His tongue was hot and invading, dueling with hers when he wasn't taking tiny bites of her lower lip. She jammed her hands in his wet hair as Lucas spun, setting her on the counter and sliding his hands beneath her shirt.

Without hesitation she broke the kiss, leaned back and jerked her shirt over her head. She'd have worn the black lace if she'd known this would happen today, but Lucas didn't seem to mind the white satin with colorful stars. He was looking with his hands more than his eyes, and Sid thought she might die from the sensations assaulting her.

Desperate to feel his skin against hers, to run her tongue over the muscles bunching and flexing under her touch, she slipped her hands under the hem of his shirt, pushing the wet material over perfect abs until she could take a nipple between her teeth. Lucas growled and pulled her core hard against his hips. He cradled her ass, lifting her off the counter so he could take her mouth again.

Seconds later he'd moved to her earlobe, rolled his tongue down her neck, and licked the top of her breast above the confining satin. "Where's your room?" he asked, his voice thick and heavy.

Reveling in the feel of his hot breath between her breasts, Sid wrapped her legs tighter around his waist, anchoring against him, and wound her arms around his neck. "Through the living room. Blue door. Right."

Lucas found the room without breaking the lip-lock. Bless the man for being a multitasker.

The lack of electricity rendered the light switch useless, but her alarm clock battery had kicked on, the large glowing numbers illuminating the room enough for Lucas to find the bed. When he did, they toppled down together, him throwing his weight to one side, seemingly to keep from squishing her, but Sid was having none of that.

She shifted further onto the bed and urged Lucas to move with her. He was hard and ready against her thigh, sending waves of panic coursing alongside the overload of adrenaline already drowning her brain.

What if she did this wrong? What if he could tell she didn't know what she was doing? What if she was awful at it?

In that instant, Lucas rose off the bed and Sid feared she'd aired her doubts aloud. But then he pulled his shirt over his head and her brain shut down. Good Lord, the man was gorgeous. Like rock star gorgeous. Even in the dim blue light of the clock, Lucas was a god.

And he was reaching for the button on his pants.

Panic took hold again, sending Sid scooting back against the headboard. Lucas froze.

"What's wrong?" he asked. "Do you want to stop?" The words were barely audible through his heavy breathing. The tension in his body as he fought for control was palpable.

Sid shook her head no.

"Then why does it feel as if you're about to run out the door?"

Sid shook her head again.

"We're not going to do anything you don't want to do, Sid. I don't think I can make it home now, but I'll go stay on the couch."

"No!" she yelled, more afraid he'd leave than stay. "I'm just . . ." She was just what? If she told him she didn't do this much, he'd bolt for sure. This was supposed to be casual. She was supposed to be good with casual sex. "I just wish it wasn't so dark in here. I want to see you."

That part was true. She'd give anything to see him in full light, naked in her bedroom.

"I want to see you too," he said, his voice dropping an octave. "We'll just have to make sure we each get a good look when the sun comes up." Leaning over until his hands were braced against the mattress, Lucas grinned. "Come down here, Sid."

As if pulled by an invisible string, Sid scooted down the bed, powered by the wave of lust that had brought her this far. "You want to do this?" he asked, nuzzling along her jawline. "A summer fling could be fun."

She had no doubt a summer fling with Lucas would be the most fun she'd ever have in her life. But what would happen when summer rolled into fall? When the fling was over and Lucas was gone?

"I did promise to show you a good time," she said, with more swagger than she felt. "Are you up for the challenge?" Was she up for the heartbreak?

Lucas crawled back onto the bed until Sid was prone beneath him and ground his hips against her thigh. "I'm up, Sid. I'm definitely up."

He took her mouth slowly this time, savoring her. Tasting and teasing, his hands on the bed beside her head instead of where she wanted them, on her body. Her hands explored at will, showing Lucas what she wanted in return. The muscles of his upper arms were rock solid as he held himself above her, leaving too much space between them. When she reached up and tugged on his neck, he kept the distance, but ground his hips once again.

An odd sound filled the air and Sid realized the animal moan had come from her own throat. A kind of purr she'd never uttered before. For a brief second the sound made her wonder where Drillbit was, but then Lucas rolled his hips once more and thoughts of the feline fled.

When he left her mouth to shift attention to her neck, Sid begged. "Touch me, please."

"Patience. We have all night."

Sid did not have all night. If he didn't touch her in the next five seconds, she would burst into flames and die without ever feeling Lucas inside her. With a move honed from years of wrestling a giant of a brother, Sid locked her legs around Lucas's waist and flipped them both until she was on top.

Hands braced on his shoulders, she stared down into startled eyes and smiled.

"*I'm* the one showing *you* a good time, remember?"

"By all means," he said, sliding his hands over her thighs. "Present your case, Ms. Navarro."

Sitting up taller, Sid reached back and freed her hair. She'd always seen chicks look hot doing that in the movies, and hoped she was pulling off the same effect.

"I love your hair," he whispered, a potent hoarseness in his voice. "I've wanted to yank out that ponytail for a week."

She wiggled one finger before his nose. "There will be no hair pulling."

His grin turned wicked. "We'll table that one for further discussion."

Sid's stomach clenched as Lucas thrust up off the bed. Her hands hit his shoulders again, draping the both of them in a mass of dark waves. As he moved it away from her face, their eyes met. "You're beautiful," he said.

And for the first time in her life, Sid believed the words.

"So are you," she said, needing to make him feel what she was feeling. "You always have been."

His body stilled and he pulled her face down for another hungry kiss. This time, they kissed each other, taking and giving in turn, thrusting, parrying, breaking contact only when breathing became absolutely necessary.

With the flick of one hand, Lucas unhooked her bra, the satin sliding down her arms and disappearing somewhere near the dresser. Cool air caressed her nipples for only seconds before the brush of coarse hair and hot skin replaced it. She pressed down as Lucas squeezed tighter, neither able to get close enough. Her body was a coiled spring, threatening to snap and send her flying across the room.

Lucas took charge again, rolling until he was once more hovering above her, then lavished detailed attention on her breasts. The right, then the left, each forlorn when his lips wandered away to the other.

Between nibbles he said, "We'd better get out of these wet clothes, don't you think?"

Sid nodded, then remembered he couldn't see her with his nose pressed between the girls. "Yes. Please."

Lucas rolled to the side, far enough for her to reach between them. "Undo the button. Please. I need you to touch me, Sid."

Pushing through her growing panic at how fast they were moving, she watched his eyes as her fingers steadily did as he asked. Sliding a hand down behind the open zipper, she found no further material in her way.

"You're not wearing underwear," she said, as if discussing the absence of personal clothing were an everyday thing.

"I never do unless I'm running," he mumbled between gritted teeth. His eyes were closed, and judging by the muscles in his neck, he was ready to snap.

A sense of power mixed with lust was a heady cocktail. Sid stopped thinking about her lack of experience, as she'd never pleasured a guy, for lack of a better word, with her hands before. Instead she let instinct take over, pushing the cotton down over his ass until what she wanted sprang free. Whoa. That was more than she'd expected. Fascinated, she ran a hand down the side, then gripped the base.

Very interesting tool. And it fit nicely in her hand.

"Are you trying to kill me?" Lucas asked, dropping his head on her shoulder and bracing himself half on top of her.

She'd almost forgotten the rest of him was there.

"You don't like this?" she asked, knowing to tease was cruel, but having too much fun to stop.

After rolling over to kick the pants onto the floor, Lucas returned to Sid's side in all his pride and glory. And glorious he was. "Time for me to return the favor," he said, making short work of removing her jeans and thong, tossing them through the air to join the bra somewhere on the floor. Sid tried to stay relaxed, fending off the feeling of complete and utter vulnerability.

She hated feeling so exposed and defenseless, but then Lucas began exploring and Sid's body tensed for a totally different reason. One nimble finger found what turned out to be the magical spot, sending Sid soaring through the air with surprising speed, her scream of raw pleasure rattling the walls.

As far as first orgasms went, Sid was certain of two things. She'd been missing out, and she wanted a lot more of those.

CHAPTER SEVENTEEN

Holy shit, that was awesome," Sid said, an electrical current still charging through her bloodstream. She was literally vibrating from the sensations, stretching her legs as if her body were trying to chase the ribbons of pleasure flying out her toes.

Turning toward Lucas and throwing a leg over his hip, she realized he was still as hard as a rock. He'd just given her an orgasm and they hadn't even had sex yet. Talk about skills. Sliding him between her thighs, she licked his chest and said, "How many of those do I get?"

Lucas remained still and Sid worried she'd done something wrong. Through clenched teeth he asked, "Do you have any condoms?"

Sid made another mental note. This time, to buy Will the biggest Christmas present ever for forcing her to stock up, just in case. Rolling to her left, she opened her nightstand drawer and pulled out a blue box. "We're fully stocked."

"Thank God," he said, relief and a hint of joy laced in his voice. A reaction that did positive things to Sid's ego. Positioning himself above her again, he pushed the box out of her hand, then pinned both her arms over her head. "Now where were we?"

Sid coughed away a nervous giggle. "I don't know about you, but I think I was just somewhere around Mars."

Lucas dropped sexy kisses along her jaw. "How was the trip?"

"Hmmmm . . ." she hedged. "Good, I think. I'll need another trip to be sure."

"Then prepare for takeoff."

Their mouths met like two armies charging into battle, each trying to force the other to surrender. Lucas's hands were everywhere, and yet she wanted more. Needed more. Her hips rose off the bed through no control of her own, the brain surrendering only to the demands of her body.

The seconds it took for Lucas to open the box of condoms and sheath himself felt like an eternity in hell. Her body on fire, wanting only to get closer to the flame. She was covered in sweat, his or her own she wasn't sure, nor did she care. When his mouth returned to hers, she pulled her knees up, flattening her feet on the bed and lifting in invitation.

Lucas hesitated above her. Staring into her eyes, he gently brushed a wet lock from her cheek, then ran his thumb along her jawline. The threat of sudden tears took her by surprise. She couldn't let him see her cry.

Digging her nails into his shoulder blades, she begged, "Lucas, please. I can't take any more."

He took her mouth at the same moment he thrust inside her, her muscles rebelling and accommodating at once. The pace started slow, too slow, and she dug her nails in again. Lucas took the hint, increasing the speed, driving harder with every thrust. God, he felt so good. So right. Sex had never been like this. She'd never imagined it could be.

The bed rocked beneath them as the storm outside raged against her tiny cottage. But the storm building inside put any hurricane to shame. Her body tensed, her ankles pressed against Lucas's firm ass, encouraging, demanding. She gripped his sides, desperate to hold on, fighting the feeling she might fly away at any moment.

Lucas reached an arm behind her left knee, pulling her leg higher and thrust home, sending her off on that magical trip again. Another scream ripped from her lungs, then several thrusts later, Lucas growled in her ear and his body went straight and taut.

They remained connected, lying atop her disheveled blue comforter, panting, sweating, and in Sid's case, smiling. Lucas's nose was tucked in against her neck, his breath hot against her skin. This is where she wanted to be every night for the rest of her life. But if the next five weeks were all she could have, then she'd take them.

They'd just have to get her through the next five decades.

~

An hour later, after a brief nap, Lucas found himself curled around the hottest woman with whom he'd ever shared a bed, wondering when she'd worked her way under his skin. And how did she get in so deep? He'd been worried about Sid's ability to keep it casual, and all he could think about was spending the next fifty years in this bed with this woman.

Time to get a grip. He had plans. Plans set in Richmond with a long, profitable career as partner and a sweet-natured wife by his side. Those plans did not include a heathen for a spouse, nor did Anchor Island play a part. Not as anything more than the hometown he visited on holidays to check in with the family. Family that would someday include Joe and Beth's children.

Lucas rolled away from Sid and sat up on the side of the bed. His body objected to having to let her go, which was all the more reason to do so. She rolled onto her stomach, naked curves making his mouth water.

Sid was clearly not tormented by any unwelcome feelings. Maybe he'd been wrong about her not being the casual type. She'd offered sex and nothing more, and that's what she gave. Granted, tables could turn come morning. She might start demanding more the moment she woke. If those demands came with nights like this one, he might be tempted to meet them.

As if running from the thought, Lucas crossed the room to the small bathroom in the corner. After splashing cold water on his face, he toweled dry and felt sanity begin to return. Less than two months had passed since Elizabeth became Beth and left him for his brother.

So he'd been hurt and lonely. And maybe he still was. But he didn't feel lonely with Sid. And there was no chance of her being anything but what she was. Tough as nails. Stubborn as a mule. And sexier than any woman he'd ever met.

She had a heart too. Buried deep, but it was there. And he could break it as easily as Elizabeth broke his. So they'd keep it casual. Enjoy each other for a short while. They could do that.

His feelings on firmer ground, Lucas padded back to the bed as the wind buffeted the tiny cottage. Along the way, he pulled a white blanket from the back of a chair. The moment his weight hit the mattress, Sid turned to him, squeezing into his arms and a little closer to his heart.

He threw the blanket over them and kissed her on the forehead. *Keep it casual,* he thought. But he knew doing so was going to be the biggest challenge Sid Navarro would throw his way.

∼

Sometime during the night, Lucas had woken Sid up in the most delightful way, and proceeded to send her soaring once again. When they'd both sailed into oblivion then floated back to her room, she realized that if they didn't hook the generator up soon, there would be no hot water in the morning.

When she'd explained this to Lucas, he smiled and sleepily followed her around, hooking up wires and helping with whatever she needed. Sid had to admit, having a guy around wasn't such a bad thing. Capable and independent, she'd never understood that drive some women seemed to have to keep a man around to fix things and mow the grass.

Sid could fix anything, and what was so hard about riding a damn lawn mower? But this experience of having someone to help, to lend a hand, or even just make her laugh, had her reconsidering. She hadn't realized the potential benefits.

One in particular being Lucas's take-charge attitude in the bedroom. The day before, when they'd been boarding windows, he'd treated her as an equal. When they worked together to set up the generator, he'd let her take the lead without argument. But in the bedroom, Sid knew who was in charge, and to her utter amazement, she liked it.

Lucas didn't make her feel inadequate or unskilled. He didn't make her feel self-conscious. He was patient and passionate. Gentle until she was begging for more, then rough and demanding, dragging her into some new sexual bliss with every touch, taste, and tweak of a nipple.

He was her match in every way. They complemented each other, pushed each other, challenged each other. And she enjoyed every minute of it. Even when he was pissing her off. Which was why she found herself standing at her kitchen counter in the early morning glow of the small bulb over her stove, pouring two cups of coffee and scared out of her mind.

How the fuck was she going to pretend this was casual?

In that moment, a strong arm snaked around her waist and Sid was pulled back against a hot, firm, rock-hard body. "Good morning," he whispered into her ear. Warm breath danced down her neck as he licked her earlobe. A shiver shot through her chest, then lower. "I hope one of those is for me."

"I was going to give it to Drillbit, but since you're here, I guess you can have it." She hoped the lightness in her voice masked how much he affected her. And where her thoughts had been straying before he walked in.

Lucas scooted until his back was to the wall, taking her with him. "Where is the kitten from hell?" As if on cue, Drillbit meowed from her spot under the table. "That thing needs a bell."

Sid rolled her eyes. "I bought one, but she's too small for the collar. I'll put it on her when she's big enough."

"She could shred me by then." He released Sid and moved to the right, putting her body between him and the feared feline. To be shredded by the cat he would have to be around the cat. Which meant he expected to spend more time at Sid's place.

The knowledge made her smile. A smile she hid, not wanting to reveal too much.

"Just drink your coffee, scaredy-pants. I'll protect you."

And she would. From anything.

After shooting her a stink eye, Lucas sipped his coffee. "This is just how I like it. How did you know?"

She shrugged, choosing to wipe down the already clean countertop. "Good guess."

"Hope you don't mind," he said, "but I borrowed your toothpaste. Used my finger though. Promise." He flashed a smile. Her heart tried to leap from her chest.

"No problem," she said. Cool and casual.

He set the mug down and hemmed her in, locking her body between his and the counter. She'd slipped on a Dolphins jersey and clean thong before making the coffee. "You're wearing too many clothes," he mumbled, nibbling her lower lip.

Such dangerous ground. Sid wanted nothing more than to crawl back into bed with Lucas, but people would be out on the island, assessing the damage, helping their neighbors. The fact he hadn't gone home the night before would not go unnoticed, and Sid had no idea how his family would react when they learned of his whereabouts.

"There should be plenty of hot water by now," she said, trying to distract him, but her hands slid around his rib cage of their own volition. "One of us should take a shower."

She was lifted off the floor at that point, levitating between the counter, Lucas, and heaven.

"Excellent idea," he said.

Now she was floating through the air. "Where are we going?"

"We're taking a shower."

"Together?" she squeaked. The image of Lucas, naked, wet, and soapy, nearly made her come on the spot.

"Together," he said, then took her mouth in a kiss that promised all sorts of naughty things to come. There probably *was* only enough hot water for one shower.

She pulled back until she could see his eyes. "You wash my back . . . ?"

"Your back, your front, and all parts in between," he promised.

"Then I'll have to return the favor."

He squeezed her tighter. "I'm counting on it."

≈

The hot water turned cold before Lucas and Sid finished their shower. He'd been very thorough in his attentions; then Sid did as promised, returned the favor, and nearly sent him to his knees. Just thinking about it had him growing hard again. A condition not conducive to climbing a ladder and using power tools, which he'd be doing throughout the day.

He knew his parents would wonder where he was, seeing as he'd disappeared in the middle of a hurricane. While Sid finished getting dressed, he was lucky to find the phone working and placed the uncomfortable call. His mom answered and he'd kept the details vague. He was pretty sure she assumed he'd slept on Sid's couch, and he didn't correct the assumption.

No sense in incriminating himself, and he wasn't sure how Sid wanted to handle their situation. Were they going to be open about it? He'd be leaving in a matter of weeks, but Sid had to live here. Gossip traveled around Anchor faster than the media would out a cross-dressing judge. Personally, Lucas didn't mind anyone knowing he and Sid were an item.

But was "item" the right word? Telling people they were a fling didn't feel right. They weren't really dating, unless they were casually dating. But they weren't committed, which meant technically they could see other people. Not that *he* would be seeing anyone else, but if Sid wanted to . . .

Manny the man-boy came to mind, and Lucas nearly squeezed his coffee mug into pieces. Imagining another man touching Sid made him see red. Which was stupid since he had no hold on her. No claim. Even if he wanted one, which he didn't.

"What are you thinking about there, slugger? You look pissed off about something."

Sid wrapped a rubber band around her ponytail as she plodded barefoot into the living room. She sat in the chair to his left, a pair of socks in her hand.

"Nothing to be pissed off about here." Time to change the subject. "Talked to mom. Let her know I'm okay."

"Really?" Sid asked, pulling on a sock. "What did she say about you staying here?"

"I let her think I slept on the couch."

Sid hesitated for a split second, then pulled on her other sock. "If that's how you want to handle it." She didn't meet his eyes, but he could tell something bothered her.

"I was trying to protect you, actually. Wasn't sure how much of your business you wanted getting around."

She leaned back in the chair. "I hadn't thought about that."

Flattering, he supposed, but they'd have to face the reality after the storm. "You have to live here. We both know how the grapevine works on this island."

"Spreads like a fire on gasoline." Sid bit her lip, clearly pondering the situation. Sounding unsure of herself, which was completely out of character, she asked, "Do you care if people know? I mean, I'm not taking out a billboard that we had sex, but if we're going to spend the rest of the summer having a good time, there's no sense in hiding it."

He held out his hand. "Come here." She did as requested and he set her on his lap. "I don't regret one minute of last night, and I don't care who knows about it. But I don't live here. You do. You call the shots on this one."

The least he could do was protect her as much as possible.

She played with the top button on his shirt. "I've never given a shit what anyone thought before. Would be stupid to start caring now."

"That's what you want? To hell with everyone else?"

"Yeah." She nodded, looking more confident. "But I don't like this *fling* word."

Arguing semantics was never good. Cautiously he asked, "What would you like to call it?"

"Well." She ran a finger along his ear. He managed not to flinch. "We're kind of friends now, aren't we?"

He laughed. "I think we can say that."

"Then we're kind of friends with benefits." Chocolate eyes met his, a glimmer of challenge and triumph in their depths.

"Really good benefits." Best benefits package he'd ever been offered. "But you want to tell people that? That we're friends with benefits?"

Sid rolled her eyes. "That part's just between us. Anyone asks for details, I'll tell them it's none of their fucking business."

Lucas cringed. She did have a way with words. "One request. If my mom asks, could you phrase it a little differently?"

"I didn't think about your mom." She turned to face him, spinning on his lap until she was straddling his hips. If she squirmed any more they'd be breaking in the couch the way they'd broken in the shower.

"Like I said, she thinks I slept on the couch. But she's bound to catch on eventually." He cupped her bottom and scooted to the end of the sofa. "And if we don't get going right now, I'm going to have you on your back needing another shower in about five minutes."

Sid giggled and held onto his shoulders. "That might not be so . . ." She stopped and leaned back. "Shit. The garage."

"What garage?" The abrupt change of subject was hard to follow with no blood flowing to his brain.

"It's my . . . well, it's not mine yet. I just need to go check it out." She jumped off his lap, grabbed her boots, then sat down to put them on. "I'll have to replace the windows anyway, but I hope there's no water damage inside."

"Slow down." Lucas grabbed his tennis shoes, which were still damp but dry enough to wear. "What garage are we going to see?"

"We?" she said, sitting up, laces frozen in the air. "You're going with me?"

"If you're checking out some old garage for storm damage, I'm not letting you go alone."

"Oh." She finished tying her boot, slowly now, as if her brain were working too hard on something else to pay attention to what her hands were doing. Once both boots were secure, she stood and paced in front of the coffee table, talking with her hands except all the talking was happening in her head.

"Sid!" he said, yelling to get her attention. "What am I missing here? What's so special about this garage?"

She bit a nail as she stared at him in silence. He decided to wait her out.

"Okay, you can come," she said. "But you have to swear you won't tell anyone."

"Tell anyone what?"

"Where we're going."

"Are you keeping dead bodies in this garage?"

She tapped a foot. "Promise."

"Fine," he said, more curious than anything. "I promise. But what is this garage to you?"

Snagging a set of keys from a hook on the wall, she said, "It's my future. Now get your ass in gear and let's go."

CHAPTER EIGHTEEN

Anchor looked as if it had been through a war instead of a storm, though Sid had seen it looking much worse. Ingrid had made a hard right, tracking out into the ocean overnight, which spared the island the brunt of her power. A steady drizzle continued to fall though, the air heavy and gray in the storm's wake.

The distance from Sid's house to the garage normally took ten minutes tops, but this trip took thirty thanks to downed tree limbs littering the narrow streets. Most had been a manageable size. She and Lucas would climb from the truck, move the debris off the asphalt, then continue on their way. The one branch large enough to require more than man power they were able to navigate around.

Conversation on the way was minimal. Lucas didn't press for details on their destination, which Sid appreciated, as she teetered between giddiness and nauseous anticipation. She'd spent her adult life wanting two things: Lucas Dempsey and her own business. Even if the situation with Lucas was only temporary, she had him for now. And that was something.

The man who ten days before hadn't even noticed her, now seemed not only satisfied with their first encounter, but content to return for regular engagements. At least for the summer. She briefly pondered what would happen when fall arrived. Would everything end, or would they pick up where they left off on his rare visits home?

A glance his way got her a quick grin with long lashes hooded over hazel eyes. Her stomach dropped while her temperature spiked. A man like Lucas wouldn't stay single up in the city. He'd move on. Find the perfect dinner-party wife who wouldn't curse or wear inappropriate T-shirts. Sid would be relegated to a fling he had one summer.

She gripped the wheel hard, her knuckles going white at the thought. Casual. That's what she'd signed up for. That's what they were. No promises. No pressure. No commitments.

No regrets now.

Maybe she shouldn't have brought him with her to the garage. What if he didn't see it? Didn't get it? Sid had told no one about her plans. Will knew only because she worked at the real estate office now and then, so Sid went through her to enquire about the property.

But even Randy didn't know. This was hers and when she saw it through, on her own, she would show everyone that Sid Navarro could be more than some fishing hostess and part-time grease monkey.

She would be a successful business owner. In demand. Doing what she loved. Not just one guy's kid sister and another guy's sidekick. Sid would stand on her own.

Pulling onto the gravel road leading to the garage, she kicked the truck down into four-wheel drive to gain traction through potholes the size of craters. Like the building it fronted, the driveway needed some work.

Lucas braced himself in the passenger seat, looking perplexed about where exactly she was taking him. Sid gave him credit for not demanding answers.

When she stopped the truck ten yards from the red brick building, they both leaned forward to see the edifice. Sid left the wipers going to clear the light drizzle falling on the windshield. Looking up, she breathed a sigh of relief that the windows had held. The ones that hadn't been broken before the storm anyway.

Arms wrapped around the steering wheel, she looked over to Lucas. "Well?"

His head jerked her way as if he'd forgotten she was there. His mouth formed an "O" shape but remained silent. Then his eyes went back to the building. "It's . . . I . . ." Looking her way again he asked, "I see an old run-down building. What am I missing?"

Sid cut the engine and reached for her door handle. "Come on. I'll show you." As her feet hit the ground, she raised the hood on her jacket. Ingrid would bring rain for at least the next twenty-four hours, even as she drifted out into the ocean away from land.

Though Fisher kept a padlock on the front entrance, Sid knew the side door could be easily opened. It stuck, but with a solid smack to the upper right corner, she pushed it open. Lucas followed behind.

"Are we breaking and entering?"

"Don't worry. I'm sure you've got lawyer friends who'll take our case."

Lucas stopped just outside the threshold. "That's not funny."

She rolled her eyes. Good thing the man was hot or the goody-two-shoes act would be a deal breaker. "I'm kidding. We're fine. Come in out of the rain and close the door."

The smell of dirt filled the air as a breeze traveled down from the higher windows. The one in the back had been missing a roughly four-inch piece from the corner, and from what she could tell, that was still the only damage evident. If the storm had been any stronger, they'd be standing in several inches of water.

By now Lucas had joined her in the large garage space. His head tilted back to take in the high ceiling, grungy walls, and dust-tinted windows. "This place is a wreck. How could it be anyone's dream?"

Sid bit the inside of her cheek. She thought he'd see it. Damn it.

"You have to picture it cleaned up. New windows. Large fan up there at the highest point of the ceiling." She pointed, then crossed to the left side of the space. "This will be the work counter, where I can spread out the plans. Consult with customers and decide on colors, interiors, that sort of thing." Crossing to the other side she held her arms wide. "This will be the tool area, though some will be spread around or mounted to the ceiling, hanging within reach to work on the topside."

Lucas remained rooted to the spot where she'd left him. "You're going to turn this into a business?"

"Not just any business," she said, closing the distance between them. "Navarro Boat Repair and Restoration. I'll be able to take on the bigger jobs I can't do now because I don't have a place to do the work, but at the same time I can restore some old beauties. Something I've wanted to do for years."

Lucas did another spin in place, taking in their surroundings. "The space is good. What are the measurements?"

A rush of heat shot through Sid's chest. He was starting to see her vision. "Front to back it's just under seventy-five feet. Ceiling goes up two and a half stories." Turning to face the front she added, "The door is about fifteen feet, but I'll need to change that to make the entrance bigger."

Again Lucas fell silent, eyes darting from corner to corner as if doing mental calculations. Several seconds later, he crossed his arms. "The structure is sturdy. How long has this been here? I don't even remember it."

"Since the sixties," she answered. "It's a little out of the way, but close enough to the water to be perfect. Once the boat ramp is installed."

He shook his head. "Getting this place up and running would cost a fortune. If you found the right investors, could you really make enough to make it viable?"

Investors? She didn't want investors. "I know the price. I'll handle it."

"You'll handle it?" Lucas asked, kicking a rock with his toe to reveal a chunk missing from the concrete floor. "You have a money tree planted somewhere?"

Sid had been saving for five years for this project. Scrimped and sacrificed. Taken every job she could get, returning home at night smelling like fish or diesel or both. "The money is my business. Forget I brought you here." With a weight in her chest, she charged toward the side door. "Let's go."

"Wait," he said, catching her by the arm as she tried to pass him. "I admire your ambition, Sid. I really do. I didn't mean to imply you couldn't make this happen. It just seems like a long shot is all."

"I never said it would be easy." She pulled her arm from his grip and jammed her hands in her jacket pockets. "But I'm going to make this happen. You know as well as I do the only way to thrive on this island is to own a business. I'm not going to be a lackey for your brother forever. I have plans."

Plans she thought he'd understand. The breeze blew through again and she shivered. Why couldn't he see the potential here?

Lucas held eye contact another second, then dropped his gaze to the floor. "I get it."

Her body tensed. "You get what?"

"I get this," he said, gesturing to their surroundings. "You want to create something that's yours. To be in charge of your own life and do what you love." He met her eyes again. "I get that."

Sid hadn't realized she was holding her breath until it whooshed out. "Then you can see what this place can be. What I can make of it."

He nodded. "I do. But taking on investors wouldn't mean the place isn't yours. What about your brother? Or Joe? I bet they'd both help you out."

So much for him understanding. "You want to make partner in that fancy firm of yours, don't you?" she asked. "Are you working for that, or waiting for someone to hand it to you?"

"That's not the sa—"

"Not the same thing? It's exactly the same thing. You want to make yourself into something important." Sid crossed her arms to keep from shaking him. "Well so do I. On my terms."

"This is going to take real money, Sid."

"Law school come free these days?"

He pursed his lips. "Touché." Rocking back on his heels, he grinned. "You're a stubborn woman, Sid Navarro."

She couldn't stay angry when he looked at her that way. With frustration, amusement, and desire all mixed together. "My stubbornness paid off last night, didn't it?"

With a hard tug, Lucas pulled her into his arms. "Yes, it did." He nipped her earlobe and Sid squeaked. Heat shot through her body as she rose to her tiptoes, pressing soft curves against his hard angles. Though he stood nearly a foot taller, she couldn't help but notice how they fit together perfectly.

As if Lucas had been built for her alone. The thought set off warning bells in her brain, but then Lucas took her mouth in a hot, wet, mind-numbing kiss and the alarms faded away.

~

Lucas tried not to dwell on the fact he couldn't get enough of the woman with whom he was now officially having a summer fling. Even while trying his patience, she held the sex kitten look that made him long to sink his hands into that thick mane of dark hair. Slide his tongue along her skin, and run his hands over every delicious, mouthwatering curve.

Just as he'd suspected, this had the potential to get complicated. He'd been worried Sid couldn't handle casual, but by all accounts, she seemed to be doing just fine. Lucas was the one wanting to follow her around like a dog hot on the trail of bacon. When they'd arrived at his parents' house, after several long minutes of tasting her pretty little mouth among the dirt and cobwebs of the run-down garage, she'd nonchalantly headed off to help her brother remove the plywood from his business windows.

For a brief moment he thought to convince her to help out at the restaurant instead. To stay by his side where he could see her. Smell her. Touch her.

Now who couldn't do casual?

"Hey, Lucas," Beth said, stepping onto the porch. Her chestnut hair was held back in a clip, errant curls trailing around her face. She smiled in a way that told him this wasn't a coincidental run in.

"What is that look for?" he asked, dropping into an Adirondack chair to tie his shoes. The sneakers from the day before were still damp, so he'd grabbed a different pair.

"Noticed your car wasn't here last night. Where'd you ride out the storm?"

So the questions started already. Though Sid had said she didn't care what people thought, and it wasn't in Lucas's nature to lie, how they'd spent the night wasn't anyone else's business. And discussing sex with his former fiancée felt doubly strange.

"You keeping tabs on my whereabouts now?" He yanked the laces tighter than intended, requiring him to loosen the shoe again.

"I know I have no right to stick my nose in your business," she said, tapping a low-hanging wind chime to her left. "But Sid is my friend. I don't want her getting hurt."

Lucas kept his eyes on his shoe, took his time finishing the last knot, then leaned back in the chair. She had some nerve. "I no longer have to explain myself to you, nor do I need the 'hurt my friend and I'll kick your ass' speech. Sid is a big girl. We're both consenting adults. What we do or do not do while I'm on this island is between us."

"I didn't mean—"

"Didn't you? I'm sure Sid appreciates your concern." He glanced out to the gray clouds floating along the horizon, and thought better of that statement. "Actually, I think she'd be really pissed to know you thought she couldn't handle herself."

"Wow. That was quick."

Not the response he expected. "What is that supposed to mean?"

Beth leaned on the porch railing. "Ten days ago you barely knew Sid Navarro existed, and now you seem to know her pretty well considering the accuracy of that comment. She would be pissed. But if protecting her means pissing her off, then that's what I'll do."

A cool breeze stirred the chimes, blowing curls across piercing green eyes. Sometimes Lucas forgot Beth had a temper. He'd had such little experience with it.

"You think she needs protection from me?"

"You giving any thought to moving back to this island?" she asked.

He sat forward. "I have no intention of ever moving back to this island."

"Then all I'm asking is that you watch your step with Sid. She's not as tough as she likes people to think."

That declaration was becoming a recurring theme with these people. How could anyone question Sid's toughness? The woman could rebuild an engine, blindfolded, while barely breaking a sweat. If the ease with which she'd left him behind today didn't prove she was in no danger from their little summer escapade, then her single-minded deter-mination to turn that dilapidated old dust trap into a work-ing business did.

Sid would likely come out of this fling in better shape than he would.

"I need to get to the restaurant before the rain gets heavier." Reaching down beside the chair, Lucas grabbed his tool belt and rose to his feet. "As I've said, what happens between me and Sid is our business. And of the two people standing on this porch, I'm not the one with a history of hurting people. Careful where you cast stones, Elizabeth."

He moved to step around her but she blocked his way. "The guilt trips are going to end now," Beth said. "We both know I was never the love of your life. I didn't break your heart, I just delayed this perfect future you've envisioned for yourself. A partnership in the firm, lots of prestige and money, and the perfect hostess slash wife to round out the image. Two months ago you came to grips pretty quick with my change of heart, and had a direct hand in how things turned out."

Lucas would have defended himself if her little rant hadn't been so damn accurate. Not that she gave him a sec-ond to plead his case.

"I get that the problems at the firm landed another blow to your ego, but maybe it's time you stop blaming your brother and me for everything you don't currently like about your life."

Blinking, he tried to form a response. Which he needed to do quickly considering the look on Beth's face practically demanded one. "You're right," he said, for lack of a better answer.

"Excuse me?" Her shoulders dropped as her eyebrows shot up. "Did you say I'm right?"

The concession already tasted bitter on his tongue. The least she could do was accept his acquiescence and go. "Yes. Are we done now?"

It was Beth's turn to blink. "I guess so." She began to move aside, then stopped. "Wait a minute. How do I know this change of attitude is going to stick? I want a permanent peace between you and Joe, not a temporary one. Your moods of late seem to be subject to change without warning."

She made him sound like a hormonal woman. The epiphany she'd just thrust out of his brain needed examining. Something he could do while running power tools and barking orders, not arguing with her on this porch.

"What do you want from me, Elizabeth? You were one person and now you're another. I'm trying to deal with that, but all of a sudden it feels like I'm not the same person either. So if I'm not that guy winning cases and making partner, who am I?"

Where the hell had that question come from? Damn it, if she'd just let him deal with this crap on his own. Lucas ran a hand through his hair, smacked a porch beam, then paced the length of the hardwoods.

"Lucas, there was always more to you than that job."

He didn't feel like more than a job. Ten years chasing a dream, focusing all his energy on the big prize. Even his hobbies were about schmoozing his way to the top. What the hell had he become?

"I can't deal with this right now. I need to get to the restaurant."

"You're not going without me," came a voice from inside the house. Lucas turned to find his father standing behind the screen door. Just what he needed.

"What are you talking about? You can't help take the boards down."

"No," Tom said, stepping tenuously onto the porch as if the wrong movement could have painful consequences. "But there's stuff I can do in the office. Payroll checks need signing. Some other paperwork."

Lucas hated seeing his father so frail, but he did look better than he had a week ago. More color in his cheeks. Shoulders not so rounded. Maybe a little distraction from the pain and meds would do him good.

"Did you run this by Patty?" Beth asked.

Tom tilted his head. "I don't need permission to go to my own damn restaurant. Now if you two are done yelling at each other, we've got shit to do."

Lucas remembered what his mom had said about the cranky-ass behavior. Maybe she deserved a break as well. "Hold on and I'll help you down the stairs."

"I'm not an invalid. I can walk by myself."

Beth caught Lucas's eye with raised brows, only this time they conveyed a *better you than me* sentiment.

"Think about what I said, Lucas," Beth whispered. "You're more than a law degree and a corner office." She went up on tiptoe and placed a kiss on his cheek, then smiled and headed back to the house next door.

If her moods always shifted that fast, perhaps he'd dodged a bullet after all. He'd feel sympathy for Joe, but knew his brother was no dream to live with either. For the first time since the night he'd learned his fiancée had fallen for his brother, Lucas felt happy for the couple.

A knot in his chest loosened, as if someone pulled the thread that would let it all go. Maybe there was hope for him yet.

"You coming or do I have to drive myself?" Tom asked, jerking Lucas from his thoughts.

"Right," he said. "I'm coming." Pulling his keys from his pocket, Lucas trudged down the stairs. "You did at least tell mom you were leaving, right?"

Tom lowered himself into the BMW with a curse and a moan. "She knows. This was her idea."

The fact his mother had kicked his ailing, irritable father out of the house didn't surprise Lucas one bit. Nor did he blame her. This was going to be a long day.

CHAPTER NINETEEN

J esus, Sidney Ann, you're supposed to be helping, not trying to put me in the hospital."

Randy always had been a drama queen.

"Don't get your panties in a bunch, you whiner. I've got it now." Though she wouldn't have nearly dropped her end of the plywood if the activities of the night before hadn't been flitting through her mind nonstop. Soreness danced along places long neglected and some Sid didn't know she had.

Too bad they couldn't implement a mind-blowing sex class at the fitness center. Would be one hell of a workout, and she'd bet the class would be booked full every week.

Then again, the two other men she'd been with had not been nearly as skilled as Lucas. Since there would be no "Sex with Lucas Dempsey" class offered, she scrubbed the whole idea.

"Last screw!" Randy yelled, which for a second made Sid think he could read her thoughts and was making a prediction. Then the full weight of the plywood pressed against her shoulder and she realized the statement was a warning, not a prediction.

She stepped back to balance the board and keep it from slamming through the plate-glass window it had been protecting. "Grab your side, smart ass, or you're going to lose the window after all."

The board shifted away from her, making it possible for Sid to see her brother. He held the board with one hand, a shit-eating grin on his face. "Too heavy for the little girl?"

Sid dropped her end, forcing Randy to use two hands. "I didn't have to come over here and help you. There are a lot of other people on this island who would appreciate another set of hands."

As she lifted her end again, Sid wondered for the umpteenth time if she could make it to the restaurant before the work was done. Stupid pride had kept her from following Lucas over there. She'd wanted to stay with him all day, but gluing herself to his ass like some desperate psycho was not the way to show she could maintain the *casual* agreement.

"Other people with the name Dempsey?" Randy asked.

Sid stopped, driving the edge of the plywood into her shin. "Shit," she growled. "If you're trying to shove this thing down my throat, you're doing a damn good job."

Randy shrugged. "I'm not the one who stopped. And you're ignoring my question."

"Yes," she conceded. "I've been helping out the Dempsey family, and I'm sure they would appreciate another hand at the restaurant to get things back in order."

A deep chuckle floated from across the board. "I wasn't talking about the whole family."

"You're about as subtle as a freight train, muscle head. If you have something to say, just say it." She hoped he couldn't see the blush she felt crawling up her neck.

"Drove by your house early this morning to make sure you were okay. BMW was in the driveway."

Well hell.

"Lucas helped me get the boards on the house, and we got caught in the storm." Her voice sounded confident. Matter of fact. She hoped. "He couldn't exactly drive home in the middle of a hurricane."

"None of my business who you spend the night with," her brother said. "But—"

"No buts, Randy. You're right. It's none of your business."

Sid backed into the storage room at the rear of the fitness center and lowered her end of the plywood to the floor. Randy did the same, then leaned an elbow on the top of the board. "He's only here for the summer, Sidney. You think it's a good idea to get involved?"

Her arms hurt, her legs hurt, and if this conversation kept up, her head would hurt next. Tucking a wayward strand behind her ear, she met Randy's level gaze, spotting concern more than a nosy interest. "We're not getting involved. It's just a . . . thing. For the summer."

"A thing?"

"Yeah. A thing. Casual." She was starting to hate that word.

His lips quirked as he shook his head. "Since when do you do casual? Doesn't seem like your style."

"Not sure I have a style when it comes to this sort of thing." This sort of thing being pretending she wasn't half in love with the man sharing her bed. The consequences would suck eventually, but she'd deal when the time came. "Just trust me, okay?"

After a long pause, Randy nodded. "Your life, sis. But let me know if I need to kick his ass and it's done."

She rolled her eyes. "You've never even been in a fight, Randy. Even the drunkest idiot has enough sense not to take you on." Following him out of the building, she caught up and walked beside him.

"Shows what you know." He ruffled her hair. "Lucas breaks your heart and he'll have me to deal with. Whether you like it or not."

"You're full of bullshit today." Sid laughed, knowing Randy wouldn't squash a bug, never mind kick her lover's ass.

Her lover. Weird.

"Why don't you worry about your own love life?" she asked. "When was the last time you had a little overnight company?"

"Nice try, chica. A gentleman does not kiss and tell."

Sid laughed. "If you did any kissing, the gossip lines on this island would tell long before you had the chance. You're not getting any younger, you know."

Her brother's last relationship had been at least six years ago. Hard to forget the crazy bitch who'd tried to run him over with her riding lawn mower. He'd understandably been a confirmed bachelor ever since. A fact that drove the female population of Anchor Island damn near batty.

When he'd opened the fitness center eight years before, his personal training services had been in high demand, with clients often suggesting he do personal home visits. When a client chased him into the men's locker room wearing nothing but a towel and a smile, he finally turned the female clientele over to another trainer. A female one.

A collective estrogen-laced sigh of disappointment had echoed island-wide.

"I'm waiting for Miss Right," Randy said, holding the fitness center door open for her to pass through.

"Do you think she's just going to burst through this door?" Sid asked, stopping at the front counter.

A mischievous smile split his tanned face. "You never know."

"Is Sid in here?" Will bellowed as she flew through the entrance as if on cue. Upon seeing Randy, she stepped back, causing the door to hit her in the ass as it closed, sending her sprawling forward again. Will never seemed to be comfortable around Sid's brother. When pressed, she'd once tossed off a comment about a bad experience with some other muscle-bound guy.

"What's wrong?" Sid asked, breaking the deer-in-the-headlights look Will was shooting at Randy. "Is everything okay?"

"Yeah," Will whispered, eyes darting back to Sid's brother. If she'd been trying to smile his way, she failed miserably. Her lip curled in a bad Elvis impersonation. "I mean no. Can we go outside and talk?"

"Sure," Sid answered.

"You guys stay up here," Randy said, his voice gentle, as if trying not to spook Will further. "I'll be in the office if you need me."

Sid watched Will as her brother walked off. "If you're trying to freak me out, it's working. What the hell is wrong with you?"

"It's the garage," Will blurted.

"What about it? Is the thing on fire or something?" Her stomach turned queasy at the thought. If the garage burned down, her dream was over. At least as she imagined it. She should have checked the electrical system, but she knew Fisher had all the utilities turned off.

"It's not on fire but there's someone else interested in buying it." Will pulled a mass of dark brown hair over her right shoulder. "I was helping the real estate office field calls from tourists canceling because of Ingrid, and took the call. Some woman up in Richmond wanted to speak directly to Fisher. Said she was calling on someone else's behalf, and wouldn't give me a name."

Sid tried to process the influx of information. Someone else wanted her garage. Someone who didn't live on Anchor. But . . .

"Who would want that old garage? And how would anyone in Richmond even know about it?" She paced the length of the counter. "This doesn't make any sense." Breathing became difficult so she bent over, rubbing her palms down her thighs.

"I asked in the office and Fisher's been advertising the place on websites. No one responded before now. This lady sounded legit, Sid. The phones were so nuts, I couldn't get away to tell you until now."

Blood pounded in her temples, making it hard to think. "This could be nothing. I mean, once someone gets a look at that building, they'll never buy the thing. Right?" She shot the question at Will like tossing a hot potato.

"Right," Will said, nodding her head in agreement. "The place is a dump. Who would want it?" Sid jerked around, and Will rephrased. "I mean no one could have the vision that you have." Stepping up to the counter, she added, "Why don't you go to your brother now? He could help you with the down payment, and then you can pay him back."

"No," Sid said. She would get that garage on her own or not at all. "Did you give the chick Fisher's number?"

Will shook her head. "I wouldn't give out his information, but I took hers and said I'd pass it along."

"Then that's it. The message is accidentally lost in the hurricane chaos, and the buyer thinks Fisher isn't interested in talking. Problem solved."

The knot in Sid's chest loosened until she noticed the pained expression on Will's face.

"You didn't."

"I had to give the message to Denise," Will declared. "I'd asked too many questions about the property and she wanted to know why." Will's shoulders fell. "She sent the message off right away."

An image rose in Sid's mind. A bonfire on the beach with all her hopes and dreams going up in smoke. There were no other buildings on Anchor that would serve her purposes as well as Fisher's garage. She'd have to build from scratch. Saving for that would take another ten years at the rate she was going.

"Don't give up yet," Will said, startling Sid out of her pity party. "You're right about the building. What if Fisher wasn't honest in the ad? What if this buyer doesn't realize what he'd be getting?" Will's voice floated up an octave. "What if Fisher is asking too much?"

She had a point. Fisher wasn't the easiest man to negotiate with. Sid should know. She'd been trying for months.

"The place *is* pretty run down." Maybe all was not lost. Sid leaned on the counter. "What would someone do with it besides put in a boat shop?" She shot upright again. "Shit. What if that's what this is about?"

"We are not buying trouble." Will took Sid by the shoulders and hunched until their noses nearly touched. "This is one phone call. An inquiry. That's all. Let's stay focused here." With a shake that stirred the bangle bracelets lining her wrist, she added, "We will *not* panic."

Interesting coming from the woman who had burst through the door as if the hounds of hell were on her ass. "You're the one who got me all riled up. Why didn't you just tell the lady the place is already sold?"

Will jerked back. "Because that would have been lying." She scuffed a foot across the floor. "And to be honest, I was so surprised it didn't occur to me. But I still say this is nothing to worry about."

Sid wanted to believe that. Needed to, or she might as well take the proverbial long walk off a short pier. "Right. Nothing to worry about."

Nothing but her entire freaking future.

~

"Lucas Dempsey, I need to hire you."

Not again. He turned to see the Ledbetters charging up the front steps of the restaurant.

"I told you, I'm not for hire."

"You can tell her that all you want," Mr. Ledbetter said, following his wife—ex-wife rather—who looked much more put out this time. "She don't listen worth a flip, and no matter what she tells you, she doesn't have a case anyway."

"Let my lawyer be the judge of that." Gladys's blue eyes were not dancing this time, and her brown hair looked as windblown as the trees covering the island. "This good-for-nothing's hammock is up on my roof, and he won't get it off. I told him to tie it down, but as usual, he wouldn't listen."

"There's a hammock on your roof?" Lucas asked. This story might be worth hearing.

"*His* hammock!" she yelled, pointing to the hammock-owning offender. "Not like we didn't know a hurricane was coming. I told him three times to strap that contraption to the porch."

"How many times do I have to tell you? We're not married anymore." Mr. Ledbetter smiled when he said those words. "I don't have to listen to your damn orders, woman."

Meaty hands landed on rounded hips. "That thing could have killed someone."

Frank chuckled. "That would have been an interesting headline in the paper. 'Woman killed by flying hammock; assumed she didn't duck fast enough.'"

Lucas stifled the laugh. "I think *tragic* is the word you're looking for, Mr. Ledbetter." He turned to Gladys. "Other than finding someone to help get the hammock off the roof, there isn't much I can do for you, Mrs. Ledbetter."

"That's Ms."

"Yes. Right." Lucas wondered if he could render himself unconscious with one good hammer blow to the head. "Have you considered moving?"

"Tell him to get that damn hammock off my roof," she demanded, ignoring Lucas's question. "Before the thing slides off and kills me."

"Heh," Frank said, stretching his considerable girth along a bench on the porch. "That puppy's clamped onto the chimney good and tight. It's not sliding anywhere any time soon." In a lower tone, he added, "More's the pity."

"What's the ruckus out here?" Tom asked, exiting the restaurant with a beer in his hand.

"Are you drinking that?" Lucas asked, knowing his mother would skin him alive for letting his dad have alcohol.

Tom shot him a look that said *Don't be an idiot* and joined Frank at the bench. "Thought I heard your voice. Here." He handed over the beer, then waited for the man to move over before dropping onto the bench beside him. "Now, what's the problem?"

"Lucas won't tell Frank to get his hammock off my roof," Gladys said, speaking more calmly. "He handled that tree thing for us. He needs to settle this one."

"You handled a tree case?" Tom's tone reminded Lucas of a judge instilling order from the bench.

"I . . . They . . . Ah, hell."

"I lost that one," Frank said. "But I'm not losing this one."

"Is your hammock on her roof?" Lucas asked.

"Lucas Dempsey, are you calling me a liar?" Gladys charged forward. "You think I'd come all the way over here and make up some cockamamie story about a hammock on my roof?"

Lucas would need something stronger than a beer when this was over. "I'm not calling you a liar, Ms. Ledbetter. I'm just trying to get Mr. Ledbetter's side of the story." Addressing the bench again, he asked, "Mr. Ledbetter, is she telling the truth?"

The defendant looked down at his shoes. "It's up there. But it ain't hurting anything right now. I'll get it down . . . eventually."

"Get the damn thing off her roof, Frank," Tom said. "We all know you just make her mad so she'll talk to you. She's talking, now go on and do the right thing."

Lucas looked back and forth between the bickering Ledbetters. Gladys looked flattered and Frank was blushing. This couple gave new meaning to the word "dysfunctional."

"Alright," Frank finally said, easing off the bench. He tipped the longneck up, drained its contents, then handed the bottle to Tom. "Let's go, Gladys. I'll get it down."

To Lucas's utter amazement, the pair walked off toward a rusted-out green pickup, arm in arm. Turning to his dad, he said, "They're nuts."

"Nah," Tom said. "They've been in love since high school. Just stubborn is all." Pushing off the bench, he headed back inside. "They wouldn't make you much money." He watched the pickup drive away. "But they'd make sure you weren't bored."

"I wasn't bored at what?" Lucas asked, bristling at the not-so-subtle implication. How many ways could he say he was not moving back to Anchor?

Tom met his gaze, then shrugged. "I just meant any lawyer around here. Didn't mean to imply that lawyer might be *you*." As he jerked open the door of the restaurant, he mumbled, "Heaven for-fucking-bid."

CHAPTER TWENTY

By five o'clock, Sid was tired, covered in sweat, and teetering between pissed off and pitiful. The high of sex with Lucas, followed by sharing the dream she was determined to make a reality, fizzled quickly after Will showed up at the fitness center.

She'd tried to cling to Will's words. The call was just an inquiry. No offer was on the table, and no sane person, especially a non-islander, would make an offer after seeing the building in person. But what if they only wanted the land? The building could be demolished for little expense. Someone with plenty of money could build something new.

The future she'd set for herself could be wiped out with one phone call.

So much for staying positive.

By seven, Sid had showered, slipped into pajamas, and killed half a six-pack. She hadn't stopped at Dempsey's because she didn't want to seem too needy, and in her present mood she wouldn't have been good company anyway.

They hadn't made plans. Didn't say when they'd see each other again. While she'd been working with Randy, Manny had asked if she and Lucas were an item. Sid hadn't been sure how to answer. Did having a casual fling make them an item? Were they exclusive, or free to fling with anyone they wanted?

Sid didn't want anyone else, but couldn't think of a casual sounding way to tell Lucas that. He might bolt then, and losing both him and the garage in the same day would suck way more than she wanted to think about.

With that thought, a knock sounded at the door along with the words, "Anyone home?"

Lucas. Sid hopped up, catching her toe on the leg of the coffee table.

"Shitgoddamnsonofabitch," was followed by every other curse word she knew as Sid bounced around on one foot. The pain subsided before the profanity ran out. Hobbling, she bent over and checked her hair in the TV. Still wet from the shower, the black mass was pulled into a clip on the back of her head with several wisps falling around her face.

Guys liked that, right? With a huff, she blew a lock off her forehead and headed for the door. "Screw it. If I'm lucky he won't be looking at my hair."

"Hey," she said, opening the screen door. "Come on in."

Lucas stepped through, and a hint of cologne filled her senses. Just having him close sent her temperature up several degrees. His hair looked damp, as if he'd recently showered, too. Standing just inside the door, he held out an envelope.

"Today was payday. Since you didn't come by the restaurant, I thought I'd bring this over."

She'd forgotten all about the paycheck. Now that the target was gone, there wasn't much point in saving. "Thanks."

An awkward silence fell between them. Lucas looked uncomfortable, leading Sid to assume he was afraid she'd expect him to stay. Sid didn't know what she expected anymore.

Common sense told her not to make a fool of herself, but she asked anyway. "You want something to drink? I've got beer, soda, wine."

"Soda's good," he said. Of course. If he intended to drive home, he shouldn't have alcohol.

Worried he'd see the disappointment on her face, Sid headed for the kitchen. Not until she reached the fridge did she realize Lucas had followed. After sliding the cold can across the Formica, she popped a top on another beer for herself.

"Sid?" Lucas said, choosing to remain silent until she met his eyes. "If I don't touch you soon I might spontaneously combust."

To her own credit, Sid didn't react. At least not where Lucas would be able to tell. She gently set the bottle on the counter. A tilt of the head was added to give the effect she was debating her response.

With what she hoped was a sexy grin, Sid said, "So what's stopping you?"

∼

Lucas exhaled for the first time since stepping out of his car. He had to be flashing the goofiest smile, but didn't care. The only thing that mattered in that moment was the adorable pixie standing before him in oversized pajamas that covered every inch of the delectable curves he knew lurked beneath the cotton.

Taking those things off was going to be more fun than he could stand. But first things first. With one step forward, he cupped her face, tilting her head back and staring into milk chocolate eyes.

"Hi," he said, enjoying the slide of silky curls along his knuckles. Feeling her heartbeat steady against his fingertips.

"Hi," she answered. Her voice, low and breathy, vibrated through his whole body.

Slowly he leaned in, taking his time, enjoying making her wait. He knew from the night before Sid was not the most patient woman. A soft nip, then another before he pulled back. Her lips moved forward, trying to follow. Another nip and her hands slid up his arms as her body melted into his.

His own patience waned and he took her mouth full on. Heat spiked through him as her hands jammed into his hair. Wrapping his arms around her back, he lifted her off the floor as they tasted each other. This is what he'd been longing to do all day. Where he'd longed to be.

With Sid. Beside her. Touching her. Teasing her.

This was heaven, and he never wanted to be without it. The thought jarred him like a punch to the temple. He broke contact but continued to hold Sid off the floor. Staring into dark brown pools of lust, Lucas set her down gently. This was too much. Too fast.

He couldn't think straight, and the blood flow headed south wasn't helping. Putting air between them should have been his next move, but his arms were ignoring the messages coming from his brain. Bottom line, the organ upstairs was no longer in control.

"That was a pretty good greeting," Sid said, sounding more girly than he'd ever heard her. She shifted against him and he went hard. Or rather, harder.

"How was your day?" he asked, taking her by the hand and heading for the couch. Talking. Talking should help. Casual talking.

"Oh," Sid said, struggling to keep up. "It could have been better." Lucas sat down, pulling her onto the cushion beside him. How he managed not to pull her into his lap, he didn't know. "How about yours? When will Dempsey's be ready to reopen?"

"If the delivery Vinnie put in to replace the lost meat comes through on Sunday, we should be up and running on Monday. Distributor said Highway 12 through Hatteras held up, so we should be good."

He wanted boring talk and this was definitely it. Then Sid's words sank in. "Did you say your day could have been better? What happened?"

"Just something I might have to deal with later." Sid threw a gray pajama-clad leg over his knee. "Did you come all the way over here to discuss our days?"

Grasping for a distraction, he asked. "Are those . . . flying piggy banks on your pants?"

Sid shrugged. "Yeah. I thought they were cool. And the message on my shirt is not intended for you, of course."

The shirt read, "I'm not antisocial, I just don't like you."

"Good to know." Had someone kicked on the heat? Lucas turned his body until Sid's leg dropped off, then draped an arm across the back of the couch. "What do you know about Willow?"

Sid froze. "Will? What about her?"

"She's been on the island for a while, right? Works at O'Hagan's, I think she said?"

"Among other places." Sid scooted away and crossed her arms. "But I don't think Will is looking for a man."

What did that mean? "I'm not trying to give her a man, I want to give her a job."

The sudden cold front coming across the couch thawed. "You want Will to work at Dempsey's? Is this your way of telling me you're going back to Richmond before your dad recovers?"

The thought *I'm not going anywhere* sprang to mind. He shoved it down with the other unwelcome thoughts and stuck to his purpose. "I'm talking about when dad is recovered. He can't run that bar by himself anymore. It's too much. I haven't talked to Willow—"

"Will," Sid corrected. Seemed like an odd thing to be a stickler about.

"Right. Will. If she tends bar at O'Hagan's, then she knows what she's doing and is used to handling the tourists and crowds. Do you think she'd be qualified as an assistant manager?"

Sid relaxed, pulled her legs up and squeezed them to her chest. "I don't know. Will is like the island temp, bouncing around nearly every business on Anchor. Except for Randy's. She doesn't like Randy, for some reason."

"Why not?"

"She has this weird phobia about big guys or something. But she might like having one full-time position instead of hopping around to half a dozen shops." Sid hugged her knees tighter. "Just to be clear. You're only interested in giving her a job, right? Not slipping her anything else?"

Not slipping . . . Lucas took a full five seconds to catch on. Where did she get these ideas?

"Sid. Where was I last night?"

She tilted her head. "Is that a trick question?"

"And where am I right now?"

"Have you been drinking?"

"Are you going to stop asking stupid questions?"

She huffed and dropped her gaze. "It's not so stupid. I mean, we're not *committed* or anything. Not exclusive." Scratching a spot on her PJs, she mumbled, "You can do whatever you want."

Unnerved by her lack of confidence, Lucas didn't know what to do with Sid's vulnerable side. Surely she knew how desirable she was. Challenging. Driven. Flat-out hot.

Maybe she didn't.

With one finger under Sid's chin, Lucas brought her eyes back to his. "Do you plan on sleeping with anyone else in the next few weeks?"

She shook her head.

"Good. Me neither." He tucked a wayward lock behind her ear. "Come here, Sidney." He caved and pulled her onto his lap. "Do you think I should ask Will if she'd take the job?"

"I do." Her smile created a knot in his chest before she switched to pensive again. "Shouldn't you talk to your parents first though? Would they want someone else helping run the place? Someone who isn't family?"

"I don't know. Dad came to the restaurant with me today, and I've never seen him so mean. Mom said it's a side effect of the heart attack. All I know is he can't go back to running the bar on his own." He flattened his hands on her thighs, then tilted his head back on the couch. "Mom's worried about losing him, and so am I. I think they both need a break." He brought his head back up. "Will is your friend, so that tells me we can trust her."

"You get that through me?" she asked, absently running circles on his stomach with one finger. Sending more heat down to lower regions.

"I trust you, and you trust her, so I trust her." That sentence probably didn't make sense, but brain function was deteriorating by the second. "Before I forget, do you care if I check my e-mail from here?"

"No, but I'd have to turn the computer on." As if they weren't having a mundane conversation, Sid leaned in and dropped a moist kiss at the base of his neck. "I'd rather turn something else on." Another kiss and her hands slid beneath his shirt.

"It's okay," he practically moaned. "My iPad is in my bag in the car."

Sid stopped the kissing and sat up. "You have a bag in the car? Like an overnight bag?"

"Yeah." Time to see if his presumptions were wrong. If her body language was any indication, he didn't think so. "I wasn't sure you'd want me over, so I didn't bring it in."

The rare occasions Sid hit him with a full-on smile had felt like getting punched in the gut. This one, which he would forever deem her sex-kitten look, felt like getting hit by a train. And he'd gladly jump in front of this locomotive any time.

"I definitely want you over," Sid purred. "And under and any other way I can get you."

Lucas rose to his feet, taking Sid with him. She yelped and threw her arms around his neck. "You're going to get tired of carrying me around."

"Never," he answered, then stopped in the middle of the floor. The look on her face reflected the same shock spiking through his system. Where had that answer come from?

Tightening her grip, Sid ground against his stomach. "Didn't you want to check your e-mail?" One hand slid into his hair as she trailed kisses along his jawline.

"E-mail can wait," he growled, taking her mouth with all the passion he'd been holding in check. Without breaking contact, he moved them both to the bedroom, where, as he'd predicted, removing Sid's funky pajamas was the most fun he'd had all day.

Hours later, as the clock turned over to midnight, Lucas got around to checking his e-mail. Of the dozen or so messages, one caught his eye first. Davis Holcomb, the partner who had suggested he take some time off, didn't e-mail often. This had to be important.

Opening the message, Lucas found the words he least expected.

We need you for a case. When are you coming back?

CHAPTER TWENTY-ONE

Summers on Anchor could never be considered scorchers, but by mid-August the humidity had spiked, making eighty-five feel more like ninety-five. In the shade. After tossing two large garbage bags into the Dumpster behind Dempsey's, Sid caught a drop of sweat headed for her chin and stretched out the muscles in her back.

In the last week, she'd gotten more of a workout than she ever had hitting the gym. Lucas had stamina to spare, and quite the imagination. Good thing she trusted him or she might never have been willing to try that chair maneuver the night before. A move likely illegal in several states.

But the payoff had been worth the bending and twisting. Her teeth still tingled when she thought about it.

Eight nights with Lucas in her bed, and Sid woke every morning afraid she might be dreaming. After the weekend, she'd assumed he'd want some time apart. That he'd stay at his parents' house during the week. But Lucas had followed her home from work every night, and by midweek they realized what a waste it was to drive two vehicles to the same place.

They started driving in together and if anyone found it odd that she and Lucas were suddenly joined at the hip, they kept it to themselves.

Contrary to Sid's own expectations, she enjoyed having a man around. His hot, solid body tangled with hers as she fell asleep. Hazel eyes and a stubble-covered chin the first thing she saw in the morning. Though if this arrangement ever became permanent, she'd need to install a bigger shower, as they'd become strict practitioners of water conservation.

Two people saving the planet one shower at a time.

But this *wasn't* a permanent arrangement. Something Sid had to remind herself on a regular basis. Lucas would be leaving in four weeks. Not that she was marking the days on a mental calendar or anything. The two or three brief moments when she imagined waking up alone again, waterworks threatened. Tears were not an option. Sid Navarro did not cry over something as stupid as a man.

To preserve her sanity as well as her dignity, the winding river of denial had become her mental happy place.

"Sid, wait up," Will said from the front corner of the building, pulling Sid from her wayward thoughts. "I was hoping to catch you." The lanky brunette crossed the distance between them, then shoved her hands in the pockets of her jeans, setting off a cacophony of bangle bracelets. Her eyes looked everywhere but at Sid.

"Should I be sitting down for this?" Sid asked, assuming the worst. "There's been a formal offer on the garage, hasn't there?"

Will jumped and met Sid's gaze, eyes wide. "No. Not that I know of."

"Then what are you acting so weird about?" The woman looked ready to leap out of her own skin.

"I . . ." Will started, then looked around as if making sure they were alone. Leaning forward she whispered, "Do you know why I'm here?"

She thought she did. "Lucas called and asked you to come, didn't he?"

Will took a step back. "And you're not pissed?"

"Why would I be pissed?" Sid had encouraged Lucas to make the call. They'd been so busy through the week, and distracted with each other, that he must have only just gotten around to it. If Will was going to become the new assistant manager of Dempsey's Bar & Grill, they needed to ask her first.

"But you two have been together all week? I get that whatever you have is casual, but it's still weird that he would ask me out while he's seeing you."

"What the hell are you talking about?" There would be no sharing of Lucas. She may have to give him up when summer ended, but fuck all if Will thought she could have him now.

Will crossed her arms. "The guy you're sleeping with called and asked me to meet him here on a Friday night. I assumed . . ."

When she put it that way. "So Lucas didn't tell you *why* he called you here?"

"He said he wanted to talk to me." Will shrugged one shoulder. "I tried to tell him no, but he insisted and said it was important." Will took a step back when Sid started to laugh. "Is that your crazy 'I'm going to cut a bitch' laugh? Because I swear I had no intention of—"

"Relax," Sid said, holding her side and snorting again. "He wasn't asking you out. He wants to offer you a job." She sobered and leaned against the railing. "And if it were the other, I *would* kill you both. So lucky for you it's not."

Will rubbed her forehead. "I'm so confused. What kind of a job could Lucas offer? He doesn't even live here."

Sid gestured toward the building. "He thinks Patty and Tom need help running this place. Someone to take some of the load off. Figured with your experience, you'd be the person for the job." As Will's lips moved but no sound came out, Sid added, "You don't have to answer right away, but something full time would be better than flitting around to every business the way you do, don't you think?"

"It's a great offer," Will said, eyes on her shoes. "But I don't know." Backflips of excitement weren't necessary, but Sid had expected a more positive response.

"We haven't talked to Tom and Patty about it yet. Lucas thought we should ask you first before taking the idea to them." She'd thought Will would jump at the chance. So much for that. "If you're not interested, then just forget it."

Sid wasn't sure why she felt betrayed. It wasn't as if she'd be working the tables after Tom and Patty returned. What did she care if Will took the job or not? Silence loomed, tension crackling in the air.

"I'd better get back inside," Sid said. "If you want I'll tell Lucas you're taking a pass."

"Wait," Will said, stopping Sid as she turned back toward the kitchen door. "I didn't say I don't want the job. It's just that . . ." She hesitated, biting her lip. "I'm not sure how long I plan to stay on Anchor."

That announcement hit like a blow. Though Will had been on the island less than a year, she'd never mentioned wanting to move on. She, Beth, and Sid had spent hours talking over desserts at Opal's, and never had the topic of leaving Anchor come up.

Maybe they weren't the good friends Sid had thought. "By all means, don't let us tie you down." This must be how puppies felt when kicked. Stupid puppy kicker.

Sid was pulling the kitchen door shut behind her when Will stuck her foot in the way. "I didn't say my bags are packed. It's just complicated. I like it here, but things could change. I can't plan things long term."

What the hell was she talking about? It was starting to sound like the woman was in the witness protection program. "Look, Will, I don't know what all this mystery stuff is about, but if you ever run into trouble, you have friends here. We take care of our own."

"You consider me part of 'your own'?" Will asked, brows raised.

Sid nodded. "Damn right."

Will lingered in silence for several more seconds. Stared at the floor. Chewed her lip. Then she caught Sid's eye and nodded. "Then I'd like to talk about the job."

As if the floor had just tilted and then reset itself, Sid felt her world settle back into place. She'd spent most of her life without any close friends, and never thought twice about it. Now, in one week, she'd gone from not needing a man or friends to realizing she had both and liking it that way.

Sid held the door open wide. "Then let's go get you a job."

∼

I'm not sure how much longer they're willing to wait, Lucas." Calvin Bainbridge's words were clipped with impatience. "You've been gone a month already."

"I've only been down here two weeks and I wouldn't have been off at all if Holcomb hadn't insisted. My dad had a heart attack, remember?"

"And we all feel bad about that, but how many people does it take to run some dinky restaurant?"

Red flared behind Lucas's eyelids. "My family does not run a *dinky* restaurant. And considering the number of lawyers working in that firm, how could this case possibly require my participation?"

"It's the prosecutor," Calvin said. The sound of rustling papers traveled down the line. "Dannon has been given lead in the case. You've singed his ass three times in the last year and that makes you the go-to guy on this one."

"You worked those cases too, Cal. Surely you've learned something from me by now." Lucas paced the tiny confines of the office. Georgette was covering the bar, but she'd need to return to the floor soon. "I need another couple weeks down here. Take it through discovery and I'll be back before the trial starts."

Calvin sighed. "Holcomb's not going to like this. Did you know there's a pool going around for who's going to get your office?"

Lucas stopped. "What are you talking about? No one is getting my office. I'm not quitting."

"You quitting is not the reason people think the office will be up for grabs." A female voice could be heard in the background, then Calvin continued. "Look, man, we need you up here and we need you now."

"My family needs me down here," he said, wondering when his coworkers had become so callous. Or had they always been that way? "I'll deal with Holcomb when I get back."

Lucas was not looking forward to that conversation.

"You're putting your career on the line here," Calvin warned. "I hope you know what you're doing." With that message, the line went dead.

Did he know what he was doing? Part of the reason for taking time off had been to figure out his priorities. Lucas had lost Beth because his job came first. Because he'd been too blind to see what he had when he had it. He didn't want to make that mistake again.

"There you are," Sid said, sticking her head into the office. Upon seeing his face, she stepped further in. "Are you okay? Georgette said you had a phone call. You don't look happy."

He didn't want to make that mistake again.

"I'm fine," he said, setting the phone on the charger and trying to pretend he wasn't debating his entire future. "Someone at the firm needed one of my old files and they couldn't find it. It's all good now."

Sid looked dubious, but didn't press. "Will is here and I had to tell her what this is about since you didn't bother." Sid moved in closer and toyed with the collar of his polo shirt. "You need to stop calling other women and sounding all hot and bothered on the phone. She thought you were asking her out."

The lack of air between them made it difficult to concentrate on her words. "I thought we were clear about this.

You're the only woman getting me hot and bothered." He nearly added the words "these days" but that would have been a lie, as he couldn't imagine another woman ever having this kind of effect on him. Even long after he'd left Anchor Island.

Lucas sat on the desk to bring himself closer to Sid's level, which gave her the opportunity to drop a kiss in the opening of his collar. "If you keep that up, someone is going to walk in here and find us in a very compromising position."

"Compromising for who?"

"For whom," he corrected, before he could stop himself.

Sid drew back. "Way to kill the mood, fancy pants." As she moved toward the door, taking her heat and heady scent with her, a bitter sense of loss swept over him. Like the warm sun going behind a thundercloud of doom.

How was he going to tell her he was leaving early? Throwing away the career he'd worked so hard to build wasn't an option. This wasn't a matter of fucked-up priorities. He and Sid had agreed to a casual fling. They always knew he'd have to leave at the end of summer. What difference would a couple weeks make?

"I've got to get back on the floor." Sid reached the door, then looked back. His thoughts must have shown on his face because she asked, "Are you sure you're okay?"

No.

"Yeah. Everything's fine."

"You're not flaking out about tonight, are you?"

Tonight? What was tonight? A quick memory check brought the answer. "The Smuggler's Ball?" he asked. Too bad dressing as a pirate wasn't his only worry. "No way. I'm ready for my eye patch."

Sid rewarded that statement with a full-press smile. "Good, because you will not believe the getup Curly talked me into wearing. You coming up to talk to Will or do you want me to send her back?"

Getting the Will situation settled would help him get back to Richmond sooner, which made him want to tell Sid to send her away. "Give me a minute and I'll be up. I just have to make a quick call."

Sid's brows drew together but she didn't pry. If he were leaving early, there was one other thing besides the family business he needed to take care of.

CHAPTER TWENTY-TWO

The eye patch was a bad idea. Lucas had nearly run off the road trying to drive with the thing on. And a dull sting prevailed after his mother's stunt of pulling the patch out and letting it snap back against his face. Joe had warned him she might try that.

After she'd already done it.

Lucas wasn't sure why he was dressed as a pirate to begin with. From what he understood, the Anchor festival planners had added this Smuggler's Ball to bring in more late-season tourists. The larger pirate festival in June, to which Joe typically wore the outfit Lucas was now sporting, brought in the highest numbers of the season.

Vacationers loved their pirate lore. Most claimed the allure was due to Blackbeard's historical ties to the area, but Lucas blamed Johnny Depp. If anyone else had asked him to don a costume and act pirate-y, he'd have said absolutely not. But Sid had played dirty. She'd asked while lying gloriously naked atop his chest.

Regardless, scheduling a visit for June to see Joe at the helm of his fishing boat, while wearing this ridiculous getup, would be more than worth the drive. The thought reminded Lucas that in order to come back, he first had to leave. Not that he'd thought about much else since the call from Bainbridge. Between ponderings on how to prolong his stay were the even less successful contemplations on how and when to tell Sid he'd be leaving early.

She'd given no indication they'd gone beyond casual, nor had she even hinted at the idea of him staying permanently. During one brief moment of insanity, he considered asking her to move to Richmond, but returned to his senses almost immediately. Not only would Sid hate the city, she'd never fit into his world.

Sid just didn't fit the mold. Partner's wife. Smiling hostess. Pleasant and diplomatic. Strolling into the office for a lunch date wearing a shirt that read "Life's a bitch and then you marry one" would not go over well. A thought that made him feel disloyal even as he knew it was true.

Admitting she was not wife material did not mean he wanted to change her. Lucas liked Sid just the way she was. The attitude and chip on her shoulder didn't tell the whole story of his lusty little pocket pixie. Sid was smart, ambitious, and took shit from no one. All qualities he liked, but the last was most refreshing, and the one trait he never expected to want in a woman.

And their relationship was not just about sex. They spent several evenings the past week lounging on Sid's couch, Drillbit digging her claws into his thigh like a baker kneading dough, and her owner reading a book while tucked in close against his side.

He'd checked his e-mail, or read the news, content to be exactly where he was. To enjoy the silent company of the one he was with.

By the time he pulled into Sid's drive, Lucas still had no clue what the hell he was going to do.

"You can come in, but don't go past the couch," Beth barked as Lucas stepped into Sid's cottage. "We'll be out in two minutes."

His former fiancée was the reason Lucas had to get dressed at his parents' place instead of at Sid's. Something about being Sid's fairy godmother and making sure Cinderella looked right for the ball. He'd assumed it was all a joke, until Joe let him know she was quite serious. They'd even shared an amicable laugh about the two women, which was a nice change from their usual interactions.

"It's easier to go along," Joe had said. Going along with insanity didn't sound rational, but Lucas did it anyway. After all, Sid *had* promised to repay his cooperation in a most generous fashion.

Lucas plopped down on the couch, barely remembering to flick the sword aside before turning himself into a Popsicle. Drillbit took her place on his leg, claws extra sharp as if she'd filed them for his benefit.

"Not tonight, fur ball," he said, setting her gently on the floor. From there, the cat climbed to the back of the couch and started kneading his shoulder. He was struggling to remove her claws from the linen when Beth breezed back into the room.

"Are you ready?" she asked, eyes twinkling and rubbing her hands together like a mad scientist.

He stopped with the kitten in midair. "Ready for wha . . ." The rest of the sentence fell away as Sid appeared behind Beth. Fairy godmother, my ass, Lucas thought. Instead of a princess, she'd turned Sid into every man's sexual fantasy. On steroids.

A thin piece of red material barely covered Sid from shoulder to upper thigh, with some corset-like strip of black leather cinching in her already narrow waist, making the classic hour glass curves more pronounced. What he supposed passed for sleeves gaped open with slits from shoulder to elbow and then elbow to hand. As if enough flesh weren't already showing.

Fishnet stockings trailed into black boots that started just below her knees and a black bandana covered with tiny skull-n-crossbones topped off the look. The thick mass of dark curls had been pulled to one side and hung in disarray over her left shoulder.

Every circuit in Lucas's body went on high alert as his brain screamed *Mine!*

"What did you do to her?" Lucas moved closer, holding a squealing kitten against his chest. "She looks . . . That outfit . . ." Turning to Beth, he demanded, "Where's the rest of it?"

"You don't like it?" Sid asked, her face falling as she tugged at the top of the dress. Which did absolutely nothing to cover the more than ample cleavage. Lucas's mouth watered.

"I didn't say that." He backtracked, trying to get a grip on the sudden intense desire to drag the blanket off the back of the couch and cover her up. Which warred with the Neanderthal reflex to throw her over his shoulder and head for the bedroom. "You look great. Really great."

"My work here is done," Beth said, looking much too pleased with herself. "You kids have fun. I better get back to Dempsey's before Joe has a cow."

Lucas would be having a talk with Beth before he left Anchor Island. She was never to dress Sid in this fashion again. Especially not when he wasn't there to let every other man know exactly to whom she belonged.

"That reminds me," Sid said, taking Drillbit from his grip. "I need to feed her before we go."

As Sid sashayed into the kitchen, Lucas took several deep breaths. He did not own this woman. In a couple weeks, he'd be gone and she would be entitled to dress like a pole-dancing pirate for anyone she wanted. Just as he would be entitled to drive back to the island and kick that anyone's ass.

"Okay, I'm good," Sid said, snagging her keys off the end table. Her smile hit like a bolt of lightning. "You're rocking that pirate look pretty good yourself, by the way."

~

Sid made a mental note to suggest Lucas go without shaving more often. The dusting of whiskers suited his high seas adventure look perfectly. She never remembered Joe looking so delicious in this outfit. The pirate standing in her living room looked good enough to eat.

Since Joe was slightly broader in the shoulders than his brother, the normally loosely fitting shirt billowed even more on Lucas. She recognized the black pants as his own. Joe's wardrobe would never include a pair this fancy, but the knee-high boots added a hint of sexy that made her forget why they were heading out the door instead of down the hall to her bedroom.

"If you don't stop looking at me like that, we'll never get

out of here," he said, then crossed the distance between them and slid his hands up to cup her face. "Not that I'd have a problem with that. I hate the thought of any other man seeing you dressed like this."

Before she could respond, he took her mouth in a way he never had before. This wasn't just a kiss but a claiming. A man staking out his territory in a manner that brooked no argument. And Sid had never experienced anything so arousing.

"We don't really have to go." The words were breathed more than said as she dropped her head back and enjoyed the sensations of Lucas's tongue sliding along her skin. When he reached the top of her breasts, she thought her entire body might go up in flames.

"Aren't you supposed to help Opal with her dessert table?" Lucas asked, between the tender bites he was dropping along her shoulder.

Damn it. She'd forgotten about that. "We don't have to stay long though, right?"

His attention returned to her face, his hazel eyes a deep, mossy green as he ran a thumb along her bottom lip. "An hour tops. I don't think I can take more than that."

"Deal," she said, taking his mouth for another scorching kiss. Pulling back, she took his hand and reached for the door. "Let's go then. We're killing time."

～

Rows of tents formed a frame around the city park, which was little more than a wide open area bordered by towering oaks, whose branches brushed the ground as if bowing to the guests. Young pirates flitted through the crowd, stopping now and then to parry and thrust their wooden swords in battle with an enemy.

The older buccaneers, some dressed more elaborately than others, carried giant drumsticks and tankards of what had to be nonalcoholic ale, as no adult beverages were permitted in the park. Johnny Roger and his Mutineers provided traditional tunes for the swashbucklers looking to twirl around the dance floor.

Business at Opal's dessert table had been steady for half an hour, making it difficult for Sid to keep tabs on Lucas. Kinzie, Opal's granddaughter and apprentice of sorts, worked the end opposite Sid, looking adorable in a long black skirt, red corset cincher, and puffy white blouse. A hint on the plump side, the pastry-chef-in-training fit the role of pirate wench turned ship cook perfectly.

Sid had always thought of Kinzie, with her ready smile and pleasant disposition, as her polar opposite. Sunny. Happy. Friendly. All things Sid was not. Which made it odd that they got along so well.

"We might have to hire you to wear that outfit and work at the store, Sid," Kinzie said, laughter in her voice. "Grandma's cakes are good, but you're the hot cake bringing in the customers tonight."

Opal handed a large cupcake to a blushing teenage male, who nearly dropped his booty due to not taking his eyes off Sid. "We could just put you out front on the porch and we'd sell out every day."

Her two tablemates giggled, and though Sid knew they were only teasing, she couldn't help but feel conspicuous. She'd tugged at her neckline, which rested way too many inches below her neck, to no avail. Lifting the top only raised the bottom, and the fishnets Curly had insisted she wear didn't exactly provide much coverage either. She feared her own booty was in danger of flashing the entire crowd. Or at least anyone standing behind her.

"I didn't realize the dress would be so small when Curly put it on me." Another tug up. "I feel like an idiot."

"Oh, we were only teasing," Opal said, giving her a reassuring pat on the arm. "You look beautiful and we're just jealous. Don't mind us."

But she did mind all the male eyes that kept sliding over her body as if she were wearing nothing at all. "I think I need to go home and change. Do either of you see Lucas?" Sid craned her neck to look through the crowd.

"You mean your pirate protector who has been standing twenty feet to our right shooting mental daggers at every man who's smiled your way?" Kinzie took two dollars from a kid who looked no more than ten, and handed over a slice of apple pie. "Two hands, little man. No replacements if you drop that."

Sid glanced to her right to find Lucas standing with his feet apart, arms crossed, and brows together. He looked ready to tear someone apart.

"Has he been there the whole time?" she asked. A ribbon of heat snaked through her system, but instead of the shot of lust she was used to, this one went straight for the heart.

Oh, that wasn't good.

"The whole time," Opal said. "Like an angry Adonis. Too bad men don't dress this way anymore." The older woman sighed, drawing Sid's attention. Did she just call Lucas an Adonis?

Sid glanced Lucas's way again. Opal did have a point, but it was the look in his eyes more than the outfit that was doing funny things to Sid's sense of balance. Her world was tilting and she had no idea how to get her bearings.

You don't get to keep him, girlfriend. Do not get too attached.

But it was too late. Sid was definitely attached.

"No wonder there are so many desserts floating around this crowd," Manny said, stepping up to the booth. "The sweetest piece in the room is hiding behind this table."

The sweetest piece? He better not be talking about her.

"Hi, Manny," Kinzie all but purred. Her face was an odd shade of pink and she seemed to be bouncing on her tiptoes. "I made some meringues for you." A box of fluffy white concoctions appeared from under the table.

"Hey," he said, pulling the box across the table. "Is this my grandmother's recipe?"

"It is," Kinzie beamed.

So that's how things were.

Sid pondered the possible couple. Kinzie and Manny were the same age but that's where the similarities ended. Then again, she and Lucas were about as different as a tuna and a marlin so who was she to judge?

"How much do I owe you for these?" Manny asked, reaching for his wallet.

"Since you gave me the recipe, we'll call it even. I'm sure they're not as good as your grandmother's, but I hope they're close."

He shot the blushing pirate wench a smile and took a

quick swipe off the top of one of the delicacies. Popping the taste in his mouth, his eyes rolled back. *"Al igual que la abuela."*

Sid assumed that meant the white puffs were good.

Manny cradled the box against his chest. "Thanks, Kinzie. This gives me a little taste of home."

Pride beamed from the happy baker until Manny turned Sid's way. "Why don't you take a break and come sit with me for a while." He held up the box. "I'm willing to share."

Oh, no. Sid looked over to Kinzie in time to see the woman practically deflate to the floor. Manny could not be this dense. "I think the one who made them should get to have some, don't you?" she asked, nodding her head furiously in Kinzie's direction.

Manny didn't get the message. "Come on. Don't you want some of this?" By *this* he clearly didn't mean the desserts. Men were so damn stupid.

"Time's up, Sullivan. You're holding up the line." Lucas appeared at the end of the booth, standing as close to Sid as possible with three feet of table between them. She could feel the anger rolling off him.

"What's up with you, man? Don't you need to get back to that fancy lawyer gig of yours?"

On a normal day, Sid would expect laid-back Lucas to ignore the challenge in Manny's voice and bring a rational, mature end to this ridiculous scene. But a crowd was gathering and Lucas looked neither laid-back nor rational.

"I think it's time to dance," she said, hopping over the side of the booth, hoping she hadn't just flashed her girly parts to the crowd at large. "Come on, Lucas. Twirl me around the floor."

Sid was not a dancer. She'd never twirled around anything, never mind a dance floor. But unless she wanted to see the typically bored Anchor Island Police Department, all two of them, be called into action, she had to think quick.

When they reached the dance floor, she pulled Lucas into the crowd, hoping to put obstacles as well as distance between the two men. Not two seconds after reaching the middle of the floor, the toe-tapping number came to an end, and another song, slow and mournful, began.

For several seconds they stood unmoving, eyes locked, surrounded by tension. Sid bit her bottom lip and raised her brows. "You going to leave me hanging?" she asked.

"I don't want to," he said, hands at his sides.

"You don't want to dance?" This was not how she expected the night to go. "We don't have to . . ."

Before she could wind her way back off the floor, he caught her hand and pulled her against him. "I don't want to leave you hanging," he said, as if the statement made any kind of sense. "I need you to know that."

Okay. Now she was completely confused. He held her so tight, she had to push away from him just to lean back far enough to see his face. When he finally looked down, she said, "What does that mean?"

He ignored the question, laying his forehead against hers. "Can we get out of here?" he asked.

They'd begun to sway to the music and Sid realized dancing had something going for it. Hips pressed together.

Lucas holding on tight. The music floating around them as their bodies moved in time as if melded together.

"Can we finish this song?"

Lucas smiled, though his eyes remained dark and stormy. "Yeah. We can do that."

CHAPTER TWENTY-THREE

Sid didn't say much on the way home, which was good since Lucas didn't have the words to explain whatever this was spinning through his system. Her scrap of a dress didn't include pockets so he'd carried the keys. Reaching the truck, they seemed to decide he would drive without either of them saying a word.

With Sid curled against his side on the bench seat, Lucas absorbed the feeling of having her close. A memory he could bring to mind once he was back in Richmond. It would be a while before the scent of watermelon made him think of anything other than Sid in his arms.

Once they reached the house, Lucas circled the truck to lift Sid out. Even with no one around, he didn't want her jumping out wearing the handkerchief Beth considered a dress.

"I've never let anyone drive my truck before," she said, as if talking about the weather instead of revealing how much she'd come to trust him. Lucas's chest tightened.

"I can see why. There's a lot of power under that hood. Takes a steady hand." He slid a knuckle along her jawline, knowing he wasn't talking about the truck. Recognizing the understanding in her eyes.

"Right." Sid looked down but didn't move. "I need the keys to unlock the door."

"I've got it," he said, following her to the house, his hand possessive on the small of her back. As he slipped the key into the lock, Sid stopped him with a touch on his arm.

"I appreciate this chivalry thing, but I've been taking care of myself for a long time." She hesitated, as if searching for the right words. "Playing the passive damsel doesn't sit well with me."

In the fading light he could see uncertainty in her expression. As if walking a thin line, worried it might break. "I'm sorry," he said, stepping back to give her access to the door. "You're right. I'm acting like a caveman."

Lucas had never been the grunting, Neanderthal type, but something changed when he was with Sid. He wanted to take care of her. Keep her close and send a message that she was taken.

Which, of course, she wasn't. At least not beyond the next couple weeks. Which didn't feel nearly long enough. For what, he didn't know. He only knew thinking about leaving made his gut feel like it was being shoved through a meat grinder.

Sid pushed into the house and Lucas followed. She dropped her keys on the end table, then waited for him to reach the couch.

"What happened back there?"

Lucas shrugged and sat down to remove the ridiculous black boots. "I didn't like the way Manny was talking to you."

"I got that," she said. "We all got that. I admit this jealousy thing was flattering at first. I've never had a guy get riled up on my behalf. But now it's just annoying."

She had every right to be angry, though he'd have expected a more brilliant display of temper. A good fight would lead to make-up sex, with the bonus of heightened intensity. Not that having sex with Sid wasn't already the most intense thing he'd ever done in his life.

"It was a knee-jerk reaction. I'll control it better from now on." With one boot off, he moved to the next.

"Have I given off the 'helpless' vibe?" Sid asked, ripping her own boots off. "Something that says I need to be taken care of?"

She flung the boots to the floor and started untying the leather piece around her waist. Lucas crossed the room and stilled her hands. "Listen to me. There is nothing helpless about you. Nothing. My stupid male ego just takes charge and I turn into a grunting idiot." He pulled her with him until he was sitting on the coffee table, saving her from straining her neck to see his face. "I'm sorry if my actions made you feel weak. You're the strongest person I know." Resting his head against her stomach, he mumbled, "Stronger than I am."

She had been the one to keep things casual, after all. Something at which he'd failed miserably.

With a firm touch beneath his chin, she forced him to look up. "Why would you say that? You've worked your ass off to become a powerful lawyer. You did it all on your own. And you came down here without a second thought to help your family when they needed you. When they needed your strength the most, you came through."

A thousand arguments ran through his mind, but he didn't want to fight with Sid. He wanted to love her.

With great care, he dropped a kiss in each of her palms, then pulled her closer, until she was sitting sideways in his lap.

The distraction worked because Sid gave up the fight and said, "I don't think this table can hold the both of us."

"Then we'd better find a surface that can." He took her mouth as he rose to his feet. Standing there, in the middle of Sid's whitewashed cottage, Lucas made a silent vow that tonight would be different. Tonight would be about more than sex.

Tonight, Sid would know that she was loved. He couldn't say it with words, but he could show her with his body.

~

By the time they reached her bedroom, all of Sid's typical moves to get Lucas to speed things up had failed. The man was determined to take his time, and once he laid her gently on the bed, sending Drillbit hissing from the room, she decided to let him. Instead of ripping her clothes off, their usual first step, Lucas undressed himself, slowly, while maintaining eye contact. His shirt went first, then the pants.

She never failed to be amazed by how beautiful he was.

Sid had a death grip on the comforter by the time he returned to her. But Lucas never looked away. As if he were trying to tell her something important. Make her understand what he was thinking.

If the blood hadn't all rushed out of her head, she might have been able to download the message. However, brain function wasn't operating at the highest levels in that moment. The only thoughts running through her mind were of the *good God this is going to be good* variety.

Lucas reached out a hand and like an obedient child following the Pied Piper, Sid gave her own and was pulled off the bed. She'd half untied the cincher and now Lucas proceeded to unlace it the rest of the way. With no urgency whatsoever. She'd thought him totally unaffected until his hands brushed her breasts and he moaned.

Moaning was a good sign.

The leather fell away and Lucas moved to her shoulders, sliding the dress down little by little. The material slid over her now sensitized breasts, lighting fires across her skin as if every nerve ending were exposed. The dress finally dropped, the cool air fluttering along her body raising goose bumps everywhere. Or maybe that was the anticipation of what would happen next.

The way Lucas was handling the situation, it was hard to tell what he had in mind. He had to know by now seduction was unnecessary. Not that she was going to remind him. Why spoil the man's fun?

And her own.

Instead of taking her mouth, he leaned down and placed a kiss on her forehead. A little chaste considering what they were about to do. Then his hands starting roaming. Taking his time, as if memorizing her, Lucas traced fingertips along her neck, over her shoulders, then his palms brushed over her tightened nipples.

She nearly came off the floor, but her reaction didn't faze him.

He continued over her taut belly, around her hips, then down her thighs, eventually dropping to his knees. By the time the contact reached her calves, this powerful man she'd had sex with countless times in the last week looked into her eyes and made her heart stop.

"I'm going to make love to you tonight, Sidney Ann."

It took everything she had not to throw herself at him. Not to lick him from head to toe, light him on fire the way he was doing to her. But something in that look stopped her. Something in his words. Love. He was going to love her.

Dumbstruck, all she could do was nod acceptance. Lucas dropped a kiss just below her navel and she shoved her hands into his hair, feeling the perspiration along his scalp. This level of restraint wasn't as easy as he was making it look. And he was doing it for her.

It was a good thing the bed was right behind her because Lucas's next move buckled her knees. His tongue slid way lower than her navel, landing Sid flat on her back on the bed. He pulled her hips to the edge, spread her legs with the slightest pressure, and proceeded to drive her mad.

A combination of torture and absolute bliss, waves of sensations slammed against her, pushing her down, lifting her up, sending her crashing and out of control. She heard a voice begging and distantly realized it was her own. Though she had no idea what she was saying. Something about *more* and *stop* and *don't stop* and *holy mother of God.*

When the final wave hit, Sid would not have been surprised to hear she levitated right off the bed. Not that she could feel the bed anymore. Everything had fallen away. Everything but the man between her legs. His hands and tongue and hot breath sending aftershocks quaking to her toes.

She felt like a live wire. Dangerous. Spitting sparks.

Finished with what Sid assumed to be the appetizer, Lucas maneuvered her further onto the bed, sliding over her, but only after kissing everything from the tip of her toes to the inside of her knee to the edge of her left hip. She'd never been worshiped before. Never thought much about the concept.

But that's what he was doing. Lucas was worshiping her body. Loving her body. How would she ever live without this?

"No thinking," he said, sliding a hand along her jaw, nudging her to look him in the eyes. With a shake of his head, he repeated, "No thinking. Not tonight."

Once again, all she could do was nod and Sid started to wonder if he'd slipped her something to make her mute. Then his mouth encircled her nipple and she quickly regained the ability to speak.

"You're trying to kill me."

The man had the nerve to chuckle, lightening the mood for the first time since they'd left the ball. "Maybe," he said, moving to the other breast. "But this would be a damn good way to go, don't you think?"

Sid couldn't answer since in that moment thinking went out the window. Along with the ability to breathe, move, and once again speak.

The whole world was centered in her breasts, until Lucas trailed a hand across her abs and settled it between her legs. Then some crazy game of sexual pinball started in her system. Surges of pleasure shooting around, bouncing through her abdomen, setting off various bells and whistles, signaling the jackpot was within reach.

Her hips rose off the mattress as she held Lucas to her breast in a death grip. She managed to mumble between pants, "I don't know how much more I can take."

"I have several more hours of this planned. You don't want to miss the rest, do you?"

Her head swung from side to side in the universal gesture for *No, no, no!*

He pulled a condom from the nightstand, sheathed himself in seconds, then braced above her, holding his weight on his elbows. His hips lowered and Sid pulled her knees up out of instinct.

That's when he stopped. Lying there, pressed against her core, bodies damp and aroused, he stopped. And Sid stopped breathing.

"What's wrong?" she asked, worried she'd disappointed him somehow.

He shook his head. "You're so beautiful. All these nights, I keep thinking I'll wake up and you will have been a dream."

"I keep thinking the same thing about you." Sid didn't want to admit as much, but she couldn't lie to Lucas. Not in that moment. "I don't know why you're here, with me, when you could have any woman you want."

Lucas smoothed her hair away from her face. "You really don't know how gorgeous you are, do you? And smart. And sweet."

She barely kept from snorting. Barely. "You think I'm sweet?"

He smiled. "You hide it well, but I've seen it. Don't worry, I won't spoil your reputation."

She returned the smile. "I appreciate that."

Their eyes remained locked for several seconds, and then Lucas leaned down. Finally. Their lips met with no urgency, leisurely exploring each other as if they'd never kissed before. And maybe they hadn't. Not like this. She was still aroused, need coursing through her, but this kiss was too good to rush. This one deserved to be savored.

What could have been minutes or hours later, Lucas began to move against her, relighting the fires that had banked down to embers. His knees spread her further, then he broke the kiss, catching her gaze as he entered her. He slid deep, slowly, allowing her to adjust to all of him. She felt awkward at first, with him watching her every reaction. Every twitch and jerk as he pulled out and drove in again.

But then she was lost. In his eyes and what he was doing to her. Stretching her body, taking her places she'd never been before. His jaw tightened and she knew he was holding back. For her.

Trailing her fingers down his ribs and around to his ass, she tried to give back everything he was giving her. "Come with me, Lucas. Come with me."

The thrusts grew stronger. Faster. His head dropped to her shoulder and she curled against him. With her legs locked around his hips, she pulled him home and experienced the most amazing orgasm of her life. She'd read a million times about bursting into a million pieces. In that moment, she understood the description.

As her body began to reassemble, Lucas jerked against her, throwing back his head with a sound of utter triumph.

CHAPTER TWENTY-FOUR

Lucas lay awake the next morning, watching sunlight pour through the window to dance across Sid's bare skin. Skin he'd spent the night touching, tasting, and memorizing for future nights when he'd be alone. He'd tried covering her more than once, but even sleeping naked, she never left the covers on for long. Sid's free spirit couldn't be held down, even in sleep.

He'd come to love that spirit as much as he loved the rest of her. Which made him a complete idiot and, oddly enough, put her further out of his reach. Sid would hate living in the city. Hate life hemmed in by all the buildings and societal rules amongst his peers. Many of the wives had careers of their own, with busy days that included lunch meetings, business suits, and keeping up appearances as much for their own careers as for their husbands'.

Forcing Sid into that world would be like putting a great white in a fish bowl. No. His world could never be hers.

Since he'd kept her up most of the night, both only nodding off shortly before sunrise, he let her sleep, leaving a note that he'd gone to speak to his parents about Will. He took the time to feed Drillbit, who had warmed to him considerably in the last week. The tiny ball of fur seemed more interested in curling up against his neck than trying to slice his jugular.

Another pint-sized female who'd managed to win his affection when he wasn't looking.

"Anyone home?" Lucas yelled in greeting, stepping through the kitchen door and breathing in the rich aroma of his mother's favorite coffee. Patty Dempsey may look like a tea drinker, but she preferred the more bitter brew in a potency strong enough to peel paint.

"You're up early this morning," Patty said, rising on tiptoe to plant a kiss on his cheek. "You don't look like you've been running, but I'd say you've been up to something."

Lucas fought the blush and lost. He was not going to talk about the activities of the previous night with his mother. "Is Dad around? I need to talk to you guys about something."

With a tilt of her head, his mother studied him. He could practically hear the gears working in that sharp mind of hers. But he doubted she knew why he was there.

"Is this about your intentions toward a certain sharp-tongued boat mechanic?" she asked, a smile crossing her face.

The question hit like a bucket of cold water to the face. What were his intentions toward Sid? The truth—he was going to love her and leave her—made him feel like the jackass that he was. Definitely not something he wanted to discuss with his mother.

"This isn't about Sid," he managed, staring through the window to watch the birds fighting over the offerings of his mother's bird feeders. "If Dad's in bed, I can come back."

"He's up." Her voice turned stern. "You're not toying with that girl, are you? She's been in—"

"Thought I heard your voice," Tom said, entering the kitchen looking healthier than he had since Lucas arrived. "Where's your little partner in crime? I was starting to think you two were attached at the hip."

What was this constant talk about Sid? So he'd lived at her house for a week. They were consenting adults. That was their business. Except he'd forgotten that on Anchor Island, everything was everyone's business.

"Sid is sleeping. She had a long night." Well shit. That wasn't the answer he wanted to give. Maybe he could leave the house and come back in again.

"I'm sure she did." His parents exchanged a knowing smile that made him feel like a schoolboy caught necking in the backseat of their car.

"I'm here to talk about something else," he blurted, desperate to change the subject. "I have an idea for the restaurant I'd like to run by you." Odd to feel nervous, but then he'd never tried to tell his parents how to run their business.

They exchanged another look, but this one he had no idea how to interpret. They didn't look angry, and neither told him to keep his nose out of things, so he took that as a good sign.

"Bring us over some coffee, Pat." Tom pulled out a chair from the kitchen table. "What do you have in mind?" he asked Lucas.

"Well," Lucas hedged, pulling a chair for his mother, then taking the next one over. "I have no doubt you'll be back on your feet soon, but this heart attack is a pretty obvious sign you can't keep up the pace you had going before."

"My pace?" Tom asked.

Lucas looked to his mother for backup, but she remained silent.

"Running the place alone, working six or seven days a week, just isn't good for you. Hell, it's about to do me in and I've only been at it for a couple weeks."

His dad leaned back in his chair. "If you're looking for time off, then just say so."

"I'm not talking about me." He was making a mess of this. "I simply think you need help. You deserve help."

Patty finally spoke up. "Are you volunteering?"

"What?" he asked, stunned by another question he didn't expect. "No, not me. Will."

"Will?" the pair asked in unison. "What does Will have to do with this?" Tom asked.

He was losing them. "Just hear me out. Will has worked for several businesses on the island and been behind the bar at O'Hagan's for nearly a year. She's also worked other bars and restaurants up and down the coast."

"What does that have to do with Dempsey's?" Tom asked, but Patty shushed him and motioned for Lucas to continue.

"You need some kind of assistant manager. Someone to take the everyday weight off your shoulders. She could work the bar. Create the schedules. Anything you need her to do."

The elder Dempseys sat silently as if absorbing the suggestion. "Have you talked to Will about this?" Patty asked.

"Yes."

"Without coming to us first?" Tom nearly leapt from his chair but Patty's grip held him in place. "You can't go around offering people jobs whenever you feel like it."

"I didn't offer her a job," Lucas defended, ignoring the knot forming in his gut. He never meant to offend his parents. Especially not the man who'd raised him like his own. "I wanted to make sure she was interested before I came to you. She understands this isn't a done deal. You have the final say, of course."

"How gracious of you to let me decide what happens in my own damn restaurant."

"Tom," Patty scolded. "He has a point. You can't go back to working so many hours. His intentions are in the right place and the idea is worth discussing."

Finally. Someone on his side.

"You'd be doing Will a favor, too. She could stop flitting from business to business, picking up hours wherever she can get them." Lucas clasped his hands on the Formica tabletop. "No one is suggesting you can't run the business, but this is an opportunity for you to relax a bit. Let someone else do the heavy lifting for a while."

"Heavy lifting takes money," Tom grumbled.

"What does that mean?" Lucas asked, confused where this reaction was coming from.

"Tom," Patty nearly whispered. "We have to tell him. We should have told the boys long before now."

"Tell the boys what?" The knot tightened and spread to his chest. "What am I missing here?"

"The restaurant is losing money," Patty said, when his dad held silent. "It's been slowing down for several seasons, but this year has been the worst."

"Are you saying we're going out of business?"

"Absolutely not." Tom smacked the table. "We'll cut

back. Wait for things to get better. Hiring an assistant manager just isn't in the cards right now. Maybe next year."

Lucas couldn't believe what he was hearing. Nearly twenty years of his life had been spent in Dempsey's Bar & Grill. He couldn't imagine Anchor without it. His family without it.

"Do you need cash?"

"We need customers, but with tourism down, the numbers aren't there." Patty rubbed a hand absently across her chest. This must have been hard on them, watching their life's work fade. Carrying the burden by themselves, pretending everything was fine.

They didn't need to carry it alone anymore.

"Let me help. I can invest in the business."

"The business is yours without your money," Tom said, dismissing the offer. "I'll mortgage this house before I'll take your hard-earned money."

"Don't be stubborn," Lucas said. "You need money and I have it."

"Are you sure about this, Lucas?" Patty asked.

"No." Tom shoved his chair back and threw his hands wide. "I won't allow it. I will not take charity from my children."

"It's not charity," Lucas argued, coming to his feet. "Dempsey's is the family business and I'm part of this family. It's time I made an official investment in my future, and I'll expect a return on that investment."

"Your future? Since when do you plan to run this business in the future?"

Tom had him there. Lucas always knew he and Joe would inherit the place someday, but never intended to come back and run it. Had his feelings changed? He considered what he'd have to leave behind and knew the answer immediately.

"I didn't say I'd be the one running it, but I will be an owner someday. That can't happen if there's nothing left to own."

Tom ran a hand through his cropped hair. "It's not right." The vehemence in his voice had softened. "I don't like it."

"Tom." Patty stood and took her husband's hands. "Lucas is right. We need a shot of capital and he's willing to give it. Better from him than someone else. Better than losing it all together."

"Listen to her," Lucas said, stepping up behind his mother and resting his hands on her shoulders. "Let me do this. No matter the amount, it won't come close to paying you back for everything you've done for me. You're always taking care of everyone else. Let someone else do the taking care of for a change."

Tom's gaze darted from his wife, to the floor, to the son he'd given his name and his love. "An investment. For a full stake in the company."

Lucas extended his hand. "Deal."

~

By Tuesday, Sid was ready to leap out of her skin. Neither she nor Lucas had talked about how things had changed after Friday night. And things had definitely changed. Any illusion of acting casual went out the window, along with Sid's final grasp on denial. She was full on in love with

Lucas Dempsey and if his actions were any indication, he'd fallen off the casual cliff right along with her.

You'd think they'd talk about it. They both knew Lucas was leaving at the end of the summer. Sid didn't harbor any great hope he'd change his mind. Lucas didn't belong on Anchor any more than Sid belonged in a beauty pageant. For all of five minutes she imagined he might ask her to go with him. Then she remembered Curly's stories about dinner parties, political events, and mindless small talk.

Sid would rather face a squall on open waters than be forced into that world.

No, she couldn't go with him. And he wouldn't stay. So they'd both avoided the subject and pretended Labor Day would never come. Or so she thought.

Until her bed partner started acting more and more odd. Happy one minute, staring off into space the next. Always with that disgruntled look as if he were passing a kidney stone while working a word problem in his head. When she'd ask him where he drifted off to during those moments, he'd just flash her a smile and drop a quick kiss on her lips before changing the subject.

They worked seamlessly during the days, then cuddled on her couch at night. The challenge of showing Lucas all there was to do on the island fell away at some point, though she couldn't remember when or why. They'd taken in another movie. One of the *Die Hard* flicks, though she wasn't sure now which installment. They also attended a Merchants Society meeting, during which Sid had whispered stories in Lucas's ear about nearly everyone in attendance.

How Floyd, who ran the Trade Store, had been courting the day-care owner, Helga, for months and finally got her to have dinner with him. To which he wore his best overalls, of course. How Sam Edwards had nearly caused a society meltdown by advertising his motels as "the finest Anchor has to offer" on his new flyers.

To be fair, Sam did have the best rooms in the village, but he'd broken the unwritten rule by actually pointing the fact out to tourists in such a highfalutin way. If there was one thing Anchor merchants strove to avoid, it was ever sounding highfalutin. Or one-upping each other. At least not on paper.

That sort of thing was reserved for the Hatteras high and mighties who liked to think they were the upper crust of the barrier islands.

By the time the meeting had ended, Lucas was caught up on all the people he once knew as well as she did, and the few newbies who'd moved in during his absence.

Speaking of Lucas being absent, he and Joe had switched shifts today for the first time in more than a week. Working without him left her torn between missing him and believing some time apart might be a good thing. He'd be gone soon and if she couldn't handle a few hours, life was going to be pretty shitty after a few days.

Everything told her to get out now. Save herself. Get the man out of her bed, even if she would never get him out of her head. Or her heart, though the thought was so sappy it nearly made her gag.

"You up for a break soon?" Will asked, surprising Sid as she loaded four beers onto her tray.

"I need to deliver these drinks, then I can spare a minute or so." Sid glanced to the clock behind the bar. "You're early, aren't you? I thought you were training with Lucas tonight."

"I'm on a break from . . . well, I'm just on a break." Will tossed dark waves over her shoulder as she backed away. "I'll wait in the office."

The office? Will needed to talk to her in the office? This could not be good. After delivering the beers, she checked on her other two tables, then dropped the tray under the bar before heading to the back.

"Since I'm assuming we're past you thinking Lucas is hitting on you," Sid said, strolling into the office, "this time it must be the garage."

The corners of Will's lips edged down and she shook her head yes.

"There's been an offer?"

Another nod.

"And Fisher accepted it?"

Will looked like she might cave in on herself. "I'm so sorry, Sid. I really didn't think things would move this fast."

Sid focused on breathing as she stared at the desk, seeing nothing as her vision was suddenly blurred. Several seconds passed before she realized the blur was caused by tears. Swiping at her eyes, she asked, "Who's the buyer?"

"I don't know. Everything has been hush-hush around the office." Will handed Sid a tissue. "Pretty sure it's the mystery buyer from Richmond. All I know is he, or she I guess, is putting up half the asking price as a down payment."

The air suddenly felt heavy, too thick to take in, and there didn't seem to be anything coming out. The room spun around her. She reached out to steady herself with the desk. A roar filled her ears before she realized the sound was coming from her throat.

"Why?" she yelled, to no one in particular. "What the fuck could a total stranger want with my garage? Tell me!" she ordered Will, who'd backed herself into the corner of the room.

"Maybe you should sit down," Will suggested, navigating Sid around the desk and into the desk chair. Then she squatted so they were on eye level. "I don't have the answer, Sid. I wish I did. Sometimes life just sucks, and there isn't much we can do about it."

Who did she think she was talking to? "I'm not a child, Will. Don't treat me like one." Sid blew her nose, making a sound like a dying pelican. "I'm sorry. This isn't your fault. I was so close, you know? So fucking close."

Now she would never have her business. And she'd never have Lucas. Not for real. Could life get any worse?

Just then, Daisy showed up at the office door. "You'd better get out here, Sid."

"Why?" she asked, pausing to blow her nose again. "Did a meteor hit my house or something?"

Daisy's eyes cut to Will in a look of obvious concern, though for herself or the crazy woman at the desk Sid couldn't be sure.

"Um, not that I know of. But some idiot just backed into your truck."

CHAPTER TWENTY-FIVE

Where was Artie? Lucas had left the old lawyer a message two hours ago to meet him at the bank. The documents he'd drawn up were sound, but he still wanted another lawyer to take a look. His parents deserved an impartial review. And the other documents were more complicated, requiring someone familiar with legalities on Anchor.

Pacing the small conference room where the bank manager had suggested he wait, Lucas thought about all he needed to do in the next few days. In a couple weeks he'd be driving back to Richmond, returning to the life that now felt foreign and far away. Which was the problem with Anchor Island. It deluded a person into forgetting about the outside world. Made a man believe life could be simple and satisfying without all the trappings and chaos inherent elsewhere.

Complete nonsense. Life happened in the city. That's where ambitions could soar. Endless opportunities around every corner waiting to be snatched and wrestled to the ground.

So why did his mind keep harping on the fact that there was no Sid in the city?

"No coffee, Maxine," Artie said as he was shown into the room. "I've had my one cup of the day." With a smile and a nod, the older gentleman dismissed the manager and turned to Lucas. "Sorry for the delay. Popcorn machine took longer to repair than I'd expected."

Lucas had been waiting due to a broken popcorn machine? This was exactly the kind of thing that didn't happen in the city.

"Not a problem," he lied. "I need you to review some paperwork for me. Everything is in order but as the circumstances involve myself and my parents, I'd feel better knowing their interests were protected by an unbiased party."

Hands in his pockets, Artie glanced between Lucas and the folders spread out on the conference table. "No can do."

"Excuse me?"

Artie smiled. "I'm retired."

"I know that," Lucas replied, clinging to patience by a thin thread. "But you don't stop being a lawyer simply because you close your practice. You're still licensed. You have the knowledge to review these documents and give a legal opinion."

"I do," Artie nodded. "But I'm retired."

Lucas squeezed the bridge of his nose and took several deep breaths before addressing the man again. "I'm asking you for a favor, Mr. Berkowitz. I don't have the time to find another lawyer in the county, and you're here. If payment is the issue, I fully intend to compensate you for your time."

Now the smile tilted a bit, the weathered eyes flashing something akin to disappointment. "This isn't about money, Lucas. My work was never about the money." With slow but deliberate movements, Artie pulled out a chair and lowered his considerable girth onto the cushion. With a nod, he gestured for Lucas to do the same.

When both were seated, Artie joined his hands on top of his stomach and spoke. "When I first retired, this happened a lot. Everyone needed a favor. I was right here. I'd been the person who answered all their questions for years. Why couldn't I just do this one favor? So I gave in. Did the favors and before I knew it, I was working more than I had before hanging the closed sign on the door. Not much of a retirement if you're working all the time."

"But this—"

"But this is different?" Artie asked. "This is what every citizen on this island needs, Lucas. A lawyer practicing here." He shook his head. "I'm no longer that lawyer. No exceptions. This is my life and my time. I've put in the work to get here and I'm going to enjoy it."

Though the smile remained, Lucas recognized the unbending tone in the words. "I'm sorry I've taken up your time then," Lucas said, rising from his chair and collecting the folders.

"Lucas," his mentor said, halting his actions. "There's a hole on this island that needs to be filled. No fancy high-rise offices. No ladder to scratch and claw your way up. But there is an opportunity here. A good one. A fulfilling one. Think about it."

Before Lucas could rebut with what should have been an instant "No thank you," the older man lumbered out of the room without a backward glance.

Why hadn't Lucas refused immediately? There was nothing to think about. His career was back in Richmond. That's where he belonged. That's what he wanted.

This has been a visit. Temporary. But Artie did have a point. Lucas could help these people. And he would. As soon as he was back in Richmond, he'd find a solid attorney looking for a slower pace. The hole would be filled and he'd be back in Richmond. Everyone would be happy.

Or so he kept telling himself.

~

Sid woke the next morning, surprised to find Lucas next to her in bed. When they'd changed shifts the night before, she'd explained she wasn't feeling well. Losing the garage, coupled with the realization she'd fallen too hard for Lucas, made her want to curl into a ball and hide from the world. Add the new dent in her left rear quarter panel, which would be a bitch to fix but doable, and distance from humans in general felt eminently necessary.

She hadn't actually told him not to come over. Hadn't even locked her front door to keep him out. She just assumed that dropping the hint there would be no sex would result in no sleepover. But she'd been wrong.

Desperate to be alone, but unwilling to kick Lucas out of her house, Sid slid from the bed, got dressed as quietly as possible, then planned to go for a run by herself. She needed to go back to doing things alone, and a run along the beach with nothing but the birds for company would give her time to figure out what to do next. What to do with the rest of her life, since opening her own boat restoration business on Anchor was now a long lost dream.

"Morning, gorgeous," Lucas said, handing Sid a cup of coffee as she attempted to sneak out of the bathroom. "Glad you're up. I've got something I want to show you."

As much as she enjoyed sex in the morning, Sid wasn't in the mood. "I was heading out for a run. Figured I'd let you sleep since you worked late."

"Ten minutes," he said, as if she hadn't turned him down. "Give me ten minutes to shower and I'll be ready."

Shower? Before sex? "Ready for what?"

"Don't ask so many questions," he said, dropping a kiss on her nose. "Drink your coffee and I'll be ready to go in a flash."

The man seemed chipper about something. And he'd spent the night sleeping beside her without even trying to have sex with her. As if just sleeping next to her was enough. She'd been pretty sure he'd sunk as far into this relationship as she had, but a sleepover with no sex almost confirmed the fact.

Then what was he going to show her? There wasn't anything on Anchor Sid had never seen. Were they going off island? They couldn't go far and be back in time to open the restaurant. The guessing game only heightened the headache she'd gained from the brief cry she'd allowed herself in the shower, so Sid opted to feed the cat and load the dishwasher while waiting for Lucas.

"What the hell is he up to, Drillbit?" she asked her pet, who ignored the question and continued to devour the smelly gook in her bowl. "I hope it's good. I could use some good news today."

∾

It had taken a full five minutes to convince Sid to let him drive her truck. Another five to get her to wear the blindfold. A brief shower the night before meant the road ahead would be too treacherous to navigate in his car. He couldn't blame her on either count. The truck had taken a hit the day before, though the damage was only cosmetic. But getting by Sid's inner control freak to put the blindfold on had been the real test.

Lucas had used all of his manly wiles, which he wasn't proud of. Nor would he ever admit to the thought of having manly wiles.

"Are we almost there? This thing is making my head itch."

"Two more minutes," he said, which he'd been saying since the first time she'd asked, at the end of her driveway. "Not long now."

He turned onto the road leading to their destination and dropped the truck into four-wheel drive. They bounced from side to side and he reached out to brace Sid so she wouldn't land on the floorboards.

"If you hurt this truck I will kick your ass," she declared, with complete conviction in her voice. He laughed and focused on avoiding the potholes ahead.

When they reached the building, Lucas cut the engine and leaned forward to see the sign hanging on the brick wall. Just as he'd ordered. Lot would get an extra fifty dollars this week.

"Finally," Sid said, reaching for the bandanna covering her eyes. "Get this thing off."

"Not yet," he argued, halting her movements. "Let me get you out first."

"Are you kidding me?" Sid tried to smack the dash and missed, but Lucas caught her before her nose took the hit.

"Just scoot over here. There you go." With little effort,

he lifted her to the ground, turned her to face the building, then stood behind her. "You ready?"

"This better be good," she grumbled. But when he remained silent, she surrendered. "Yes. I'm ready. I'm beyond ready."

"Good." With a sweep of his hand, Lucas removed the bandanna, and waited. For what he wasn't sure. Sid wasn't the squealing and happy dancing type, but this was a pretty big surprise.

Silence reigned. No squealing. No dancing. He leaned around to see her face. No smiling.

"What the fuck did you do?" she asked, her eyes locked on the sign that read NAVARRO BOAT REPAIR & RESTORATION. "You need to get that down. Now."

Not the reaction he expected. "What are you talking about? That's only a temporary sign. We'll get a more permanent one when the renovations are done."

"We won't do shit. Get the fucking thing down." Sid turned with her hand out. "Give me the keys so I can back the truck up and tear the thing down myself."

"But why?" he asked, refusing to hand over the keys. "I don't understand. Why are you so mad?"

"Because it's not mine!" she screamed. "This doesn't belong to me. Someone else bought it. It's not for sale anymore. The boat business isn't going to happen."

"Wait." How could she know? Everything had been done in secret. "You know that someone bought this garage?"

"Yes, damn it. Will told me yesterday. Some fancy ass from out of town bought it, and he'll probably tear it down for all I know." She stomped over to the truck. "I can't be here. I need to get out of here."

"Hold on," he said, spinning her around. "You knew that someone else was trying to buy your dream, and you didn't tell me?"

"What difference does it make? I set out to buy it and I failed. Telling you wasn't going to change that."

"But you could have counteroffered. I could have helped you come up with the money to buy it."

"No way. I'd never do that." She swiped away a tear. "It's over. The garage belongs to someone else now. Just please let me go home."

His heart nearly broke watching her stand strong and proud, knowing she must have been dying on the inside since getting the news. With a gentle hand, he nudged her chin up until their eyes met, wiping away another wayward tear with his thumb.

"This garage doesn't belong to someone else, Sid. It belongs to you. I bought it for you."

They stared at each other as the words sunk in, a myriad of emotions running through him. Then Sid snapped.

∾

Shoving against his chest, she screamed, "Why would you do that? Why would you take this away from me?" Sid had never been stabbed, but the feeling of a knife slicing through her heart made her long for the real thing. At least she could heal from a knife wound.

"I didn't take anything away from you," he argued, reaching for her but she batted his hands away. "It's yours. I'm giving it to you."

"I don't want it! Not like this." The tears flowed freely now, more from anger than the loss she'd felt moments before. "What part of doing this on my own did you not understand? I was close. I'd have had the money by Labor Day. Just a few more weeks."

Lucas kept crowding her, trying to force her to let him in. "I didn't buy it outright. There are still payments to be made. I only provided the down payment. This way you can use your money for the renovations. And you can make the payments on the remaining mortgage."

"Only the down payment?" she asked, remembering what Will had told her. "You paid *half.* Is this my consolation prize? Is this what I earned in the last couple weeks?"

Lucas jerked as if she'd slapped him. "What is that supposed to mean?"

"I think it's pretty clear." She laughed, a hollow, empty sound. "I gave you me and you give me a garage. Something to remember you by after you're gone."

"That's crossing a line and insulting to both of us. What we have is more than that."

"Really? What do we have, Lucas? A casual fling, right? That's all this is supposed to be." Sid opened the truck door. "It's clear that's all this is because if you knew me at all, cared about me at all, you wouldn't have done this."

She climbed in and waited. He still held the keys so she couldn't drive off without him. Which she sorely wanted to do. After what could have been a minute or an hour, Lucas climbed into the passenger seat and set the keys on the bench between them.

Sid drove back to her place, numb and empty. He could

have the damn garage. She'd let it rot before taking his charity. When they reached her driveway, she kept the motor running.

"Get your stuff and lock the door behind you."

Lucas didn't move to get out. "Can we talk about this?"

Sid shook her head, too drained to say anything more. Unable to look at the man beside her. The man she loved, even now.

With a sigh, he finally opened the door. From the ground, he said, "I never meant to hurt you," and closed the door.

The sobbing started again. She threw the truck in reverse, spewing gravel against her garage door as she backed out. Sid wasn't sure where she was going. She just knew she had to go.

CHAPTER TWENTY-SIX

Lucas did as Sid asked. Packed his things. Gave Drillbit a pat good-bye. Locked the door behind him. Then he sat in his car in her driveway, unable to turn the key.

She'll come back, he thought. She'd realize he only wanted to make her happy. To give her what she wanted most. If he could do that for her, why wouldn't he?

But Sid didn't come back, and eventually he had to admit the truth. He'd fucked up. He didn't know exactly how, but that's what he'd done. Even after he started the car, Lucas remained there in the driveway, staring at the little beach cottage he'd begun to call home. Not a permanent home, since the cottage was on Anchor, and Anchor wasn't his home.

But the cottage meant Sid and Sid felt like home.

With little thought to what he was doing, Lucas drove the short distance to his parents' house, checking his watch after pulling into the drive. He'd need to be at the restaurant in less than two hours. Would Sid come to work? Would she talk to him? Would she listen to him?

What would he say if she did? He couldn't pretend nothing had happened, and he knew Sid would never put on an act. She was incapable of being disingenuous. One of the many things he loved about her.

Well, shit.

Lucas pressed back against the headrest. Maybe this was for the best. Leaving would be easier this way. For both of them. If anything, Sid would be relieved to see him gone. She could be rid of him. Maybe she'd turn to Manny as an alternative. The thought made him want to rip the steering wheel off and throw it out the window.

"Hey there," came a voice from outside, startling him out of his misery. Lucas looked up to see his dad hovering on the porch. "You going to stay out there all day?"

Just what he needed. Captain Cranky-pants. Grabbing his duffel bag from the passenger seat, he stepped out. "I'm coming in, if that's all right?"

Tom stared, face pinched. "What kind of a question is that?"

He just could not catch a break this morning. Embracing his right to remain silent, Lucas climbed the stairs and followed his father into the house. "Got any coffee?" he asked, dropping his bag beside the doorway to the living room.

"Help yourself," his dad said, taking a seat at the table. "Rough morning?"

"You could say that." Lucas searched for the sugar, but it wasn't in the usual place.

"She's hidden everything I'm not supposed to have," Tom explained. "There's a bunch of those yellow packets in the top drawer."

Lucas needed the swift kick of bitterness anyway. "I'll pass, thanks." Bringing his mug to the table, he pulled out a chair. "Where's Mom?"

"Ladies Auxiliary meeting."

"Oh." Lucas sipped the coffee. Definitely bitter. "Went to the bank yesterday. Money is ready for transfer as soon as the papers are signed, but I want to run them by another lawyer first."

Tom huffed. "Aren't you a lawyer?"

"Last I checked," he said. "But you deserve to have an unbiased legal review. Someone looking out for your interests."

Tom huffed again. "That's a load of crap. Bring me the damn papers and I'll sign them."

Lucas considered arguing, explaining the risks and intricacies of the situation, but his dad was right. Believing he'd ever not protect his parents' best interests was a load of crap.

"They're in my car. I'll bring them in tonight."

"Tonight? So that and the bag mean you're back, huh? Want to talk about it?"

The last thing Lucas wanted to do was discuss his relationship.

"I don't think so," he said, cringing as he took another sip of the tar in his mug. "Did you make this or did Mom?"

"I made a new pot after she left. You don't like it, don't drink it."

Lucas pushed the mug away. He preferred to keep the lining of his stomach intact. "I'll just let it cool."

The two men sat in silence, Tom scratching his chest while Lucas picked at the corner of his place mat, searching for something to talk about.

"When you buy someone something they really want, aren't they supposed to be grateful?" he asked, choosing to broach the subject with a hypothetical.

Tom shrugged. "That's the protocol. What'd you buy Sid?"

So much for hypothetical. "Something she said she really wanted."

"Did she ask you to buy it?" Tom asked, hitting close enough to the mark to make Lucas uncomfortable.

"No. She said she wanted to buy it on her own, but this way she can have it sooner."

Tom shook his head. "Classic mistake. Though I'm not surprised." He crossed his arms, flinched, then rested his elbows back on the table. "Sounds like something you'd do."

"What's that supposed to mean? And are you still in that much pain?"

"I just forget and it pulls sometimes," he said, waving away Lucas's concern. "Even as a kid, you'd barrel through with your own agenda, regardless of what anyone else was trying to do. Probably a good trait to have in the courtroom, but that shit doesn't fly out here in the real world."

Not the most flattering assessment. "You make me sound like an inconsiderate jerk."

"Nah. Not inconsiderate. Most of the time, your heart was in the right place," Tom said, cracking a smile for the first time since Lucas arrived.

That's exactly how Beth had described him. The guy who barreled ahead without ever stopping to ask what *she* wanted. Sid hadn't needed to be asked. She'd made it clear the garage was something she wanted to do on her own. Only he hadn't listened. He'd brushed off the words as if what she wanted didn't matter.

He *was* an inconsiderate jerk.

His head dropped into his hands. "How do I fix this?" he asked. "How do I make this right?"

His dad stayed silent long enough to draw Lucas's gaze. Brows drawn together, Tom rubbed his chin, deep in thought. "Don't think I can answer that. Being with the same woman more than twenty years means I know that particular woman. Rest of the species is still a mystery."

Not the answer Lucas was hoping for. "I can withdraw my offer on the garage," he said, thinking out loud. "Seems like that would be taking it away, but in a weird way, I'd be giving it back to her."

"You bought Sid a garage?" Tom asked, surprise taking his voice up an octave. "One of those steel building things?"

Lucas shook his head. "No, an actual garage. It's off Pamlico Shores. Red brick. Run down. She has plans for a boat repair and restoration place."

"I'd forgotten all about that place. It's been empty for decades."

"Looks it too." Lucas remembered he'd just shared Sid's secret. "But don't tell anyone. Not even Mom. Sid doesn't want anyone to know." He ran a hand through his hair. "And now I know why. She was afraid someone would butt in like I have."

"I thought maybe you bought her a tool or something." Tom leaned forward. "You tried to buy her a building?"

"It's an old, dilapidated garage, not the Taj Mahal. She has her heart set on opening this business, but she's insisting on doing it all by herself. She won't take money from her brother or Joe, which I suggested." She'd definitely made her intentions clear, and he ignored them. Such an asshole move. "I thought if I could give this to her, then . . ."

"Then what?" Tom asked, as Lucas trailed off. Excellent question.

Lucas shook his head. "I don't know."

"Lucas," Tom said, his voice quieter. "Do you plan to stay here on the island?"

"What? No. My life is in Richmond."

"Then do the girl a favor and walk away."

The words were like a gavel upside the head. He'd given her the garage because he couldn't give himself. Because he had to leave. Because he loved her.

"I can't," he said. "Not yet. I need to make her forgive me. Show her I understand and that I screwed up, but I'll fix it."

Tom laid his hands flat on the table and sat back with a sigh. "You kids always insist on learning things the hard way." With that, he rose and grabbed a newspaper off the island. "Don't forget that paperwork. And exactly how much money do you have floating around that you could afford to buy that garage after investing in the restaurant?"

Lucas shrugged. "Enough."

Tom snorted. "That's a first."

"A first?" Lucas asked, feeling another insult coming on.

"Nothing has ever been enough for you, Lucas. That's why you went running off this island chasing your fancy partnership." He smacked the paper against the table. "There's something to be said for being happy with what you have. Looks like you're choosing to learn that one the hard way too."

With that parting shot, Tom left the room, leaving Lucas behind trying to decipher the Yoda-esque message his father just delivered. What was wrong with wanting something more? Why did no one in this family understand that ambition was not a character flaw?

And how had he made such an unholy mess of his life in less than three months?

～

The smell of Opal's chocolate cake was almost enough to make Sid forget she felt like roadkill. He hadn't listened to a word she'd said. So much for him understanding how important her independence was. She'd pay him back every penny he put down. Only she'd been saving up for twenty percent, not fifty. If she used all of her savings, the garage would sit empty for who knew how much longer until she could save back up for the renovations.

It would be like not owning the place at all. Trying to make the mortgage payments while not making any money from the building would see her broke within a year.

That business was all she would have after Lucas left. Without him beside her, in her bed, in her life every day, she'd need the distraction. Something to keep her from focusing on the pain in her chest. Sid sighed. Nothing was going to block out that pain, and she was foolish to think any differently.

"Hey there, darling. You're in early today," Opal said, appearing at the front counter. She took one look at Sid and said, "Have you been crying?"

"No," Sid said, shaking her head hard. "I don't cry." The tears started again, pissing her off even more. "Goddamn it!"

"Oh, baby." Opal waddled out from behind the counter,

arms spread wide. "Come here, sugar. That's all right." As Opal's arms enveloped her, a feeling of comfort spread through Sid's chest.

Maybe it wouldn't hurt to cry on the older woman's shoulder. Just a little.

She tried to say something about Lucas ruining her dream and breaking her heart and how stupid she'd been to think she could ever let him go, but what came out was a high-pitched squeal—like a dolphin on helium.

"Let's get you in the back and get some tissues. Come on now," Opal said, herding a snorting and squealing Sid toward the kitchen. "I'm guessing this has something to do with that man of yours."

"He's not mine," Sid whined, then blew her nose on the towel Kinzie handed her. "I was stupid to ever get involved. God, am I an idiot."

"Every woman in love is an idiot, darling." Opal turned to Kinzie. "Put on some of that orange blossom tea and bring out the tub of chocolate buttercream."

Kinzie went off to do as she was told and Sid asked, "What's the buttercream for?" Maybe some homemade remedy for red, puffy eyes.

"To eat, honey child." Opal handed over a spoon. "If we're going to talk about heartbreak, we're going to need a heaping helping of chocolate to get us through."

At the mention of heartbreak, Sid snuffled up again. "This wasn't supposed to go this way. It was just sex!"

"Few women can manage to have sex and not fall in love," Opal lamented. "We've all tried it a time or two, and have the scars to show for it."

"You tried having a casual fling and fell in love?" Discussing Opal's sex life should have seemed odd, but the woman looked unfazed by the topic.

"I haven't always been an old lady, my dear. The seventies were wild times."

"I wasn't alive in the seventies," Sid pointed out, belatedly realizing this probably wasn't the right thing to say.

"Yes, well. Let's stick to the present situation then." Patting Sid on the shoulder, Opal yelled, "Where's that buttercream?"

"I'm coming, Granny. Hold your horses." Kinzie dropped a large white tub on the stainless steel counter and peeled off the lid to reveal the biggest batch of frosting Sid had ever seen.

"Wow," she whispered in wonder. "That's like the Holy Grail of chocolate." Looking at Opal, she asked, "Are we really going to eat this?"

"Not the whole thing, of course," she said. "And just remember, there's no calories in anything we eat standing up." Sid moved to slide her spoon across the top, but Opal stopped her. "Wait. We can't contaminate the whole batch. Let Kinzie scoop some into a bowl first."

The words sent Kinzie into action. Once the bowl was filled, she put the lid back on the tub and stepped back.

"Aren't you going to have some?" Sid asked.

Kinzie shook her head. "I'm trying to lose weight."

"Please tell me this isn't because of Manny."

"How did you know?" Kinzie gave her grandmother a stink eye. "Did you tell her?"

"I didn't tell anyone anything." Opal took a scoop of frosting, then said around the spoon, "I'm innocent."

Kinzie pouted. "You're far from innocent."

"She didn't have to tell me," Sid said. "I could see it at the ball last Friday. If Manny can't see how awesome you are, then that's his loss. I'm convinced that boy couldn't spot a bluefin tuna if it jumped out of the water and poked him in the ass."

Opal laughed and nearly spit buttercream across the counter. Kinzie turned pink. "But he's so gorgeous. And those eyes."

"Eyes that can't see how great you are." Sid took a taste of the buttercream and felt her shoulders relax. Chocolate really could cure a broken heart. Or at least numb it a bit. "If you want him, make him earn it, Kinzie. Better yet, screw him. Screw all men."

She reloaded her spoon and went on with the rant. "They don't listen. They're always looking for something more than what's standing right in front of them. And we make it so easy." Sid slapped a hand on the counter. "They flash those hazel eyes—"

"They're blue," Kinzie interrupted.

"—and we sigh and thank the Lord he's noticed us at all. They kiss us and we fall into bed with them."

"I haven't fallen into bed with anyone," Kinzie argued.

"Hush," Opal said. "This is getting good."

"Then we fall in love with them!" Sid yelled to the rafters. Her own words echoed in her ears, and the heartbreak returned, stronger than before. "I fell in love with that son of a bitch." Tears spilled over as she leaned on the counter, chin dropping to her chest. "What am I going to do? This hurts so much."

Gentle hands lifted her face. "You have to make a choice, honey."

Sid wiped a tear from her chin. "What choice do I have? He's leaving in a few weeks."

Opal tucked a hair behind Sid's ear. "You can let him go, or you can fight for him." She winked. "You've always struck me as a fighter."

Sid wanted to fight, but the odds were stacked against her. How could she compete with life in the city? The important people, foreign cars, and fancy dinner parties? And she hadn't even decided if she was willing to forgive him for trampling on her dream yet.

Which was an idiotic thought. She'd forgive him anything if it meant being with him.

"Are you saying I should go after him? Beg him to stay?"

"Heavens no." Opal stuck her spoon in the buttercream. "That's the last thing you need to do. Keep your distance would be my suggestion."

Sid glanced at Kinzie, who shrugged in a no-idea-what-she's-talking-about way.

"How would keeping my distance be fighting for him?"

"If my instincts are correct," she said, tapping a finger against her chin, "and they almost always are, that boy is just as in love with you as you are with him. Stay away and he'll be at your door in less than twenty-four hours."

This did not sound like a good plan. She'd kicked him out of her house. Told him to get his shit and go. Why would he come back? Especially if she stayed away. Then he'd believe she was still pissed, and leave her alone.

"Are you sure about this?" Sid asked. "Wouldn't that just make *him* stay away?"

"You have much to learn, grasshopper," Opal said, spooning chocolate into her mouth. "He's going to miss you something awful. The longer you're silent, the more determined he's going to be to win you back. Mark my words. Less than twenty-four hours."

Sid hadn't decided whether she wanted to report to the restaurant or not. She was still mad about the garage, and spending the day pretending she wasn't for the sake of ungrateful tourists didn't sit well.

"Then it's a plan." Sid loaded her spoon with a double helping. "But if he doesn't show up at my house by this time tomorrow, I'm never taking your advice again." Licking the spoon clean, she added, "And I'm taking a bowl of this to go. I'm going to need it."

CHAPTER TWENTY-SEVEN

Lucas had gotten his answer when Sid didn't come to work. Instead, Georgette showed up with the message Sid had gotten a repair call. Interesting timing for the first call she'd gotten in nearly three weeks. Maybe there was no call at all, and she was just avoiding him.

Then his conscience slapped his ego with the thought *Not everything is about you, idiot.*

Sid wasn't the type to lie. If she didn't want to work, she'd have said so. Though the timing was either convenient or coincidence. Either way, his plan to apologize throughout the day was scrapped.

Plan B was to drive to her cottage after work and make her listen. But then he was being the arrogant asshole who barreled over people and demanding life happen on his terms. So he gave her the evening, had dinner with his parents, then tossed and turned all night, unable to sleep without Sid curled up beside him.

That was going to be a problem once he was back in Richmond. Maybe his dad was right. Maybe he should let her go now. Save them both from any more heartbreak.

As if anything was going to make leaving easier. Then again, for all he knew, Sid would give him a wave and get on with her life. At least after the calls he'd made yesterday, she could get on with the life she'd planned. The way she'd planned it.

Now he needed to make sure she'd remember their time together with something other than hurt and anger. Even if this summer would never be more than a memory, he'd be damned if that memory would be one she'd regret.

That meant plan B would have to work. Will had agreed to cover for him at Dempsey's, because what he had in mind would take all day to execute. Pretending Will needed training had gotten old quick. The woman was more capable than anyone he knew. She could mix two drinks one-handed and total out a bill in her head before he could unlock the screen on the computer.

That freed Lucas to unleash what he deemed Operation Sweep Sid Off Her Feet.

The rain that set in overnight had slowed to a steady drizzle by daylight. He knew because he'd given up trying to sleep around four and watched the steady downpour taper off to a misty fog by dawn. By six he'd showered. By seven, he was headed for Sid's.

By seven fifteen he was sitting in her empty drive, cursing his own stupidity. Where would she have spent the night? Not Joe and Beth's or he'd have seen her truck. Would she have stayed with her brother? Or Will? Not that he knew where either of them lived.

The worst hit. What if she'd gone to Manny?

No. Sid would never do that. Or would she? Then he remembered her old routine and his grip on the steering wheel loosened. Running. She had to be on the beach.

Lucas didn't breathe again until he slid the BMW up next to Sid's truck. Thank God the woman was a creature of habit. He spotted her thirty yards away heading in the opposite direction. Good. He could catch up before she saw him.

When he reached her, she stopped, but he kept going. Sid's competitive side would get her moving again. Or so he'd hoped. Sadly, he was wrong. Ten yards up he stopped too and turned around to find her in the same spot, hands on her hips.

As he trudged through the sand between them, Lucas tried to gauge her mood. For once, her face was unreadable. *Now* she had to master the art of bluffing? Really?

"Hey," he said. Not the powerful intro he'd planned, but the urge to touch her was shorting out his brain.

Sid shook her head. "No shit," she said. Then she looked down. "Less than twenty-four hours. I can't believe it."

"I know it's only been a day and you're still mad," he said, taking advantage of her calm response to his presence. "I just wanted to let you know the garage is yours."

"Did you hear nothing I said yesterday?" she asked. "I wanted—"

"I heard you. I mean I withdrew my offer." Lucas put his hands in his pockets to keep from pulling her in. "The paperwork wasn't signed so I told the Realtor I changed my mind. It's all yours," he added. "On your terms."

"Withdrew your offer?" Sid shifted, glancing over to the waves pounding against the beach. "So it's on the market again? Free and clear?"

"That's right."

Her shoulders relaxed a bit, but her eyes stayed on the water. "You're walking away?"

Lucas held silent, waiting for her to meet his eyes again. When she did, he said, "From the garage, yes." He stepped closer. "But not the other. Not yet."

Sid dropped her gaze again, but didn't back away.

"I hope you're not ready to walk away either." He lifted her chin with one finger. "I want to make this up to you. Will you let me?"

She stared into his eyes as if trying to determine whether he meant the words or not. He put every feeling he had out for her to see, and took her reluctant grin as a good sign.

"You're not going to buy me a truck or something, are you?"

"No more buying. This time, I'm going to make you something."

Sid raised a brow. "You? Make something?"

He couldn't fault the skepticism. He hadn't shown her any of his skills outside of the bedroom. Time to correct that.

With relief flooding his body, Lucas moved closer and slid his hands around her waist. "I'm sorry," he said. "I should have respected your wishes."

She moved her hands up his chest. "Yeah. You should have. Do you understand why I need to do this my way?"

Lucas still wasn't sure he agreed with her plan, but he did understand. "It's hard for me to see you want something and not do what I can to give it to you. I hope you know that my intention was never to take the dream away. Quite the opposite. But I respect your decision. And I respect you for it."

A light shone through her eyes as if he'd just given her the world. "Thank you." She lifted on tiptoe and took his mouth with hers. Leave it to Sid not to wait for him to make the move. God, he loved this woman.

The thought had him ending the kiss before they wound up horizontal on the wet sand. Which, now that he thought about it, was how this whole thing had started. As he pulled back, Sid came forward.

"What's the matter?"

He dropped a kiss on her nose. "Be home by sunset," he said, ignoring the pouting lips begging for more attention. "And don't be late."

Leaving Sid standing there took enormous effort, so he broke into a jog to keep from turning back.

"What about the restaurant?" she asked, raising her voice over the wind and surf. "Who's going to run the bar?"

"Will is covering today," he yelled over his shoulder. If he turned around, he was toast.

"What are you going to do?"

He did turn then. Sid's face split in a bright smile and his heart landed on the sand. "Don't worry about it," he said, watching her dark hair whip in the wind. She looked like a goddess of the depths. Or would, if her shirt didn't read "I can't help it you're a douche bag."

She propped a hand on one hip. "This better be good, pretty boy."

If everything went to plan, good would be an understatement. "Hey," he yelled. "Leave the door unlocked, okay?"

Sid nodded agreement, then waved as she went back to her run. Mission one accomplished. On to mission two.

~

"I know you know so just freaking tell me already." Sid had repeated similar statements since arriving at work that morning, but Will refused to confess, claiming she didn't know anything.

Bullshit.

"This is the last time I'm going to say this. I have no idea what Lucas is planning." Will slammed the tap shut, cutting off the beer that had been flowing into the tall, chilled glass. "Ask me one more time and I'm shoving a bar rag down your throat."

Sid didn't scare easy, but Will did look like a woman on the edge. And she had the advantage of height, if not weight. Hard to tell what the lanky ones were capable of.

"Fine. I'll stop asking." Sid hefted the loaded tray onto her shoulder. "But not because I believe you."

She heard a huff behind her, but kept walking. Crowds had been thin considering the official end of the summer season was still a month away. Tourists always straggled onto the island well into fall, but the real money that sustained everyone through winter was made in June, July, and August.

Thinner crowds meant fewer tips and that slowed her down a bit. Sid hoped Fisher losing out on a potential sale would make him more desperate. Then she could swoop in and take the place off his hands for a price well under asking. She sent up a silent prayer to whatever higher power might be listening. A little divine intervention never hurt.

"Explain this to me again," Will said, when Sid returned to the bar. "Lucas tried to buy the garage *for* you? I can't even get a guy to buy me flowers, and you've got a BMW-driving lawyer buying you whole buildings. You must have seriously made that man see God."

"I am not discussing my private life with you. At least not here. But yeah, he tried to buy the place." Sid stuffed her latest tip in the pocket of her apron. "Everybody's giving ones today. I need to shove some of this in a drawer in the back before I lose it."

"Go for it," Will said. "We're good up here."

Sid dropped her tray behind the counter, then swung through the kitchen. As she reached the office door, the phone rang.

"Dempsey's. How can I help you?" she answered.

"Lucas Dempsey, please." The voice was male, clipped, and not one Sid recognized.

"He's not here right now. Can I take a message?"

"This is Davis Holcomb of Bracken, Franks, and Holcomb, Mr. Dempsey's employer. Is there another number at which I can reach him?"

Sid considered her options. If she said no and this was an important call, she could screw up Lucas's gig back in Richmond. But then, in all honesty, she had no idea where he was. Calling his cell was clearly not a possibility.

Then she remembered he'd asked her not to lock her door. It was a long shot, but the man was welcome to try. "There are a couple of numbers I can give you. The first is for his parents' house."

"I tried," the man interrupted. "He's not there."

She was trying to help the guy out. The least he could do was use a friendlier tone.

"Then you can try the other." Sid shared her home number, then let the cranky caller read it back.

"That's right," she said. In case he wasn't there either, she asked, "Would you like me to take a message in case he doesn't answer?"

"Yes. Tell Mr. Dempsey either I see him in my office on Monday, or he can forget coming back at all."

With that bombshell, the line went dead. Sid dropped into the desk chair and stared at the phone in her hand as if it might start talking again. Hopefully to say, "Just kidding."

Only this wasn't a joke. And Sid definitely didn't feel like laughing. She felt like crying and screaming and calling the phone company to disconnect her service before hateful Holcomb got through to Lucas. Maybe he wouldn't be there. Which meant Sid would have to give Lucas the message.

How in the hell was she going to do that?

~

After a morning setting the scene, then pilfering his mother's cupboards to find everything he needed, Lucas stood in Sid's kitchen chopping shallots and mushrooms for chicken marsala. By some miracle, the sun had burst through the clouds shortly after he'd left Sid on the beach. It was as if the universe approved of his plan, and decided to lend a hand to make it perfect.

As he gathered the bits of mushroom against his knife to transfer to the bowl, Sid's phone rang. Normally, he'd ignore it. But a quick glance at the caller ID, more out of habit than nosiness, revealed a familiar number.

"Shit."

After wiping his hands on a tea towel, he turned his back to the counter as he answered. "Hello?"

"You're not an easy man to track down, Lucas Dempsey." Holcomb.

"Sorry, sir. There's no cell service here on the island."

"How the hell do people live down there?" his boss asked, voice laced with disgust. "Do they have electricity and indoor plumbing or is that too civilized?"

Lucas remained cordial. Barely. "We have all the other amenities, yes sir."

"I'm sure you know why I'm calling," his boss continued, getting right to the point. "Calvin Bainbridge tells me he's explained the situation we have here."

"Yes, I know about the case. Sir, my father is still recovering from his heart attack. Surely you understand that I'm needed here."

"Since you're not working in this family restaurant today, which is supposedly the reason you're there, I can only assume they no longer need you."

Lucas didn't even question how his boss had gotten Sid's number. He must have called the restaurant first. But who had he spoken with?

"We've hired some new help so I'm able to take a day off, but that doesn't mean I'm not still needed." But he wasn't. Will could handle his shifts from here on out. There was no real reason for him to stay.

But one.

"Do you think I'm calling you personally to debate whether you need to be washing dishes or running this defense team?" Davis Holcomb rarely raised his voice. Just as he rarely made his own calls. "You've been an asset to this firm, Lucas, with a promising career ahead of you. But our patience will stretch only so far. We need you on this case and we need you now."

"Sir, are you saying if I don't return immediately—"

"We're giving you until Monday. Wrap up whatever you need to do down there between now and then."

Three days just wasn't enough time.

"If I could have one more week."

"Monday, Lucas. Or you can return a week later and collect your things."

He'd never actually believed they'd fire him. Not after everything he'd done for the firm. The days, weeks, years he'd given to make sure they almost never lost a case. His record was better than any other lawyer on the payroll.

And it would all have been for nothing if he didn't go back.

"Yes, sir. I understand." Lucas looked down to see Drillbit rubbing against his leg. "I'll be there Monday morning."

CHAPTER TWENTY-EIGHT

Sid pulled into her drive, tired and in dire need of a shower. She hadn't gotten much sleep the night before. Having the whole bed to herself again should have been liberating. Instead it felt wrong. The weight missing on the other side. The lack of heat pressed against her back. She'd have to buy one of those body pillows once Lucas left for good.

Which would apparently be sooner than expected. She still didn't know if the Holcomb guy had found him. Her heart told her not to ask. Not to pass along the message. But her head, or maybe her conscience, argued how wrong it would be not to say something.

The question was, would she sabotage his career to keep him? That was an easy answer. Absolutely not. Besides, he'd hate her if she did and then she'd lose him anyway.

Sid hoped she had time to clean up. Surely he didn't expect her to face his big surprise smelling like french fries and beer. The front door was open and the scent of something delicious hit her before she'd even stepped through the screen. Definitely not fries or beer. As the door slammed shut behind her, Lucas appeared from the kitchen.

"You can't come in here."

"Excuse me? This is my house. I can go wherever I want."

Lucas rolled his eyes, which made him look like a teenage drama queen, and herded her toward the bedroom. "I mean you can't come in the kitchen. Take a shower. I've laid out some clothes on the bed."

Sid applied the brakes. "You what?" she asked, spinning around. "Since when do I need you to pick out my clothes?"

She could almost see him mentally counting to ten. "Fine. The clothes are merely a suggestion. Wear anything you want." Then he mumbled something that ended with "stubborn ass."

"Aren't you supposed to be making up to me? Rolling eyes and name calling isn't going to do it."

Before she could say another word, he met her mouth in a kiss that sent heat down to her toes, and made her feel as if gravity had lost its effect on her body. When he pulled away, she was out of breath and not sure where she was.

"Now," he said, forehead pressed to hers. "When you're done with your shower, we'll get this evening started."

Sid nodded, the will to argue gone. "I'll be quick."

Lucas chuckled. "Take your time. I have a few things to finish up."

His order to stay out of the kitchen combined with the awesome smell in the air finally registered. "Are you *cooking*?"

"Don't look so surprised. A bachelor has to eat, and I don't do fast food."

"Not even pizza?" Sid asked, perplexed as to how anyone could not like pizza.

Lucas gave her a gentle nudge. "Pizza doesn't count as fast food. Maybe tomorrow I'll make my focaccia bread pizza with roasted tomatoes and black peppercorns."

That sounded . . . fancy. "Wait," she stopped just before her bedroom door. "Why have you not cooked before now? You've been here every night for two weeks and only now decide to show off your cooking skills. What gives?"

"Would you go take a shower," he huffed, heading back to the kitchen. "If my sauce is burned . . ."

Sid couldn't hear the rest of the rant, but wondered when her live-in lover had turned into a Dockers-wearing Julia Child. When she returned to the living room fifteen minutes later, wearing the black wraparound number Lucas had left on the bed, he was nowhere to be found. The only clue to his whereabouts was a Post-It note stuck on the range hood.

Dinner awaits on the pier.

The pier? What the hell were they . . . ? But then she stepped out on the back deck and her breath stopped. She should have known Lucas would never do anything simple. As she walked across the yard in bare feet, feeling awkward with the dress whipping around her legs, she held her hair out of her eyes and took in the scene.

A table stood at the foot of the pier, a patio umbrella posted at each end leaning in, presumably to protect the diners from the elements. Or maybe to dissuade the birds. There were two tablecloths—the white one brushed the boards of the pier, while a shorter, blue square hung only halfway down.

Wine glasses reflected the setting sun, and as she arrived at the table she spotted silver domes covering each plate. He definitely hadn't found those in her kitchen. How much trouble had he gone to? No one had ever done anything this nice just for her.

"I wanted the setting to be as beautiful as the woman it was for," Lucas said, stepping out from under the far umbrella and sliding his hands into his pockets. "But I should have known better." He'd changed into black pants and a white dress shirt, the sleeves rolled nearly to the elbows. It was as if he'd stepped out of her dreams.

"I'm afraid I can't compare to all this," she said, feeling small and inadequate. Lucas was the epitome of sophistication. Her opposite in every way.

"There is no comparison," he said, pulling out her chair. "Thank you for wearing the dress."

That's when she noticed they matched, except Lucas wore shiny black dress shoes. "I didn't have any shoes—"

"It's perfect," he said, then leaned forward. "You're perfect."

A snort threatened, but the look in his eyes said he meant the words. Butterflies the size of seagulls took flight in her stomach. "Thank you," she whispered, sinking as ladylike as she could into the seat he offered.

Sid wasn't used to accepting compliments. This one went down like a sardine can, odd-sized and hard to swallow, but she did her best.

"Would you like some wine?" he asked. "I have beer in the cooler, if you'd prefer that."

She was not about to ruin his elegant evening by drinking a beer. "Wine is fine, thanks."

Sliding the linen napkin across her lap, Sid wished she'd known what Lucas had been planning so she might have asked Curly how to behave. This whole setup was out of her league. More proof she did not belong in Lucas's life on a permanent basis.

"How was work?" he asked, dropping his own napkin across his lap. "Busy?" Lucas poured and Sid considered mentioning the phone call, but the timing didn't feel right.

"Not really, which is strange. The crowds are usually much bigger in August."

"Do you remember what it was like last year?" he asked, seemingly very interested in her answer.

She thought back. "Thinner than the year before, but not this bad."

"That's what I was afraid of."

"What do you mean?" Sid sipped the white, surprised by the smooth, buttery taste.

Lucas sat back and swirled the liquid in his glass. "Nothing," he said, failing to meet her eye. "Time to unveil the main course."

Not the most graceful change of subject, but she let it pass as Lucas reached across the table and lifted her silver dome away. An earthy hit of goodness nearly overwhelmed her senses, causing her mouth to water instantly. "This explains why the house smells so good. Did you really make this?"

"I did," Lucas said proudly. "I've been perfecting this recipe for about two years. Surprising how easy it was to find all the ingredients here on the island."

"Yes," she said, fork in hand. "What a surprise to find fancy ingredients on a little speck of dirt like Anchor." Before digging in, she asked, "Are there onions in here?"

"No onions," Lucas replied with a sheepish grin. "For obvious reasons."

"If you mean because I'm allergic, then yeah, obvious."

"Wait," Lucas leaned toward her. "You're allergic to onions?"

"Just cooked ones. I can eat them raw, which makes no sense, but it's true."

"That's awful." The concern on his face was almost comical.

"Not really." Sid picked up the butter knife to cut her chicken, but it fell apart with the first stab of her fork. "I haven't eaten anything this fancy that wasn't cooked in a restaurant since before I left Florida."

"Did your mom cook a lot?" Lucas asked, then took his first bite. "Man, I amaze myself sometimes."

Sid chuckled. "Your modesty is astounding. Yeah, mom cooked, but my grandmother on my dad's side was the real queen of the kitchen. She was half Italian and half Puerto Rican, so it was this weird fusion of flavors."

"Sounds wonderful." Lucas took another bite and his eyes rolled. She'd never seen a man enjoy his food in quite this way.

"Are you having some kind of food-gasm over there?" Then she took a bite and got an extra hit of flavor. "Holy shit, this is good. I just got a bite of something . . . smoky?"

"Probably the prosciutto. That I had to steal from Mom's kitchen." He licked his lips. "Which means I risked my life to make you this meal. Hope you'll remember that while you're deciding how to thank me."

His brows wiggled up and down, earning a giggle from Sid. Something she only seemed to do when Lucas was around. "So you were at your mom's house today?"

There was no way she could enjoy the dinner until she knew if he'd gotten the phone call.

"Just this morning," he said, reaching for his glass. "Then I hit the grocery store, and swiped the umbrellas from the coffee shop."

"Swiped?" How did one steal patio umbrellas without getting caught? "Wouldn't it look bad for a lawyer to get busted for umbrella theft?"

"It would probably be bad for anyone to get busted for umbrella theft. Technically, I borrowed them."

At least she didn't have to worry he'd be arrested any minute. "Good to hear you stayed on the right side of the law. So you were here in the afternoon then?"

"Sure. I did the cooking here." He speared a piece of asparagus. "Drillbit wanted to help, but I suggested she stick to observing."

"My kitten offered to help you make dinner?"

"That's what I assumed when she clawed her way up my leg and hopped onto the counter before I could wipe off my hands."

"She didn't."

"She did," he nodded. "Twice."

Lucas didn't sound mad. In fact, there was a hint of affection in his voice. "You like that little fur ball, don't you?"

He set his fork on the table, wiped his mouth with his napkin, and sat back. "Not as much as I like her owner." This declaration should have been accompanied by Lucas's best bedroom eyes, but the look on his face said something else. Something she didn't want to believe, not if he would be leaving in a matter of days.

"You got a call at the restaurant today. I gave him this number." She pushed a piece of chicken around her plate. "Did he get a hold of you?"

Lucas's fork stopped halfway to his mouth. "Um . . . yeah. He did." He lowered the bite back to the plate. "Just a work question, that's all."

A chill filled her chest as Sid stared at her plate. Questions raced through her mind, but she kept them to herself. He wasn't going to tell her.

~

He hated lying to Sid. Hadn't intended to do it, but his brain backfired when she mentioned talking to Holcomb. Lucas refused to let that call ruin Sid's night. He'd gone to a lot of trouble to make the evening special, and she deserved all of it after what he'd done.

His efforts at conversation had fallen flat through the rest of the meal. Sid seemed preoccupied, but when he asked if something was wrong, she'd claimed to be fine. Lucas may not have been a master at reading women, but even he knew the word "fine" never really meant fine.

After dinner, he'd pulled the radio from under the table and proceeded to dance with Sid on the pier. Stars filled the sky as if he'd flipped a switch to create the perfect mood lighting. As they swayed, her soft curves pressed along his body, Lucas breathed in the scent of salt air and Sid's fruity shampoo. He wanted to hold her there forever.

Two more days. He'd have to fit forever into the next forty-eight hours. He had to tell her. Sid deserved to know that he was leaving early. Maybe in the morning. Just not tonight.

When the CD finished and the music faded, Sid stepped back. "Let's go inside," she said, taking his hand and pulling him behind her. With a combination of slow deliberation and frantic need, they'd made love with the full moon shining through the window. There were no words. No teasing or laughter. No questions or promises.

Just a woman holding nothing back, and a man saying good-bye.

~

"Order up!" The words came through the kitchen window and Lucas set down the glass in his hand to move the food over to the pickup station. As if some tourist god had answered his silent pleas, Dempsey's was a madhouse this morning.

The rain probably had more to do with it than divine intervention, but whatever the reason, Lucas was happy to see the dining room full. Sid and Annie were being run to death so they'd called Daisy in an hour before, which lightened the load a bit. He and Sid didn't talk much before work that morning. They'd cleared the table off the pier before the rain got heavy, then worked together in the kitchen until all evidence of the previous night was cleaned and put away.

He kept meaning to tell Sid that he was leaving. The words hovered at the tip of his tongue several times, but then she'd give him a smile and he'd swallow them again.

Would she be angry? Or hurt? Would she ask to go with him? Ask him to stay?

She'd be miserable in the city, and him staying on Anchor was out of the question. He couldn't abandon his life and career in Richmond. He'd worked too hard to throw it all away.

"I need three Millers and a Coke for table eight," Sid said, breezing away to deliver the food order.

She hadn't joked with him today. Hadn't called him "fancy pants" or "sweet cheeks" like she usually did. He chalked it up to being busy, but something still felt off. Sid just wasn't acting like Sid.

"Did I miss a tour bus outside or something?" Will asked, stepping behind the bar and shoving her bag in the drawer under the register. "Got to love a rainy day."

Daisy stepped up to the bar and Lucas asked, "Could you cover back here for a couple minutes? I need to talk to Will."

"Sure," Daisy said, setting her tray down. "What do we need?"

Lucas repeated Sid's order, then nodded for Will to head toward the office.

"You're not firing me already, are you?" Will asked, walking into the office in front of him.

"What?" Lucas said. "Why would I fire you?"

"I don't know," she shrugged. "You look like you're about to do something you don't want to do."

She had that part right. "Do you think you're ready to handle the bar on your own?"

Will's brows drew together. "I'm ready whenever you need me to be. But why?"

Lucas closed the door. "I haven't told my parents or Sid yet, so I'd appreciate it if you'd keep this to yourself until I do. I'm going back to Richmond on Sunday."

"You're what? What do you mean you haven't told Sid?"

"I didn't know myself until yesterday. I'm going to tell her today."

"But why? I don't understand," Will said. "You're supposed to be here for six weeks until your dad recovers. You can't just walk away now."

"Will, I don't have a choice." He wished he did. "And no offense, but I don't have to justify my actions to you."

"You sure as hell have to justify them to Sid. What are you going to tell her?"

That *was* the million dollar question. "I'm going to tell her I have to go. She always knew I wasn't here to stay. I'm just leaving a little earlier than planned."

"A little?" Will's eyes flashed. "Weeks, Lucas. And don't talk about her like she's something you can toss away. She's a person, not a used-up pair of socks."

He'd had enough. "Can you run this bar or not?"

"I said I can."

"Then we're done here."

He opened the door and motioned for Will to exit, but she didn't move.

"Don't hurt her," she said. Three words that sliced him in half.

"I won't," he replied, but something told him the promise would be difficult to keep.

307

CHAPTER TWENTY-NINE

"Thanks, Daisy. I can take it from here." Will tied an apron around her waist, mumbling under her breath.

"What's wrong with you?" Sid asked, loading the drinks onto her tray. "O'Hagan give you flack about quitting?"

"No," Will said, jerking a knot in her apron strings. "My *former* employer is not the problem today."

Sid watched her struggle with the strings another ten seconds. "Come over here and let me fix that." She squeezed her tray between her knees. "If it's not O'Hagan, who is it?"

At that moment, Lucas stepped through the kitchen doorway. The dull ache that had been sitting in Sid's chest since taking the phone message the day before flared to life. As it did every time she looked at him, knowing he wouldn't be around much longer.

The apron secured, she glanced up to see Lucas and Will exchange an unfriendly glare.

"What's up with you two?" It wasn't like Will or Lucas to be outright hostile, especially to each other.

Another brief hesitation and Will finally said, "Nothing. I'm good." Grabbing a rag from beneath the bar, she asked, "How about you, Lucas? You got anything you want to say?"

The tone of her voice made it clear *nothing* was *something.*

"No, Will," he ground through a clenched jaw. "Thanks for asking."

She'd definitely missed something, but preferring to let the pair work out whatever spat they were having on their own, Sid turned to go back to the floor and nearly ran into Beth.

"Hey," Beth said. "You guys look crazy busy in here."

"You think?" Sid asked. "What was your first clue?" Now she was doing it. "Sorry. What's up?" Realizing the time, she added, "Aren't you supposed to be at the art store?"

"Unlike here, that place is dead," Beth said. "But Lola is there."

Sid blinked. "Lola who is in New Orleans?"

"*Was* in New Orleans. They came back a week early."

"Seems a lot of things are happening early around here," Will mumbled, loud enough for everyone around to hear.

Now Sid caught on. So Lucas had told Will before he'd told her. She supposed Will did need to know since he'd be dumping the bar in her lap.

"Will," Sid said. "I need to see you in the back."

"Why not," Will huffed, throwing her rag on the bar. "Maybe I'll just work from the office today." Then she marched into the kitchen.

Before Sid could follow, Beth caught her arm. "Wait. I came to ask you and Lucas to come to breakfast at Patty and Tom's place tomorrow morning. Can you guys make it?"

Sid looked over to Lucas, who shrugged. "I don't see why not. What time?" he asked.

"Nine." Beth gave Sid a hug, then pulled back, eyes beaming. "Okay. See you later."

As Beth practically waltzed through the front door, Sid turned back to Lucas. "What the hell was that about?"

"I don't know," he said, moving glasses into the chiller. "But you've got Will waiting in the back."

"Shit." Sid left her tray on the bar. This was not going to be fun. "I'll be right back."

When she stepped into the office, Will was sitting behind the desk, jaw tight, arms crossed. Sid shut the door.

"I know he's leaving," she said, seeing no reason to dance around the issue.

Will stood up. "You what? He said he hadn't told you yet."

"He hasn't." She'd realized during their dinner the night before that Lucas's leaving had always been inevitable. If she'd fallen too hard too fast, that was her own fault, not his. Lucas never made any promises about sticking around. She'd known what she was getting from day one.

"And you're not mad?" Will asked, leaning on the desk. "You two have been playing house for weeks and now he's just leaving without any warning? Doesn't that piss you off?"

What Sid felt was far from anger. But then she'd always been forgiving of Lucas. Clearly to her own downfall.

"It's been two weeks and we both agreed this was a temporary, casual fling. The temporary part was supposed to last a few more weeks, but he was always going to leave."

"But he—"

"He what? He made me feel special? He made me giggle?" Sid sat down in the chair behind her. "The man made me giggle, Will. Do you know how many times in my life I've giggled?"

Will looked like she was considering her answer. "I'm guessing not many. In fact, I'm trying to imagine it right now and can't do it."

"Exactly." She shook her head. "I can't ask him to stay here. Opal said I should fight for him, but Lucas doesn't belong here. He's meant for bigger things than Anchor can give him."

Will squatted in front of Sid's chair. "Anchor can give him you. Or you could go with him. Not that I want you to leave but—"

"I could never live in the city. I hated Miami with a passion. All those people and the noise." She exhaled, shoulders falling in resignation. "Besides, I'd only embarrass him at those fancy dinner parties Curly talks about. I don't think greasy work boots and profane T-shirts would be acceptable attire."

Will rose back to full height. "So he won't stay and you won't go. Man. This is a cluster and a half."

"That's one way to describe it," Sid said, dragging herself out of the chair. "Just cut him some slack, okay? And don't tell him I know." She opened the door. "He'll tell me when he's ready. At least I'll be prepared when he does."

❧

By the next morning, Sid was ready to shout the words, "I know you're leaving!" The strain of keeping it in, pretending she didn't know, had her shoulders aching. She may have even been grinding her teeth in the night, considering how badly her jaw hurt when she woke up.

Lucas had looked ready to tell her several times. When he set the homemade pizza on the coffee table. While they were doing the dishes. As he handed her a cup of coffee that morning. But every time, he seemed to tense, flash an empty smile, and keep silent. Why wouldn't he just tell her already? How long was he going to wait?

They didn't have sex, but Lucas held her all night, as if he were afraid she might disappear if he let go. A part of her wanted to push him away, but the other part, the one aching in her chest, made her hold on. Lucas had become her drug. Quitting him cold turkey was going to feel like hell, but she'd take the trip and hopefully come out the other side only slightly singed. Now she knew what Georgette had meant by the permanent mark comment.

"Good morning, you two," Patty said, as she and Lucas walked into the kitchen. "Coffee is hot and the food will be here shortly."

Lucas reached for a mug. "You're not cooking?"

Patty shook her head. "This is Beth's little get-together. I'm just providing the table."

Sid wondered what this was about. Will claimed not to know, and Curly wouldn't give any clues when she showed up at Dempsey's to work the dinner shift the night before. Even Joe was tight lipped, which wasn't unusual, but he smiled more than normal, which made the whole thing feel even more ominous.

Could Beth be pregnant? Would they be happy to announce that before they'd even set an official wedding date? It was clear they were both ready for "till death do us part," even if Joe hadn't put a ring on it yet.

Wait. Maybe that was it.

"Good morning, everyone," Beth trilled, prancing through the kitchen door with a large aluminum pan in tow. "Lucas, can you go help Joe with the rest of the food?"

"Sure," he said, and dropped a kiss on Sid's forehead as he passed her by.

One more thing she was going to miss after tomorrow.

"The table is almost set," Patty said, grabbing a pile of forks and butter knives, then following Beth into the dining room.

Sid felt about as useful as four-wheel drive on a golf cart. "Is there anything I can do?" she asked, stepping into the dining room.

"You could fill some glasses with orange juice," Patty said. "And pour what's left of the carton into the pitcher that's in the cupboard over the fridge."

Sounded easy enough, until Sid tried to open the cupboard over the fridge. Maybe if she pulled up a chair.

"What do you need?" Lucas asked, setting a smaller aluminum pan on the island.

"I need the pitcher out of that cupboard." Sid indicated the correct door. Lucas didn't even have to stretch. The man came in handy in so many ways. "Thanks," she said as he handed it over.

"Any time," he responded, then his eyes clouded. He couldn't reach things for her any time because after this weekend, he wouldn't be around. They both knew it, only he didn't know she knew and was apparently not ready to tell.

Sid considered pouring an extra glass of juice for the giant elephant they'd brought along with them.

"This is the last of it," Joe said, stepping through the door as Beth and Patty returned to the kitchen. Dozer shot between Joe's legs. "Damn it, Dozer. I almost dropped the bacon."

"That was probably his intent," Beth said, grabbing the big mutt's collar. "If you hadn't given him four pieces already." She dragged the dog to the door. "Outside, Dozer. This food is not for you."

Dozer pressed his nose to the screen and whimpered. Amazing an animal that big could look so forlorn and pitiful.

"Did somebody say bacon?" Tom asked, appearing in the doorway to the dining room.

The gang was officially all here.

"No bacon for you," Patty said, shooing Tom back in the direction from which he'd come. "Egg whites and whole wheat toast. I've put the butter substitute down by your plate."

Butter substitute? Poor Tom.

"Everyone take a seat." Beth took the pan Lucas had carried. "Breakfast is served."

Twenty minutes later, the eggs were nothing but a memory, the bacon a mere scent lingering in the air, and three sausage links huddled against aluminum as if in fear of their lives. And rightly so, as Joe grabbed them all with one stab of his fork.

"So why are we all here?" Tom asked, garnering a harsh look from Patty. "What? There has to be a reason, other than torturing me with food I can't have."

All eyes turned toward Beth and Joe. Her cheeks were pink, and Joe wore the same look he'd gotten when they'd landed a record-size marlin off the coast last year.

Beth slid her right hand into Joe's, turned to the eager audience, and held up her left hand. There, on the third finger, had appeared a dainty rock that could mean only one thing.

"Joe asked me to marry him."

Well duh, Sid thought. That part was obvious. *About time* was her second thought, then she looked to Lucas, expecting the same tension as when they'd all gathered in the hospital weeks before.

But it was nowhere to be found. He was actually smiling. Who was this imposter and what had he done with Lucas?

And then the entire table exploded. Patty was crying and Beth was crying. The men shook hands and did a lot of back slapping. Sid considered going out to congratulate Dozer, since no one was paying much attention to her.

Then Curly pulled her out of the chair and into a bear hug, in the middle of which she started jumping up and down. "You're going to rip my head off, woman." Sid extricated herself, but when she looked into Beth's shining eyes, she felt her own grow misty.

"I wondered when he was going to get around to this," Sid said, smiling and dabbing the corner of her eye on her shoulder. "Let me see that ring."

Weren't girls supposed to ooh and ah over the ring? Sid *was* a girl and Beth deserved the expected response. "That's really pretty. Why does it look so old?"

Beth teared up a little more. "It was Joe's mom's. I still can't believe he trusts me with it."

"That's pretty damn romantic," Sid said. "I didn't think Joe had it in him."

"Cute, smart-ass." Joe pulled her into a hug, then punched her on the arm as if reaffirming their standoffish male-type relationship.

"Listen up, everyone," Beth said, wiping at her eyes with her napkin. "We wanted to have this breakfast for the family, but tomorrow, we were thinking we could close up

Dempsey's to the public and have a celebration dinner for the staff and all our friends. We'll pay the rental fee, of course."

"The hell you will." Tom threw his arm across Patty's shoulders. "The place is yours for the night and don't mention money again."

"Did you say tomorrow night?" Lucas asked. Sid tensed.

"Yeah," Joe said. "Around six o'clock."

Lucas rubbed a hand across his forehead. "I won't be there."

"What do you mean you won't be there?" Beth asked.

Silence settled into the room like a fog blanketing the bay.

"Why won't you be there?" Joe asked, gripping the back of his chair until his knuckles were white.

Sid knew what was coming next.

~

"Because I'm going back to Richmond tomorrow morning," Lucas said. He hadn't intended to drop the words like a live grenade, but keeping them in was killing him. And now, with the dinner planned, he had to be honest.

His mother gasped. Beth dropped into her chair. Tom cursed under his breath, and Joe continued his vise grip on the buffed oak.

Sid didn't react at all. Why didn't she react?

"I don't understand," Patty said. "You're supposed to stay a few more weeks. Why now?"

"Yes," Joe all but growled. "Why now?"

"Something came up at work." The words felt lame on his tongue. "They need me."

He didn't see any point in sharing the detail regarding his job security. They'd all think he'd jeopardized his career to come down here, and he didn't want anyone feeling guilty on his behalf. He'd made his own choices.

Now he had to make another one.

"If they need you for a case, then you have to go," Beth said, gripping Joe's hand. "If we'd known—"

"I didn't know until a couple days ago," Lucas said. "It all happened pretty fast."

He had yet to make eye contact with Sid. Afraid of what he'd see in her eyes. Would she hate him? Would she care? When he finally glanced her way, the look on her face was inscrutable.

"If you all don't mind, I'd like to talk to Sid outside."

Lucas wanted to make sure she didn't think he was leaving because of Beth and Joe. What he and Sid had the last two weeks was special. He'd never leave her believing she'd been a stand-in for another woman. She deserved to know how much she meant to him.

No one spoke. Sid nodded, pushed her chair further back, and walked out of the room. Lucas followed. When he stepped onto the porch, Sid was standing at the rail looking out toward the towering oaks.

"So this is it," she said.

"I wanted to tell you before."

"But you just found out yourself." She turned, face placid. As if they were discussing the weather. "You'll need to pack up your things. Get an early start on the drive."

"Sid," he said, and waited for her to meet his eyes. "I'm sorry."

She raised one shoulder. "For what? We always knew you were leaving."

"But what we've had." He moved toward her. She shrugged him off and dropped into a blue Adirondack chair.

"What we've had is a casual fling. That's what we agreed on."

Why was she being so callous? Didn't she care about him at all?

"That's how it started. But—"

"You don't have to worry about me. I promised I could handle casual and would be fine when it was time for you to leave." She picked at a spot of loose paint on the arm of the chair. "So it's a little earlier than we planned. Shit happens."

Shit happens? *Shit happens?*

"You're right," he said, a dead weight filling his chest. He'd done it again. Fallen for a woman who didn't fall back. "We had a good time for a couple weeks. I hope it was as good for you as it was for me."

The words were cruel. He shouldn't have said them.

"I have no complaints," she said, rising out of the chair. He thought he saw her lip quiver, but when she turned his way, her jaw was set, eyes dry. "I mean, there was never any chance of you staying. Right?"

"Right. There's nothing here for me." Her chin flexed as if she'd taken a punch. Lucas fought the urge to break everything on the porch. "My life is back in Richmond. That's where I belong."

Sid nodded. "I forgot I told Randy I'd help him with something this morning." She charged down the steps.

"The door is unlocked so you can have someone run you over to the house for your things. You should probably stay here tonight. Get a good night's sleep so you'll be awake for the drive."

She was in the truck seconds later. He wanted to go after her, tell her he was an ass, but what good would that do? He was still leaving. A piece of gravel pinged off his knee when she backed out of the driveway, but Lucas didn't move. He just watched her drive away.

Leaving him before he could leave her.

He'd never know she pulled off the road half a mile away and cried until she couldn't breathe.

CHAPTER THIRTY

The gut-wrenching cry took a full five minutes before Sid could pull back onto the road. There was still enough drizzle in the air to keep the tourists off the streets, thank goodness. By the time she found herself in the parking lot of Anchor Adventures, she'd pulled herself together as much as possible, blown her nose on some napkins from her glove compartment, and ruled out having Randy kick Lucas's ass.

Partly because she didn't believe her brother should fight her battles, but mostly because she knew she'd hurt Lucas as much as he'd hurt her. Maybe this was exactly what they needed to do to get him off the island. No tearful, sappy good-bye, see-you-next-time scene for them. Better to cut it off at the knees and kill it dead.

Which was probably why she felt like roadkill.

Sid slipped in the back door, hoping to reach Randy's office without encountering anyone else. She may have pulled it together, but she wasn't stupid. Her eyes were red and puffy, clear evidence she'd been crying.

With great relief, she reached the office unnoticed.

"Morning," Randy said, pen poised over some papers. "I didn't know you were coming by today."

Sid sniffed. "If anyone asks, yes you did." She didn't make a habit of lying, which is why she'd driven to Randy's at all. Because she'd said that's where she was going.

Randy's eyes narrowed. "Where is he?"

"Who?" Sid asked, examining the back of her hand as if something new had grown there.

"Is he still where I can reach him, or was he smart enough to hide?"

"If by *he* you mean Lucas, he's still on the island. For another day anyway."

"I see." Her brother crossed the office and wrapped her in his arms.

And Sid fell apart. Again.

Several minutes later, Sid held a bottle of water in one hand and a tissue in the other. Her breathing was returning to normal and Randy sat beside her, patient and silent. He was using his Zen crap on her. She could feel it.

"Don't do that."

"Don't do what?"

"Sit there all silent and meditative."

Randy chuckled. "Would you rather I rage against the walls on your behalf?"

Sid sniffled. "You couldn't rage if you tried. I'm just not in the mood for deep thought right now. I want to wallow and not have to hear about how I should get in touch with my inner being and find peace with this situation."

"For the record, all I'm doing is sitting here. But I would recommend you try some steady breathing to stop that hiccupping." Sid took a deep breath and Randy asked, "Want to tell me what happened?"

321

Did she? Did she even know what happened? "It's kind of a long, complicated story."

"I'm not going anywhere," he said, crossing his arms, which was a feat considering his chest was nearly as wide as the doorway. "Did you have a fight?"

"Not exactly." If anything, they'd had an anti-fight. Agreeing with each other while saying cruel things. "Lucas is going back to Richmond tomorrow. I've known since Thursday, only he didn't know I knew."

"How did you know?"

Sid pulled her legs up and hugged her knees. "His boss called the restaurant looking for him. Left the message that if he wasn't in the office on Monday, then he shouldn't bother coming back at all. I gave the guy my home number because I thought Lucas might be there and he was, only when I asked him if the guy found him, he said yeah and that it was nothing."

"Ah," Randy sighed. "So neither of you told the truth."

When he put it that way. "It's not like we lied. Well, I didn't lie. I just omitted a bit of information."

"And he omitted the same bit of information."

"Whose side are you on?" she asked, twisting to face him.

"I'm always on your side. You know that. So what happened today?"

Sid blew her nose, then took another deep breath. "We all had breakfast at Tom and Patty's place so Joe and Beth could announce they're engaged." Wait. Was that supposed to be a secret? "Maybe I wasn't supposed to mention that."

"I knew," he said. "Go on."

"Oh." Of course he knew. Randy was Joe's best friend. "Anyway, they're planning a dinner tomorrow night to celebrate with everyone else, at Dempsey's, and that's when Lucas announced that he wouldn't be there."

"How did they take it?" Randy asked.

Sid flashed back to that moment in the dining room. "Not well. It looked like Joe assumed it was because of the engagement, but I don't think Lucas is pining for Beth anymore."

Randy reached for another tissue and passed it over. "I would hope not. Considering." He raised one brow and she had to admit he had a point. Had she helped Lucas get over Beth?

"I just realized," Sid said, "he never told them why he had to go back. Never mentioned the ultimatum or the threat of losing his job."

"What does that matter?"

"They couldn't be mad if they knew he didn't have a choice."

Randy shook his head. "He had a choice."

Sid dropped her feet to the floor. "No, he didn't. They threatened to fire him."

"Lucas wouldn't be the first person ever to lose his job," Randy said, returning to the chair behind his desk. "From what I've heard, he's excellent at what he does. Some other firm would take him on."

Loyalty pushed her to defend him. "You don't know that would happen."

"And he doesn't know that it wouldn't." Randy leaned back in his chair, eyes cutting to the wall on his right covered in pictures. "Why do you think I settled down here?"

Sid felt an old guilt tighten her spine. "Because of me. You couldn't drag a fourteen-year-old around the globe and up every mountainside."

He smiled and leaned forward. "You were only part of it, Sidney. Aunt Roberta offered to take care of you. I could have continued chasing the next ride, the next climb. But I chose you and this island."

Her body loosened. Tears threatened again. "Why didn't you ever tell me that?"

"There wasn't a reason before. You're my little sister and I love you. You were more important than the life I had at the time." His brown eyes, identical to hers, held her gaze. "I've never regretted that decision. Every man has a choice, Sidney. Even Lucas."

She thought about those words as the tissue in her hand turned to a pile of shredded fragments between her feet. "I don't blame him for choosing Richmond," she finally said, knowing to the tips of her toes that she meant it.

Randy picked up his pen. "Maybe someday you should tell him that."

~

Lucas couldn't bring himself to ask anyone to drive him back to Sid's house. He'd had a hard enough time explaining why she'd left. Unwilling to endure the disappointed looks coming his way, he opted to walk.

Packing didn't take long, even though he'd had to remove Drillbit from the duffel bag three times. She seemed to be the only creature in his life who didn't think he was a piece of shit at the moment. Maybe he'd get a cat when he got home. His own little ball of fur to keep him company.

Though with his hours, the animal would be alone most of the time. Based on Holcomb's tone on the phone, he'd have to bust his ass even harder to get back in the good graces. The partnership wasn't even a consideration until he straightened this mess out.

Not that he regretted a moment he'd spent on the island. His family needed him and he was there. He'd done his duty, and now was leaving the restaurant in capable hands to return to his life. Earlier than planned, but that couldn't be helped.

When he stepped outside, pulling Sid's front door closed behind him for the last time, Lucas was surprised to see Beth standing in the driveway.

"If you're looking for Sid, she's not here."

"I know," Beth said.

"Then why are you here?" he asked, tossing his duffel bag into the car.

She ignored his question. "You didn't have to walk. I'd have driven you over."

"I didn't want to bother anyone."

Beth propped a hip on the front corner of her Civic. "I don't blame you," she said, pinning him with her eyes. "For leaving that is. They ordered you back, didn't they?"

Why couldn't anyone leave well enough alone? "There's a big case. They need me."

She nodded. "Right." Her eyes slid toward the water. "Sid has a nice spot here. I've always liked it. Very peaceful."

"Sure," he agreed, looking out to the waves, spotting a seagull swoop down for a meal. "Probably one of the nicest spots on the island." There had to be a point to this conversation. A reason Beth had followed him. "I doubt you came over here to admire the view."

"She loves you, you know." Beth kept her eyes on the water. "She doesn't let many people get close. See how vulnerable she is." She pinned him again. "But she's different with you. Open. Trusting. And I think she could make you a better man."

Beth obviously didn't know her new friend as well as she thought. Sid didn't love Lucas.

"That's a nice speech. I'll try not to be insulted."

"Don't try on my account." Beth slid the sunglasses from the top of her head onto her nose. "You're still the sweetest and smartest guy I've ever met, Lucas. How you can be so stupid at the same time is such a mystery."

He watched her drive off. She had the nerve to wave from the road as if they'd just exchanged recipes and made plans for tea. This had to be some kind of record, even for Lucas. The two women he'd had the misfortune to fall for had both cut him at the knees in less than an hour's time.

Maybe he'd been a douche bag in a former life. He made a mental note. Any future pet would be of the male variety.

After the encounter with Beth, Lucas had no desire to head back to his parents' place so he sat in his car and debated where to go. Whether out of habit or due to newly developed masochistic tendencies, he chose Dempsey's as his destination. Might as well settle things with Will to make sure the restaurant would be good without him.

His early departure should have no effect on the business. As Will had proven more than capable, he had no concern on that front. The visit was more his version of closing a case. Tying up loose ends so he could put the file away without a second thought.

Right. As if he'd ever be able to file away the last three weeks and forget about them. This visit to Anchor had changed him. For better or worse he had yet to decide. The corner office and fancy gadgets seemed less important now. He'd lived on Anchor for three weeks without his atomic clock, cell service, or a golf course in sight. And he hadn't missed any of it.

Quite an unexpected development.

"I was wondering if you'd show up today." Will turned her eyes to the clock. "About time. Sid called off so I pulled Annie in to cover."

"I'm just here to make sure you have everything you need." He started pulling chairs off the tables. "Have Beth or Joe talked to you about tomorrow?"

"You mean about you leaving?"

Lucas nearly dropped a chair on his foot. "No," he said, counting to ten to keep from throwing the chair out the window. "They're planning an engagement party tomorrow night. Here. The staff needs to know. I'm sure they're all invited, but someone will have to cook and serve."

"Beth didn't mention it," Will said, stacking glasses. "I'll call Lola's later to get the details."

They worked together in silence for fifteen more minutes. Until Lucas decided Will didn't need him and he didn't need the "fuck you" vibe she was sending. It seemed every woman on this godforsaken island intended to make him feel as low as possible.

So he did what any self-respecting man would do. He went home to his mother.

～

TERRI OSBURN

Sid strolled into Dempsey's thirty minutes after opening time and grabbed an apron.

"I thought you were taking off today," Will said. "I called Annie in to cover."

Leave it to Will to be efficient. "I didn't feel good, but now I'm better."

"And now you're not needed." Will removed the cap and placed a beer in front of her. "Beth told me about this morning."

"Curly has a big mouth." Sid grabbed the bottle and plopped down on a stool.

Will tossed the cap in the garbage. "She's worried about you, and so am I. Are you okay?"

That *was* the question of the day. Sid didn't have an answer. "I've had better days, but life goes on. Like I said, this was always a temporary thing." She picked at the label on the bottle. "Randy made me feel a little better, even if he was talking out his ass."

"If your brother really wanted to help, he'd kick Lucas's ass from here to Currituck."

Sid appreciated Will's loyalty and indignation on her behalf. "Randy wouldn't hurt a fly."

Will snorted. "Are we talking about the same person? The big guy who looks like he could give the Hulk a run for his money?"

"They may be similar in size, but Randy *really* wouldn't hurt a fly. I know it's a cliché, but in his case it's true. I've seen him catch them in a glass and let them go outside. Once he even herded one out an open window."

Will leaned her elbows on the bar. "How do you herd a fly? And if he's that friendly, why does he bench-press tugboats in his spare time?"

328

Another good question. "I don't know," Sid said. "It's just his thing. He's all into being healthy. Goes with the Zen thing."

"Zen? Like meditating?"

"Yep. He's even a vegetarian."

Will's jaw fell open. "No way."

"Yes way. And look here. We've been talking about something that has nothing to do with my once again nonexistent love life. See? Life goes on."

"Uh huh." One brow shot up. "That's why your eyes are all puffy and red. You want to hang out here, I'm good with it. But we don't need you on the floor today." Annie rattled off an order for three sodas from the end of the bar. As Will filled the first glass, she said, "Crap. I can't believe I forgot to tell you. I heard that offer on Fisher's garage was a no-go. Buyer changed his mind or something."

"Really?" Sid said, feigning ignorance. "How did Fisher take that?"

"I believe the phrase Deb used was 'mad as a hornet.'" Will filled the second glass. "Started ranting that he wants this place off his hands. If you can, I'd suggest you make a move now."

Sid nodded. That had been her plan. To focus on the garage once Lucas was gone. Tips had been good, and with Fisher desperate and frustrated, she could probably talk him down.

"Maybe that's what I can do today. I'll check out the numbers and give Deb a call."

Sid backed off the stool into a solid chest behind her. Spinning, she looked up to see Manny.

"Oh," she said. "Hey, Manny."

329

He was smiling down at her, blue eyes alight. "I heard pretty boy is headed out."

The Anchor grapevine. Fastest gossip line on the planet. "That's the rumor." She didn't want to talk about Lucas, especially not with Manny. Why couldn't he go bark up Kinzie's tree? Didn't men have a thing for women who could cook?

"So how about dinner? Artie's got a *Godfather* marathon going tonight."

Wouldn't a *Godfather* marathon take days? Gangster films were never her thing. "Aren't you supposed to be at work, Manny?"

"The rain grounded the parasailing." He shifted from one foot to the other. "So what do you say?"

Sid shoved her hair out of her face. It was time to set the boy straight. "Manny, I appreciate the offer, but it's a no. It's a no tonight, a no tomorrow, and it'll still be a no every day after that. Get the idea?"

His face fell and Sid felt as if *she'd* just kicked a puppy.

"Right. That's cool."

She squeezed his face in one hand. "Manny. Listen closely to what I'm about to tell you. Ask. Kinzie. Out."

"Kinzie?" he asked. Or tried to through his scrunched-up lips.

"Yes," Sid said, letting him go. "Now. How about you go buy some cupcakes?"

The man looked as if she'd asked him to rattle off the number pi, so she waited. Slowly the words seemed to penetrate. Sid imagined this was what it must be like to watch chimps learn sign language.

"The guys would love it if I brought back cupcakes." Sid ran a hand over her face, ready to shake the shit out of the puppy. Until he leaned over and dropped a kiss on her forehead. "And I'll see if Kinzie is up for dinner. Thanks, Sid."

Manny exited Dempsey's like a man on a mission. About damn time. When she turned to Will, the woman was smiling.

"That was a nice thing you did there."

"Yeah, well," Sid said. "Curly isn't the only one who gets to play fairy fucking godmother. Put the beer on my tab. I've got a garage to buy."

CHAPTER THIRTY-ONE

Lucas didn't sleep well that night. He kept picturing Sid's face. That calm expression, like nothing important was happening. Like she didn't care if he left. When he did sleep, she heckled him in his dreams. Kissing him until he was on the brink of control, then walking away, laughing as if it had all been a joke. Once the laughter stopped, another scene came into focus.

Sid was bent over the front of a car, her upper body hidden behind the raised hood. When he moved closer, the car disappeared to reveal Sid straddled over Manny.

That one had jarred him awake somewhere around four a.m. He'd just gotten back to sleep when the overhead light filled the bedroom and blasted through his eyelids.

"What the—"

"Get up," Joe said. "I need to talk to you."

Lucas pulled the pillow over his face. "What the hell time is it?"

"Five thirty."

"Go away." Nothing was so important it had to be discussed this early in the morning.

"Come on." Something heavy joined Lucas on the bed. Surely Joe was not climbing in with him.

When he moved the pillow, a large, wet tongue slurped up his cheek and the foulest breath he'd ever smelt watered his eyes.

"Get your damn mutt off of me."

"Dozer, sit."

The dog planted his ass on Lucas's gut, hot breath still aimed at his face. "Fine." Lucas pulled himself up until he leaned against the headboard. He brought the blanket with him as much as the boulder on his stomach would allow. "I'm assuming the house isn't on fire so you better have a damn good reason for this early wake-up call."

Joe moved to the chair in the corner, an old rocker passed down through Patty's family. "We need to settle some things before you go."

Three weeks and they'd barely had a conversation. *Now* he wanted to talk? "I won't be leaving for hours. Can we do this after I've had a shower and coffee?"

"I've got an early charter." Joe rested a boot over one knee. "You're not leaving because of the engagement, are you?"

Lucas scrubbed his hands over his face. "No." He didn't see any need to elaborate. Best not to give opposing counsel anything to work with.

"Beth believes the only reason you'd go back early is if they threatened you. Did you put your job on the line to come down here?"

"No."

Joe stared but held his tongue. Damn it.

"I was on leave before Dad had the heart attack. There was no reason I couldn't come help. The firm had no problem with it at the time."

"At the time. But now?"

Who knew Joe would be an expert interrogator?

"Now, they want me on a case. Immediately. I tried to put them off, but they made it clear my tenure with the firm was at risk." He crossed his arms over the blanket. "They left me no choice."

"There's always a choice." Joe tapped his boot. "Beth told you Sid loves you. She got the impression you didn't believe her."

Lucas was still groggy enough to struggle with the sudden change in topic. "I'm sure Beth believes that, but she's wrong. Sid made it clear yesterday that her heart is in no danger from me." The words still rankled. He'd like to think the damage was to his pride, but the pain in his chest said otherwise.

"I don't know what Sid told you, but Beth isn't wrong. Sid has been half in love with you since high school."

"Bullshit."

"I'm still not sure how you never saw it," he said, ignoring Lucas. "She went to every baseball game you played in. Waited for you by the bike stand every day after school, always hoping you'd notice her. And you never did." Joe put the chair into motion. "Until now."

"By the time I was in high school, you were out on fishing boats full time. How would you know what Sid did or didn't do?"

"Some of us aren't as blind as you are," he said. "I went to your games. Picked you up on rainy days. What I didn't see, Mom saw. Or Dad. But not you."

Lucas leaned his head against the cast-iron headboard. "High school is ancient history. A teenager's crush doesn't have anything to do with now. What's the point of this, anyway? You don't even like me. Shouldn't you be happy to see Sid rid of me?"

The chair stopped. "I never said I didn't like you."

"Don't approve then." Joe had made it clear on more than one occasion how he felt about Lucas's life choices.

"I'm sorry about that."

Lucas shook his head. "What did you say?"

"I'm sorry for giving you a hard time about living away from here. You have every right to live wherever you want."

Maybe this was another weird dream. Any minute now, juggling clowns would march out of the closet and fill the room.

"Why the sudden change of heart?" Lucas asked, not ready to accept the new brother sitting before him.

"Beth has helped me see a lot of things." His boot hit the floor and Joe lifted out of the chair. "A couple months ago, you woke me up and told me to stop being an idiot. To go after the woman I loved. I'm just trying to return the favor. Sometimes you have to be willing to give up what you think you want to get the thing you need."

He moved to the door and Dozer jumped off the bed to follow. Lucas could finally breathe again.

"Either way, I hope you'll be willing to stand up for me at the wedding. If not, I'll understand."

Be the best man when his brother married his former fiancée? Lucas considered that twisted scenario, waiting for the bitterness to hit his tongue. All he tasted was morning breath.

"I'd be honored."

"Good. Maybe someday I can return that favor too."

Then Joe turned off the light and was gone.

~

The last of the rain and clouds cleared out overnight, leaving Anchor basking in sunshine and a warm, soft breeze. The day was perfect, which brought the tourists into the streets in droves. Lucas must have dodged ten bicycles by the time he hit the edge of the village.

Saying good-bye to his parents had been tougher than he'd expected. Though his dad was looking better every day, there was still a fragility about him. The reality that his parents would not be around forever sat heavy on his chest, making him promise to come home more often.

His bags had been packed the night before so there wasn't much for him to do after Joe left. Going back to sleep wasn't an option, what with his brain replaying Joe's words and the lingering threat of more dreams about Sid. So she'd had a thing for him in high school. That was ten years ago.

Though he did wonder how he'd missed the signs. Would he have cared if he knew? He tried to picture the Sid from high school. She'd been small. Quiet. At least around him. A memory teased at the back of his mind. A school dance. Bleachers. Lucas passed the wild horse pens on his left, and struggled to bring the memory into focus.

There had been another kid. Dean Schnitzel. A jerk, Lucas remembered. No one was upset to see him move away in the middle of senior year. But Sid would have been a junior then. Why would he remember her with Dean Schnitzel?

The scene came back to him. Dean and Sid under the bleachers. She was shoving him away, her shirt torn by the time Lucas interrupted them. How in the hell could he have forgotten that? He'd offered to give her a ride home, but fear and embarrassment shone in her brown eyes, illuminated by the field lights, before she'd run off without a word.

He'd considered reporting Dean, but that would have put Sid in the spotlight. Let everyone know what had happened, and force her to face the questions and scrutiny of the island at large.

So he'd let her go. Let her deal with the situation on her own. And Sid had done the same yesterday, run away after another asshole treated her like shit. Only this time, Lucas had been the asshole.

"Son of a bitch," he said, and turned the wheel hard.

Sid couldn't sit in the house. She kept seeing Lucas on the couch or at the stove. The bedroom was the worst. She'd given up by two in the morning and dragged a blanket out to the couch. Then she learned why they put infomercials on in the middle of the night. She'd been so tired, she actually considered buying a belt that claimed to create six-pack abs with electrical pulses.

The guy on the commercial had been wearing the thing while eating ice cream. In the light of day, it was crazy. At four a.m., the damn thing looked like a brilliant idea.

By eight she'd showered while naming every tool in her workshop in her head to keep from thinking about Lucas.

By the time she got to hacksaw, she wanted to saw her own head off. Now she was strolling through her backyard, listening to the waves and watching the gulls dip down for breakfast.

Without thinking, she found herself on the pier, standing in the same spot Lucas had served her dinner. When she closed her eyes, she saw him stepping from behind the umbrella, tanned skin glowing in the morning sun. Lips wide in that grin that made her toes curl. She dropped down onto the boards and dangled her feet over the water.

The spray misted her bare feet, but the water felt good in the heat of the day. The movement of rain out of the area meant less humidity and a warm breeze. She closed her eyes and let the wind whip through her hair. A drop of water landed on her hand and only then did Sid realize she was crying.

Not the heavy sobs of the day before. This felt more like a cleansing. A mourning. Randy was right—Lucas had a choice, but she hadn't let him know what all of his choices were. She never asked him to stay. Never told him how she really felt. Not that she believed that would have made a difference, but she couldn't blame him for going when she practically put him on the ferry herself.

Still, the tears came. She didn't have any tissues so she used the sleeve of her T-shirt. A new one she'd ordered online had arrived the day before. She was behind on laundry so she'd worn it. The phrase on this one, "The Universe abhors a vacuum . . . so don't be a sucker," seemed apropos somehow.

"Hey," came a voice from behind her, then a warm body sat down at her side.

Sid blinked, certain she must be hallucinating.

"Hey," she said, tentative. Waiting for Lucas to disappear.

He looked up at the sky. "Beautiful day."

The weather? He was going to talk about the weather?

"Yeah." She sat straight, her face turned away from him. Trying to be inconspicuous, she wiped a tear on her sleeve.

Silence prevailed, and Sid felt every muscle in her body tense. Why was he here?

"I stopped to say good-bye to Drillbit," he said, as if reading her mind. "She told me you were out here." She turned to see if he was serious and caught the grin. "I thought that might get your attention."

Lucas wiped one of her tears away with his thumb, and Sid's heart tried to fling itself out of her chest. "Why are you really here?" she asked, surprised she found the power to speak.

He looked out over the water. "I was heading for the ferry when I got this idea."

"An idea?"

"Yeah. An idea. It involves you, so I thought I'd come over and run it by you."

She'd thought any ideas involving her had ended yesterday. Her eyes dropped to her hands twisted in her lap. They were gripped tight enough to turn her fingers purple. "What's the idea?"

Would he ask her to go with him? That had to be it. She was ready to scream *yes* when he said, "I've got one more challenge for you."

Sid clamped her eyes shut. How stupid to think he'd take her with him.

"I don't think I'm up for any more challenges."

"That's too bad," he said, turning his body to face her. "This one could be a win-win for both of us."

What was the man babbling on about? Why wouldn't he just leave?

"Sid," he said, and waited. Knowing he'd sit there forever until she turned, Sid gave in.

"What is it?"

He looked very serious and a little scared. Sid's breathing slowed and the sound of waves and birds faded until she couldn't hear anything but her own heartbeat and the man before her. "I was thinking about setting up a law office on the island, but I'll need someplace to live. Do you think I could live here? With you? For the rest of my life?"

Sid sat blankly for a moment, processing what he'd just said.

Then she choked on the joy rushing through her system. She couldn't talk. She couldn't breathe. If this was a joke, she'd kill him.

When she didn't respond, Lucas scooted closer. "What do you say? Are you up to the challenge?"

"Fuck yes," she said, and launched herself into his arms.

ACKNOWLEDGMENTS

Anchor Island is a product of my imagination, but wholly inspired by Ocracoke Island, North Carolina. The layout, street names, and even the weather are liberated from this tiny island at the base of the Outer Banks. So it goes, Dempsey's Bar & Grill has a real counterpart as well. Howard's Pub is one of the first establishments you'll see as you drive into Ocracoke village. A lively restaurant with a friendly staff, welcoming atmosphere, and food that will have you coming back for more. If Anchor and Dempsey's sound like places you'd like to visit, I highly recommend scheduling your next vacation around this beautiful and historic area of the mid-Atlantic coast.

The heroine of this novel, Sid Navarro, is one of my favorite characters. She's brash and confrontational, but still vulnerable and sweet. Though she'd be quite put out to know I called her sweet. Sid sports an interesting wardrobe, and all of her (somewhat inappropriate) T-shirts can be added to your own closet if you look hard enough.

No author gets to this point alone, and I am no exception. My agent, Nalini Akolekar, is always in my corner and I cannot thank her enough. My editors, Kelli and Becky, helped me make this book the best it could be, and my beta readers (Marnee, Jeanne, Maureen, and Lynnette) are always a source of great insight and support. That said, any imperfections in this book are solely mine.

My daughter gives up much for me to pursue this endeavor, and for that I will always be grateful. The pets are not as understanding, but they try.

ABOUT THE AUTHOR

Born in the Ohio Valley, Terri moved below the Mason-Dixon line in the early 1990s after experiencing three blizzards in eighteen months. Seeking warmer climes and a career in the music business, she landed in Nashville and learned fast that getting a job on Music Row is not as easy as it sounds. Ironically, it wasn't until she left Nashville and moved to Arkansas that she found her way into radio. Being a disc jockey was the perfect job for this extrovert, being paid to talk for several hours a day, listen to endless amounts of music, and if a listener changed the channel (rejection!), she had no idea. Looking for a change, Terri moved to the East Coast, settled near the ocean, earned her bachelor's degree while raising a daughter, and joined cubicle land once again. But love of the written word pulled her into an amazing online romance community and she started putting words on the page. Five years later, in 2012, she was named a finalist in the Romance Writers of America Golden Heart contest. Shortly after, she signed with an agent and moved into publication. *Meant to Be* was her debut novel. As for hidden talents, she makes a killer lasagna.